P9-DBL-173

H130

Cast On,
Kill Off

Berkley Prime Crime titles by Maggie Sefton

KNIT ONE, KILL TWO
NEEDLED TO DEATH
A DEADLY YARN
A KILLER STITCH
DYER CONSEQUENCES
FLEECE NAVIDAD
DROPPED DEAD STITCH
SKEIN OF THE CRIME
UNRAVELED
CAST ON, KILL OFF

Anthologies

DOUBLE KNIT MURDERS

THE BERKLEY PUBLISHING GROUP
Published by the Penguin Group
Penguin Group (USA) Inc.
375 Hudson Street, New York, New York 10014, USA

Penguin Group (Canada), 90 Eglinton Avenue East, Suite 700, Toronto, Ontario M4P 2Y3, Canada
(a division of Pearson Penguin Canada Inc.) • Penguin Books Ltd., 80 Strand, London WC2R 0RL,
England • Penguin Group Ireland, 25 St. Stephen's Green, Dublin 2, Ireland (a division of Penguin
Books Ltd.) • Penguin Group (Australia), 250 Camberwell Road, Camberwell, Victoria 3124, Australia
(a division of Pearson Australia Group Pty. Ltd.) • Penguin Books India Pvt. Ltd., 11 Community
Centre, Panchsheel Park, New Delhi—110 017, India • Penguin Group (NZ), 67 Apollo Drive,
Rosedale, Auckland 0632, New Zealand (a division of Pearson New Zealand Ltd.) • Penguin Books
(South Africa) (Pty.) Ltd., 24 Sturdee Avenue, Rosebank, Johannesburg 2196, South Africa

Penguin Books Ltd., Registered Offices: 80 Strand, London WC2R 0RL, England

This book is an original publication of The Berkley Publishing Group.

FIRST EDITION: June 2012

Library of Congress Cataloging-in-Publication Data

Sefton, Maggie.
Cast on, kill off / Maggie Sefton. — 1st ed.
p. cm.
ISBN 978-0-425-24759-4
1. Flynn, Kelly (Fictitious character)—Fiction. 2. Knitters (Persons)—Fiction.
3. Murder—Investigation—Fiction. I. Title.
PS3619.E37C37 2012
813'.6—dc23
2011046661

PRINTED IN THE UNITED STATES OF AMERICA

10 9 8 7 6 5 4 3 2 1

ALWAYS LEARNING   **PEARSON**

Acknowledgments

Once again, I want to thank Kristin Aamodt of Bellingham, Washington, for the novel's title, *Cast On, Kill Off*. I had a "Name a Kelly Flynn Mystery" contest on my website two years ago and received many wonderful title suggestions. In fact, I received so many e-mails that I didn't notice Kristin had sent in two separate e-mails three weeks apart. There were nearly two hundred e-mails and literally several hundred title suggestions. So many excellent titles were submitted, I expanded the winners' categories and chose fifteen winners in all: five First Place, five Second Place, and five Third Place. I did not pay attention to entrants' names or locations, I simply chose the titles that best fit the Kelly Flynn mysteries. Last year's *Unraveled* was Kristin's idea as well. There are thirteen title suggestions remaining, so I have lots to choose from for Kelly's future adventures. Of course, all titles have to pass muster with my editor, too. ☺

The three short recipes included with this book are also contest winners. Last spring I announced an Appetizer Contest on the Cozy Chicks blog, where I post weekly with six other mystery authors (www.cozychicksblog.com). There were two categories: Hot Appetizers and Cold Appetizers. The Hot Appetizer contest winners' names are included with their recipes.

Cast of Characters

Kelly Flynn—financial accountant and part-time sleuth, refugee from East Coast corporate CPA firm

Steve Townsend—architect and builder in Fort Connor, Colorado, and Kelly's ex-boyfriend

KELLY'S FRIENDS:

Jennifer Stroud—real estate agent, part-time waitress

Lisa Gerrard—physical therapist

Megan Smith—IT consultant, another corporate refugee

Marty Harrington—lawyer, Megan's fiancé

Greg Carruthers—university instructor, Lisa's boyfriend

Pete Wainwright—owner of Pete's Café in the back of Kelly's favorite knitting shop, House of Lambspun

LAMBSPUN FAMILY AND REGULARS:

Mimi Shafer—Lambspun shop owner and knitting expert, known to Kelly and her friends as "Mother Mimi"

Burt Parker—retired Fort Connor police detective, Lambspun spinner-in-residence

Hilda and Lizzie von Steuben—spinster sisters, retired schoolteachers, and exquisite knitters

CAST OF CHARACTERS

Curt Stackhouse—Colorado rancher, Kelly's mentor and advisor

Jayleen Swinson—Alpaca rancher and Colorado Cowgirl

Connie and Rosa—Lambspun shop personnel

Cast On, Kill Off

One

Kelly Flynn looked at her reflection in the seamstress's three-way mirror. The royal blue taffeta fabric shimmered under the bright spotlights shining down from the ceiling. Kelly turned to her left and admired the lines of the bridesmaid gown. Her friend, Megan, had used her own bridal gown's strapless design to model the bridesmaids' gowns, except they weren't floor length. The skirts flared gently past the knee instead. Megan had also chosen strong vibrant colors for the dresses. Kelly's was royal blue, Lisa's was lemon yellow, and Jennifer's was shamrock green. Megan's sister Janet, who was the matron of honor, was wearing her favorite—fire engine red. Kelly had laughed when Megan told her she wanted "a bold rainbow," not those pale pastels she saw so often.

Not bad, Kelly thought to herself, admiring the fabric's shimmer as she turned to the right. She had to admit Megan had a good eye for color. The royal blue set off Kelly's dark hair and fair skin perfectly.

"How does it feel, Kelly?" the seamstress, Zoe Yeager, asked from the floor, where she sat cross-legged, dressmaker pins in her hand.

"It feels great, Zoe. You did a wonderful job," Kelly said, feeling the fabric's crisp texture beneath her fingers.

"You look gorgeous, Kelly," Megan said from the corner of the room, where she sat making calls on her cell phone. Only three and a half weeks before Megan's and her boyfriend Marty's wedding, and all the intricate plans had to fall into place. "I told you that color would look fabulous on you," Megan said as she paged through her bridal schedule book.

"Right as usual, Color Genius," Kelly bantered. "I bow to your expertise."

Zoe laughed from her spot on the floor as she ran her fingers over the hemline. "I swear, Megan, you and your friends make me laugh, especially Jennifer. She is hilarious."

"Well, that's Jennifer's specialty, making us laugh," Kelly added.

"Stand straight and don't move for a minute, Kelly. I want to give this hem a final check." Zoe scooted backward on the floor, leaned over, and peered at the bottom of the dress. "Okay, now turn in a circle slowly," she instructed.

Kelly did as she was told while Zoe scrutinized her handiwork. Kelly observed a slight blue smudge on the side of Zoe's face which she hadn't noticed before. Zoe's medium-length brown hair had obscured it.

"Looks good," Zoe decreed, rising from the floor. "Let me help you take it off, and I'll put this one on the finished rack along with Lisa's and Jennifer's."

2

Kelly allowed Zoe to unzip the dress and help her step out of it, hoping nothing would happen to the gorgeous creation once she was in charge of its safekeeping.

Zoe shook the fabric and examined it inside. Now that Zoe was closer, Kelly could see the middle-aged woman's face better. There was definitely a blue bruise along Zoe's jawline that hadn't been there before. "What happened, Zoe? Did you fall down or something?" Kelly asked, concerned. "You've got a bad bruise on your face."

Zoe looked slightly startled, then color began to stain her cheeks. "Uh, no . . . I . . . I'm just clumsy. I tripped over my back porch steps, that's all." She reached for a satin-covered hanger. "Here, let me put this away in the work closet." And she hastened from the room, taking the royal blue creation with her.

Megan approached, holding Kelly's slacks and short-sleeve top. Early September, and it still felt like summer outside.

"Don't ask her anything else, Kelly," Megan whispered when she was closer. "Those bruises are from her husband Oscar. Mimi told me Zoe had confessed to her about her husband's abuse a year ago. Mimi tried to get her to leave him, but Zoe hasn't so far." Megan glanced over her shoulder to the doorway. "I cannot understand why women stay in those relationships, Kelly." A familiar scowl darkened Megan's pretty features.

Kelly slipped on her crisp slacks. "I think it's because they're scared, Megan. Scared of what will happen if they try to leave, especially if there are young children at home."

Megan's scowl evaporated and was replaced by a contrite expression. "You're right, Kelly. I know you are, but there are shelters here in town for women to escape to with their

3

children. I just wish Zoe would think about going. She doesn't even have children."

"I'd like to think so, too, Megan," Kelly said, slipping the lightweight top over her head. "It seems everyone has a breaking point, when they decide *enough*."

Zoe came around the corner of the fitting room, a gauzy bit of ribbons and tiny silk flowers in her hand. "Here, Kelly, let's take a look with the headpiece. I finished this one yesterday."

Kelly took the delicate confection and fingered the tiny seed pearls and blue and white silk flowers that adorned the taffeta-wrapped headband. "This is so pretty, Zoe. Simply exquisite."

Zoe beamed. "Thank you, Kelly. I love working with those silky flowers. They turn out so nicely. Try it on and let's take a look."

Kelly did as directed, adjusting the headpiece's small combs into her hair. Gazing at her reflection, she almost didn't recognize herself. Kelly never wore ribbons or flowery things. But the way Zoe had arranged them, they were very flattering.

"I look like I should be going to a fairy-tale ball in some castle, rather than poring over financial statements," she teased.

"Well, wait until Steve sees you in this dress," Megan said slyly. "He may invite you to one of those fancy Denver charity balls."

Kelly deliberately didn't look at Megan. She already knew what Megan was doing. Smiling. Now that Kelly was working in Denver several days a week, she and Steve had lunch or dinner together whenever they were both in town. Conse-

quently, Megan had made it a point to offer frequent suggestions to other recreational activities Kelly and Steve could
pursue. "Suggestions," Megan always claimed. Planting seeds,
Kelly surmised.

Once Steve started driving up to Fort Connor this past
spring and summer to play baseball on his old team, Kelly
and Steve had a chance to be in each other's company on a
regular basis. *Familiar ground.* It had made it easier for them
to move to the next step of having dinner together. Of
course, Megan and the rest of the gang were careful to maintain a relaxed environment. No expectations, Kelly had told
them.

Now that she and Steve had gotten past their sudden and
dramatic breakup last year, Kelly figured both of them needed
simply to be friends right now, while they figured out what
came next. *What did the future hold in store?* She didn't know.
All Kelly knew was she enjoyed having Steve back in her life.
After all, they'd started out as friends before they became
lovers once before. Maybe they could again.

Right now, they were two friends who really enjoyed each
other's company. They talked on the phone every day, even
when Steve was traveling on business for the Denver company where he worked. Having watched his own small architect and builder business go belly-up in the recession that
followed the recent housing debacle, Steve threw his energy
and creativity into Sam Kaufman's construction company.
Sam appreciated Steve's efforts and encouraged him to follow
up on new ideas. Steve had jumped at the chance.

Zoe glanced from Megan to Kelly and back again, a smile
tweaking her lips. "Who's Steve? Kelly's boyfriend?"

Kelly didn't even have time to answer. Megan did it for

her. "He was for over two years. Then they split up last year. All of us are hoping they'll get back together." She flashed that Cheshire cat smile Kelly had seen frequently these past six months.

"I haven't heard a word from Kelly," Zoe teased. "Why's Megan answering for you?"

Kelly pretended to continue admiring the pretty headband. "Because she does it so well. Megan's got an overactive imagination."

"It's not my imagination," Megan retorted. "We've all seen you two whenever you're together. You're a matched set."

Kelly had to laugh at that, and so did Zoe. Removing the delicate headband, she returned it to the seamstress. "She makes it sound like we're bookends. Now I know what I'm going to give you and Marty for a wedding present. A set of monstrosity bookends. Maybe two huge moose heads or something."

"Please, don't. Marty would probably fall in love with them, and we'd have them on the living room bookshelves." Megan rolled her eyes.

"You are so funny, Megan," Zoe said, chuckling. "Let me put this away and check my daytimer. Now that Kelly's gown is completed, we've finished everything with three weeks to spare."

"Wonderful job, Zoe," Megan said as the seamstress headed for the curtained doorway that led to a workroom in the rear of the small shop located in a neighborhood strip mall.

Kelly checked the mirror and fluffed her shoulder-length hair. "You're right on track, Megan. I hate to sound like an anal accountant, but I am. Planning makes all the difference."

Megan drew her cell phone from her pants pocket as she returned to her chair in the corner. "You're preaching to the choir on that one, Kelly. I couldn't have done it without my lists. Which reminds me that I have to check on those caterers again."

"And that reminds me I have to finish up one of my clients' financial statements. I've got an appointment with him tomorrow."

"When will you be in Denver again?" Megan looked up from her cell phone screen.

"Later this week, and no, Steve won't be there," Kelly teased. "He's visiting some specialty building firms at a conference in Oregon."

"Too bad." Megan shot her a wicked grin before she spoke into the phone. "Hello, this is Megan Smith. Is Kevin there? I need to change my wedding reception estimate again."

Kelly felt sorry for caterer Kevin. Megan had been increasing the guest list estimate every week for a month. Kelly grabbed her shoulder bag and started for the door. The sooner she finished those financial statements, the sooner she could take a break at Lambspun, the knitting and fiber shop close to her cottage. She had been burrowed in work for several days for her Fort Connor real estate investor client, Arthur Housemann, and her Denver developer client, Don Warner.

Letting her mind return to matters financial brought another thought from the back of her mind. She needed to pay Zoe for the dress. Kelly was always scrupulous in paying small business owners by check. That way, they kept the entire amount rather than pay credit card fees. It was a small thing, but could make a real difference to a small business owner like Zoe Yeager. Her sewing business had grown substantially thanks to Zoe's creative designs. Small business success stories always made the accountant lobe in Kelly's brain buzz. Only the strongest and best survived, especially in a recession environment.

Kelly changed direction and walked through the curtained doorway that led to Zoe's workshop. She was about to turn the corner into the lighted area when Zoe's sharp voice held her in place.

"Don't give me excuses. I told you I needed that gown finished by tonight!"

Kelly didn't hear anyone reply, so she assumed Zoe was on the phone.

"I don't care how late you have to stay up. Just finish it tonight, do you hear? Or I'll take it out of your wages. You can bring it to the shop on your way to work tomorrow morning. And don't call me again. I'm busy."

Kelly quickly turned and retreated into the outer dressing room once again, not wanting to disturb what was obviously a heated conversation. She was also surprised at Zoe's tone of voice. It was sharp and dictatorial. Ugly. Whenever Kelly saw her, Zoe was always so pleasant and cheerful. Kelly couldn't help wondering whom Zoe was talking to.

Megan was clicking off her phone call, so Kelly approached and lowered her voice. "Zoe is in the midst of a phone call. I can't wait, so would you ask her to please mail me a bill, and I'll send a check right away? I need to finish some financial statements."

"No problem. She needs to send bills to Lisa and Jennifer, too," Megan said, running her finger down the smartphone's screen.

"You can add it to one of your to-do lists," Kelly said as she left.

Kelly walked across the driveway separating her look-alike cottage from the Spanish colonial beige stucco, red-tile-roofed farmhouse that had inspired the cottage's design. Once the farmhouse for Kelly's aunt and uncle, it was now a lively knitting and fiber shop. The cottage had become Kelly's when her aunt Helen was murdered nearly four years ago. That was the tragic event that had brought a transformation in Kelly's life. She'd responded to the warmth and camaraderie of the knitting shop family of regulars. They had become Kelly's family, replacing the ones who'd passed away. Kelly left her life as a corporate CPA in Washington, DC, and switched gears entirely, drawn by the warmth and friendship that beckoned to her from the friends she'd made at Lambspun.

She turned at the sound of her dog Carl's deep Rottweiler bark coming from the cottage backyard. Carl was standing on his hind feet, front paws on the chain-link fence, warning the golfers on the adjoining golf course not to trespass. Few disobeyed Carl, Kelly noticed.

Kelly admired the colorful annuals that were still blooming in the flower beds bordering the walkway that led to Lambspun's front door. Bright red geraniums and white impatiens beside deep purple petunias. Fringy dianthus alternated with sturdy orange marigolds. Colorful, easy, low-maintenance plants. The very same that Kelly had put in the planters lining her cottage walk.

She paused beside the shady patio, debating whether or not to knit here instead of inside the shop. Early September temperatures were still delightfully warm, in the low eighties. The sun shone brightly in the gorgeous blue sky that arched over the golf course. *Colorado blue*, Kelly called it. Late afternoon, and the sun hadn't even begun its descent toward the ridges of low mountains on the west side of the university town. The "foothills," as locals called them. *Beautiful* was Kelly's word.

Tempted to drop her knitting on the nearby table or wrought iron chair, Kelly decided she would first see what Lambspun's owner, Mimi, was doing. She hadn't had a chance to drop in and visit with her for several days.

Pushing the heavy wooden door open, Kelly stepped inside the wonderland of color and texture and sensuality that always greeted her whenever she entered the shop.

Yarn, yarn everywhere. Wooden crates were stacked one upon the other in the foyer. Shelves lined the walls of the adjacent room. Fat balls and loosely wound skeins tumbled forth from all of them. Tables and chests were piled high with yarns. Sweaters, scarves, and vests dangled from the ceiling and shelves. Long puffy loops of yarn draped along the walls. Wool, cotton, silk, mohair, alpaca, cashmere. Any fiber your heart desired.

"Well, hello, Kelly. It's so nice to see you," Mimi said as Kelly entered the foyer. "You haven't been here since last week." Mimi was stacking twisted coils of terra-cotta red yarn in a tidy pile beside similar yarns in the middle of an antique dry sink. Moss green, burgundy wine, copper ore.

Autumn colors, Kelly noticed. Although it was still summer outside with balmy Colorado temperatures, the Lambspun crew always had an eye for an upcoming season. Seasonal colors always appeared in the shop overnight, it seemed. She would walk into the shop and find rooms totally transformed as if by magic. Kelly attributed it to the Lambspun "elves," as she called Mimi and her two main helpers, Connie and Rosa.

Kelly fingered one of the terra-cotta red skeins. HAND-DYED, the label read. It was a merino wool, not as thick as some of the others she'd touched. It would require a smaller needle but would be perfect for making fall and winter knitted hats. Or mittens.

"How's that bridesmaid shawl coming?" Mimi asked as she gave the yarn piles a pat.

Guilt drew Kelly from her fiber indulgence. "Oh, it's coming slowly. I've been swamped with work and haven't been able to knit very much."

She headed to the adjoining main room and dumped her knitting bag on the long wooden library table that served as a meeting place for scores of fiber workers of every description. Not only knitters showed up around the Lambspun table, but also crochet lovers, or hookers, as they called themselves. Quilters turned up, too, as well as spinners, who set up their wheels in the corners. Weavers regularly worked their creations on the larger looms in the two rooms adjoining the large one.

Kelly always thought of Lambspun as an "equal opportunity" shop. Whatever your fiber tastes and inclinations, you would find someone at Lambspun to share them. And Mimi helped spread her expertise in all the fiber arts through a full schedule of classes. Kelly had noticed new classes in tatting and lace embroidery. They both sounded tricky to her.

"Would you like me to help you with it?" Mimi offered as she followed Kelly into the room. "I'd be glad to."

Now Kelly felt even guiltier. Lisa, Megan, and Jennifer had already finished their shawls. But not her. Now Mother Mimi was offering to rescue her.

"No, no, I'll get it done," she promised as she settled into a chair at the table. No other customers around. *Good*. Maybe she could get more knitting done. Interesting conversations always distracted her, she'd noticed.

She pulled the royal blue bundle from a plastic bag she had protecting it from the jumble inside her knitting bag. There were knitting needles of varying sizes, a tape measure, stitch markers, copies of previous patterns she'd worked, and not one but two plastic containers of yarn needles, perfect for tucking in dangling yarn ends. She held up the bundle which formed a large triangle and examined her work so far. It didn't look bad. The loose-knit design would be very flattering over the bridesmaids' bare shoulders.

"Look, you're halfway finished," Mimi said with her encouraging smile before she returned to straightening books on the shelves.

Kelly knew Mimi was doing her nurturing best to be kind. Normally she would make a joke, but instead a remembered thought came to mind. "My bridesmaid gown is all finished," she said, picking up her knitting stitches where she'd left off. "Megan and I went over this morning. Zoe has finished everything, including the headbands. Three weeks early, too. Megan was delighted, of course."

"Of course. Megan has to stay on schedule, or—"

"Or there'll be hell to pay. And we'll all have to listen to it," Kelly joked.

Mimi laughed her light laugh as she checked the other bookshelves. "I was going to say woe to the vendors who were not keeping up."

"That, too. Tell me something, Mimi. When I was there this morning, I noticed a dark bruise on Zoe's face and asked her about it. She got kind of flustered and said she was clumsy and tripped on some stairs. But Megan told me when we were alone that Zoe has an abusive husband. She said Zoe had talked to you about it."

Mimi turned from the bookshelves and sat across the table from Kelly. Her cheerful smile was nowhere to be seen. Worry lines appeared on Mimi's face now, showing the years of worrying about others. "Yes, that is true. It's so very upsetting. I've known Zoe for the six years she's been in Fort Connor. I remember when she first started her shop four years ago. And I noticed those bruises appearing last year. I asked Zoe about it, and she tried to dismiss my concern like she did with you. But I kept after her. Finally, she admitted that her husband Oscar had become increasingly abusive since he'd lost his new consulting business. He was trying to make it as a financial advisor so he could leave his regular job with the power company."

Mimi began to trace a pattern with her finger on the light wood of the table. "She said he started to drink heavily, and that's when he began hitting her more. Apparently he only hit her occasionally before that." Mimi's voice had acquired an edge. "I simply cannot bear it when smart women stay with men who abuse them. There were no children to worry about. Oscar had kids from an earlier marriage. I told Zoe I would take her to the battered women's shelter here in town, but she refused to go. I've told her that every time I see her.

It's gotten so she stopped coming in here to visit. She knew I'd remind her of my offer. I can't force her to go." Mimi gave a little shrug and met Kelly's eyes. "I wish I could. With Oscar drinking more, there's no telling what he might do."

Kelly had let her knitting drop to her lap. "That is so sad, Mimi. Zoe is so lively and full of energy. And . . . and so talented."

"I know, it's so—"

Her sentence was cut off by shop helper Connie, who walked into the room quickly. "Mimi, I've got that New England yarn vendor on the phone. It took me half the day calling. You wanted to talk to him."

Mimi almost leaped from her chair. "Yes! Absolutely. Sorry to leave so quickly, Kelly, but I've been trying to reach him for weeks."

"No problem, Mimi, we'll talk later," Kelly said as Mimi hurried from the room.

Kelly returned to the loose-knit shawl as she let the disturbing images Mimi had described dart around her head.

Two

Kelly walked across the parking lot in the business complex where her Fort Connor client had his real estate investor office. Glancing up, she noticed the sun still shining brightly in the afternoon sky. It was early afternoon, so maybe there was enough time to run all those errands that had been accumulating during her busy workdays. If she was lucky, she'd still have time to sneak in a workout run on the river trail before meeting the gang in Old Town.

Friday night, and the temperatures were still invitingly warm enough to meet at one of their favorite Old Town cafés or brew pubs. Pizza and Colorado microbrews beckoned.

Kelly checked her watch again as she clicked her car door lock. If she moved fast with those errands, she could definitely squeeze in a run before she met her friends at six o'clock. Sliding into the tan leather seat of her sporty red car, Kelly dumped her shoulder bag briefcase, then started the engine, her mind already plotting a route for the errands.

As she pulled out of the parking lot and into traffic, Kelly heard her cell phone's distinctive music, demanding to be answered. Kelly retrieved her smartphone from the briefcase and noticed Steve's name and number flashing on the phone screen. Surprised, she clicked on.

"Hey, there. Weren't you leaving for Oregon today?" she asked as she steered the car around a corner.

"I'm in the airport now," Steve's deep voice came over the line. Warm and familiar.

Kelly felt herself relax. It always felt good talking to Steve.

"I thought I'd give you a call before we start to board the plane. I wondered how your meeting with Arthur Housemann went. Is he going to sell that piece of land outside Windsor? How'd he respond when you asked him?"

"Actually, he was surprised that Sam Kaufman would be interested. He thought it was a little outside your Denver range. I hinted that you and Sam were dabbling in some different projects and other stuff and might be interested. He said he'd consider it."

Steve chuckled. "Thanks, Kelly. That was perfect. I don't know if Sam's friend would like that location or not, but it looks like it might be perfect. The views are great from the road. When I come back from Oregon, I may ask Housemann if Sam and I can take a walk around."

Kelly pulled to a stop at an intersection. "I'm sure Housemann wouldn't mind." Remembering something, she added, "When are you getting back? There's a fund-raiser ball game next week, and the guys are gonna join up. I'm meeting them tonight in Old Town, so I can tell Greg. He'll give you all the details."

"I'll be back Tuesday night, but I was hoping to have

other plans for that week. How'd you like to join me at the Jazz Bistro for dinner one night?"

"I'd love to," Kelly quickly replied. Old memories danced through her head as she pictured their favorite Old Town café. Great food, icy martinis, and hot jazz. She and Steve had shared many evenings there, first as friends, then as lovers.

"That's great." Steve's voice had grown softer. "Where are you and the gang meeting tonight? It's Friday night. Pizza and beer."

"At Old Town Brew Pub, assuming Lisa and Greg get there early enough to snag one of the outdoor tables."

"Don't worry. Greg will be on it. It's his favorite place." A slightly wistful tone sounded in his voice. "Maybe I'll be able to make it up there a few nights before fall turns cold."

Kelly heard that wistful tone and remembered how much Steve enjoyed relaxing with his friends in Fort Connor's Old Town plaza. Surrounded by shops and cafés, the plaza was pedestrian only and marked the center of early Fort Connor before the turn of the last century. Several of the original buildings from the late 1800s and early 1900s had been lovingly preserved and maintained over the decades, adding to the picturesque charm of the plaza.

"I hope so, too," she said. "You've been on the road a lot, so you deserve to take a break in between trips."

"That's like the pot calling the kettle black," Steve joked. "Your schedule is as bad as mine."

Kelly laughed at the expression. "That sounds like one of Jayleen's old sayings. But you're right," she admitted, rounding a corner as she neared a shopping center. "Between Housemann and Warner Development, my dance card is full."

"Well, save a dance for me, wouldja?" Steve teased. "Hey,

they're about to start boarding. Before I forget, what did you decide to do with that healthy bonus Housemann gave you? You said you'd promised him an answer this week."

Shifting away from the bantering, Kelly went into accountant mode again. "Yeah, I did. I told him I was going to start investing in the stock market."

Steve laughed. "Hey, that's great! I'm proud of you, Kelly. I also think it's smart."

His praise warmed her inside. "Thanks, Steve. I decided it was time. The money was sitting in a bank account earning next to nothing. It's time I learned how to invest money on my own. I'll have to do a lot of research, but it feels right. It's a good addition to those Wyoming gas wells pumping away."

"Those are pretty sweet royalty checks, though."

"Yeah, but they'll disappear when the gas runs out. Who knows when that will be? No guarantees, the drilling company said. I need a little diversification, as the investment gurus say." She nosed her car into a parking space in front of a Big Box store.

Steve laughed softly, bringing that warm feeling inside. "It sounds like a good idea, Kelly. Listen, gotta go. Take care."

"You, too, Steve. Have a good trip." She heard him click off and felt the letdown she had every time their phone calls ended.

"**Hey,** put that pesto pizza between Lisa and me," Megan instructed the waiter. "I don't trust the guys until the pepperoni one shows up."

"No way! I'm famished," Marty protested as he wrestled his tie over his head, then dispensed with his suit jacket.

"Yeah, not fair," Greg chimed in, taking a sip of his Colorado microbrew. "I had to work through lunch. No food. I'm malnourished."

"Malnourished, my foot," his girlfriend Lisa countered as she leaned back in her chair. "I've been to your office. Those administrative assistants bring in food every day. Donuts, brownies, muffins, cinnamon rolls, coffee cakes. It's a wonder you don't all weigh three hundred pounds."

"They don't cycle twenty miles a day, like I do," Greg retorted. "Lemme have a piece, pretty please."

"Yeah, me, too," Marty begged, his tone turning plaintive. "I've been dealing with two really demanding clients all afternoon. That's stressful."

"Stop whining, you guys," Megan said as she took a piece of pesto pizza and tore it in half down the middle. "Here, this will hold you until the pepperoni comes."

Both Greg and Marty snapped up the mini slices. Inhaling them, it seemed to Kelly.

She sank back in the chair at the brew pub's outdoor table, smiling at her friends. "You guys remind me of hungry seals snapping up fish." Noticing the waiter approach with two trays of pepperoni and cheese pizzas, she announced, "Hey, just in time. Now our pesto pizza is safe."

"Salvation at last!" Greg pulled out two hefty pizza wedges and tore into them.

"Now you're talking!" Marty cried, his eyes lighting up as he attacked the second pepperoni pizza.

Lisa snorted. "Starving dogs."

"You'd think they hadn't eaten in days." Megan separated

two slices of pesto pizza and offered Kelly one. "Here, Kelly. Eat fast before they finish theirs and try to steal ours."

Kelly didn't need any prodding. She'd raced through her errands and found just enough time to take a short run before showering and meeting her friends at the brew pub. She sank her teeth into the cheesy pesto topping and savored. *Yum*.

Taking another sip of her favorite Colorado ale, she glanced around the Old Town plaza. Every restaurant, café, and brew pub was full inside and out. All the outdoor tables were taken, filled with college students, middle-aged couples, older couples, all ages.

The balmy evening weather beguiled everyone. September was usually a beautiful time of year in Fort Connor. Early fall kept the warm temperatures and flowers blooming all over the city. And yet, the early mornings gradually grew a bit chillier as the month wore on. So, too, the evenings. Usually by mid-October, it became "too nippy," as Mimi would say, to dine outdoors in the evenings. But sometimes the Weather Gods smiled, and the warm temperatures stayed throughout October and into November.

Kelly loved the changing seasons. She could detect the scent of approaching fall in the early morning air when she took her daily workout run on the trails alongside the Cache La Poudre River, which ran diagonally through the city. The river flowed into Fort Connor from the mouth of the Cache La Poudre Canyon on the northwest side of Fort Connor. Kelly and her friends loved that canyon. It was designated a natural wilderness along with the river, which had carved a path through the canyon millions of years ago. She escaped into the canyon whenever she needed to think. She'd drive up, up, up until she found a de-

serted scenic spot with parking. Then she'd find an inviting
boulder and sit. Sit and stare at the rushing water as the river
raced past. Sit and think.

Even in the winter, beneath the ice patches, the river
flowed, heading to the east. Out of Fort Connor, joining the
South Platte River and out of Colorado, merging with the
Missouri River, which carried those rushing waters and emp-
tied them into the great Mississippi, heading south to the
Gulf of Mexico and the Atlantic Ocean.

Kelly heard the sound of Latin music coming from a club
across the plaza, and a memory surfaced, which brought a
smile.

"That sounds like a salsa beat," she said before choosing
another pizza slice. "I remember when Jennifer was dancing
outside that club one Friday night, and then danced over to
our table. Wow . . . that was my first summer here in Fort
Connor. Right after Aunt Helen's death." She sank her teeth
into the cheesy pesto.

"Whoa, that was nearly four years ago." Megan glanced
up. "You came back for your aunt Helen's funeral, and you
liked it here so much, you stayed."

"After solving Helen's murder, you mean," Lisa added
with a wink, then tipped back her microbrew.

Marty swallowed his bite of pizza then chased it down
with a beer. "Man, you were sleuthing back then?"

"Ohhhh, yeah," Megan and Lisa chorused together, then
laughed.

"Hey, I couldn't help it, the cops had the wrong guy in
jail." Kelly gave a little shrug as she turned the brown bottle
with the mountain bike label. "That was a while ago, guys.
Ol' Marty wasn't in the picture then."

Greg sank back into his chair with another pepperoni slice. "Ahhhh, those were the days. Peace and quiet. More food."

"Sounds boring to me," Marty said. "Was Megan seeing anyone then? Anybody I have to challenge for her hand?"

"Dude, you've already got her hand. And the rest of her, too."

Kelly snickered over her pesto slice as Lisa tossed a wadded napkin Greg's way. Kelly remembered before Marty came along, Megan suffered from an acute case of shyness whenever she went on a date. She froze and went mute. She was no longer the lively, talkative Megan they all knew. Until . . . Marty. Steve said Marty had sneaked up on Megan. She never even noticed he was interested in her until he'd already become a friend and tennis partner. Meanwhile, watching Marty "court" Megan had provided a source of amusement and delight for Kelly and all of Megan's friends. Megan never saw him coming. So shyness never reared its head.

"There's no one to challenge, Marty," Megan said with a knowing smile. "Before you stumbled onto the scene—"

"And broke half of Curt's Christmas tree decorations," Lisa added with an evil grin.

"And ate *all* the leftovers while Steve and I were freezing to death outside putting up the lights," Greg scowled.

"Who *me*?" Marty asked innocently, hand to chest.

"Yeah, you," Kelly said, laughing. "Spot the Wonder Dog."

They all guffawed at the memory of Marty, entertaining Curt Stackhouse's grandchildren as Uncle Marty, alias Spot the Wonder Dog, galumphing about Curt's ranch house that evening.

"Please, don't remind me!" Megan cried, hands out-stretched. "Ye Gods! I'm marrying Spot the Wonder Dog! *Ackkkk!*"

"You're a lucky woman," Marty said, wagging his finger. "Not every woman has such a multifaceted fiancé."

Greg wagged his head. "Man, you were a disaster. What a mess."

"Don't remind me. I may change my mind and call off the wedding." Megan took another bite of pizza.

"Too late. Caterers are booked. Money's been paid. Gowns bought and paid for. Wedding cakes. Music. Minister," Lisa retorted. "Besides, we've grown used to ol' Marty."

"Speak for yourself." Greg tipped back his beer.

Marty, as usual, let all insults slide off, unperturbed. His smile intact. "So there are no suitors I have to challenge? Good. They'd have to wait until I finished my pizza anyway."

A memory from the past floated before Kelly's eyes, and she couldn't resist. "Well, now that you mention it, there was that cute Wyoming cowboy up at Cousin Martha's ranch."

"You mean *your* ranch," Greg countered.

"Oh, yeah. I remember you telling us about him." Lisa looked up, eyes twinkling.

"Oh, please," Megan said, a blush starting. "He wasn't interested in me."

"Are you *kidding*?"

"That was in Megan's shy period."

"Okay . . . I gotta hear about this. Wyoming cowboy, you say?" Marty leaned his elbows on the table.

"Jennifer said he was cute as the dickens, too," Lisa teased.

"After he tasted Megan's biscuits, he was in love," Kelly said, grinning.

23

"Oh, please!" Megan protested, blush deepening.

Marty drew back with a look of horror. "You made *biscuits* for him!"

Megan simply rolled her eyes, while the rest of them laughed.

"Okay, that settles it. I gotta go challenge him." Marty pushed back from the table. "Where do I find this guy in Wyoming?"

"Marty, don't be ridiculous," Megan chided.

"Dude, don't even think about it. That guy is a real cowboy, riding herd on Kelly's cattle and taking care of her ranch. He'd beat you up with one hand while lassoing a steer with the other." Greg drained his beer.

"Not if I sneak up on him," Marty said, clearly rethinking his idea. "I'll make a plan. After I finish the pizza. And my beer."

"Actually, Curt sold off all the cattle a couple of years ago. But Chet Brewster is still managing the ranch part-time whenever there's hay to be baled and sheep need shearing. He arranges all that." Kelly twirled the nearly empty bottle on her knee.

"I thought you sold that house to the Wyoming charity," Lisa said. "How come they don't do that for you?"

"Because they're operating a home for troubled girls, so they've got their hands full with just feeding the sheep and making sure the barns are locked at night. I still own the ranch and the sheep."

"Oh, yeah, you don't want those predators getting in at night," Marty added, his last pizza slice half eaten. "I remember how upset Uncle Curt would get whenever one of my cousins slipped and forgot to lock up. Big cats are watching."

He devoured the last morsel.

"The directors of the home have told me how much the girls enjoy working with the sheep, so I just hope they stay alert at the same time. It seems to work out for all of us."

"Those Wyoming gas wells still pumping away on the rest of your property up there?"

Kelly had to smile. Those royalty checks had saved her when she was first working on her own as an accountant three years ago. After working briefly for several alpaca ranchers, Kelly was able to return to her area of expertise—financial accounting for larger businesses. She'd missed the challenge.

"Ohhhh, yeah," Kelly said, then took a sip of beer. "They're a nice cushion as long as the gas keeps flowing. But there're no guarantees. The gas could run out. That's why I joined up with those two clients, Housemann and Warner. Plus, it got me back into corporate accounting, which I'd missed."

"Plus, it's given you the chance to be in Denver more, so you and Steve can see each other for dinner or lunch."

Kelly shook her head, while the rest of her friends smiled. "You never stop, do you, Megan? Yes, that, too. Steve's out of town till next week. Off to Oregon for some special builders' conference."

"Damn, that means he'll miss the game," Greg said.

"Boy, he's really doing a lot of conference stuff or whatever these last few months," Marty said, holding up his empty bottle for the waiter to see.

"Yeah, he and Sam are expanding the business, kind of," Kelly said, claiming another pizza slice.

"Remodeling, he told me," Greg said. "I didn't know they had conferences on that."

"Actually, they've got the chance to do a new custom home for an old friend of Sam's. And the guy and his wife want a lot of the extras and high-end touches. So Steve's been checking out all the high-end builders and conferences he can find."

"Sounds like Steve," Lisa said, handing the waiter her empty bottle.

"Thorough to a fault," Megan added, snatching the last pesto slice.

"Yeah, he told me he had several conferences lined up," Marty said, then sank back into his chair and sipped his beer. Hunger apparently assuaged for a while.

"He's been to two already," Kelly said. "After Oregon, he's got another two. One in Phoenix and one in Texas."

"Sounds like you've memorized his schedule," Greg joked, lifting his microbrew.

"Accountant memory, can't help it," Kelly teased, tapping her forehead. "Besides, we talk on the phone regularly, and he tells me what he's doing."

She turned to accept another Fat Tire ale from the waiter. Meanwhile, her friends all exchanged glances and smiles.

Kelly sensed their stealth communication. She was on to them.

"I can tell you guys were smiling at one another just then. You can stop now. I swear, you're a bunch of hovering mother hens."

"Man, how does she do that?" Greg asked Marty. "That's spooky."

"Good instincts," Marty said, grinning.

"Keeps me out of trouble," Kelly said, and quickly switched

subjects. "I didn't talk to Jen yesterday or today, so I take it she and Pete are on a catering job tonight."

"Right. They're doing a big dinner at some professor's house north of town."

"Ah, yes, new academic year starting. New faculty is in town," Greg added.

"Well, at least we can all enjoy watching Jennifer and Pete," Megan said slyly. "While Kelly and Steve are still dancing around each other, driving us all nuts, we can watch sane and rational Jennifer and Pete grow closer and closer."

Kelly took a deep drink of her favorite ale. "I'm sorry Steve and I are causing you mental distress," she said in a mock solicitous tone.

"Hey, those two are perfect for each other. Pete's been crazy about her since forever," Greg added.

"Ummmm, how close are we talking about here?" Marty asked with his familiar impish smile. "Are they *really* close? I mean, close *together* together?"

They all laughed out loud at Marty's sly reference.

"Dude, you are so lame," Greg teased.

"Yes, they are *together* together," Lisa added with a wicked smile.

"Oh, good. That's one less thing to worry about," Marty said with a big grin. "Who's up for dessert?"

This time, Kelly rolled her eyes, then joined her friends' laughter.

Three

Kelly walked into the Lambspun foyer, empty of customers at the moment. Since it was only nine fifteen in the morning, she wasn't surprised by the lack of customers. They would start to trickle in over the next hour, then the trickle would become a regular flow as the day progressed.

She headed into the main room and dropped her knitting bag and over-the-shoulder briefcase onto the long table. *Perfect*, Kelly thought. She could work on her clients' accounts in the peaceful shop for a couple of hours before making phone calls. She pulled her laptop from her briefcase. Now all she needed was some of the café's strong, rich coffee, then she'd be set to work.

Grabbing her huge carryout mug, Kelly headed through the shop, angling toward the hallway which led to Pete's Porch Café, located at the back of Lambspun. The grill cook, Eduardo, made coffee exactly the way Kelly liked it—black and extra strong. Definitely not for the fainthearted. As she neared the yarn room with the extra-large loom, Mimi rounded the corner, arms filled with skeins of colorful tempting yarns.

"Hey, Kelly, good to see you here early," Mimi beamed. "Are you working in the shop today?"

"For a while. Then I have to return home for phone calls and to catch up with my own accounting. I tend to forget that," she said with a smile.

"You're entitled, Kelly. You work *so* hard for those two clients of yours. Especially that Warner Development in Denver. You're always traveling there—"

Mimi's sentence was interrupted by the sound of the shop's front-door bell tinkling, followed by Zoe Yeager rushing into the shop, looking uncharacteristically disheveled, her face flushed.

"Oh, Mimi! Thank God, you're here!" Zoe cried, rushing up to them. "I've got to talk to you! I . . . I left Oscar!"

Mimi sucked in her breath, eyes wide as saucers. "Oh, Zoe! Thank God! *At last!*" She dumped the skeins of yarn onto a nearby table and grabbed Zoe in a big hug.

"I was so scared, Mimi! I just grabbed my purse and ran out the door. Oscar learned about my winning that trip to New York for the contest, and he was *furious*! He came home after work yelling and screaming. I've never seen him so mad. I—I didn't know what he'd do, so I ran! I spent the night at Vera's apartment."

"Why don't we take Zoe into the café," Kelly suggested, hearing the front-door bell tinkle again and the voices of entering customers.

"Yes, yes, that's a good idea. A nice cup of tea would

help," Mimi soothed. Then you can tell us what happened."
She began to guide Zoe toward the hallway. "You come, too,
Kelly. Zoe needs to be surrounded by loving people right
now. Rosa can take care of customers."

Kelly followed after Mimi and Zoe into the back of Pete's
Café. Mimi selected an empty corner table in the alcove,
away from other tables. The morning rush was still going
strong. Spotting Jennifer give them a wave, Kelly hurried
over to her friend.

"Hey, I was just coming over with coffee," Jennifer said,
pot in hand.

"Listen, Zoe's left her abusive husband, and she looks
scared. We're trying to calm her down. Mimi suggested hot
tea. Why don't you bring two cups of Mimi's Earl Grey for
them, and the usual for me."

Jennifer nodded. "I'll set a tray on the nearby table, and
you can serve it, okay? That way I won't interrupt Zoe. You
can fill me in later."

Zoe was talking in an excited voice when Kelly hurried
back to the table.

"I swear, I've never seen Oscar so mad! He's never wanted
me to travel without him. That's why I didn't tell him about
winning that New York trip. I'd planned to tell him I was
helping some bride with her wedding party. I don't know
how he found out, but he came home yesterday in a rage.
Yelling at me! He said I couldn't go without him! He
wouldn't let me. I . . . . I didn't know what to do! That look
in his eyes scared me. Then a little voice inside said, *'Get
away!'* So when he went into the kitchen to get a drink, I ran
out of the house, jumped in my car, and drove off. He was
running down the sidewalk screaming as I drove off!" She put

her face in her hands. "I don't know what to do. I—I don't want to go back to Oscar. I can't anymore! I'm too scared."

Mimi grasped both of Zoe's hands, cupping them with hers as she leaned closer. "Zoe, you did exactly the right thing. You got out of that abusive relationship. He has hit you time and again, and there's no telling what he would do in a situation like this."

"But I'm scared of what Oscar will do *now*! What if he comes after me!"

"Don't worry. We'll get you to the women's shelter here in town—"

Zoe didn't look convinced. "But what if he *finds* me!"

"He won't, Zoe," Mimi insisted. "The women's shelter has an unknown address and no one except the people who work with the women know where it's located. I don't know where it is, and I've supported the shelter for years. But I know who to contact. And she'll meet us and take you there herself."

Kelly watched Zoe stare into Mimi's face, her eyes searching, clearly frightened. "Mimi's right, Zoe. I've heard Lisa talk about the shelter. She also knows some of the counselors who work with the women there. They're good people."

"You'll be safe at the shelter, while you start planning for the future," Mimi said. "I agree, you should *not* go back to Oscar. You need to talk with a divorce lawyer. Do you know any? If not, I know of several very good divorce attorneys."

Zoe looked anxious. "No, I don't. But I've got a friend who works for a lawyer. I could ask her."

Mimi gave Zoe's hand a reassuring pat. "That's a good place to start. You can call her and get some names. Meanwhile, I can get the names and numbers of the three best divorce attorneys in town."

"I think I'll take your recommendation, Mimi. You've been in Fort Connor longer than my friend. I trust your judgment."

"Thank you, Zoe, I'll give them a call and see if anyone has time to see you today," Mimi said, giving Zoe a reassuring smile. "You need legal advice, and the sooner the better. Meanwhile, I'll also contact the woman I know who works at the women's shelter and find out the procedures for getting you into their facility and protection today."

Kelly watched Jennifer set a tray filled with mugs of tea and coffee at a nearby table, then slip quietly away. "Mimi is a great source of advice, Zoe," Kelly offered. "She'll make sure you're all right. And Jennifer has brought us some tea and coffee. You could use something soothing." She pushed back her chair and retrieved the tray, setting it down in the middle of their table. "Earl Grey for you two and Eduardo's strong brew for me."

"Oh, thank you, Kelly," Zoe said, reaching for the mug of creamed and sugared tea.

"Thank Jennifer. She makes tea exactly the way Mimi likes it. Lots of cream and sugar. I hope you like it."

Zoe took a sip, then another, and she seemed to relax a bit. "Ohhhh, it's so good."

Kelly took that as an opening to ask a question and perhaps give Zoe a chance to relax a bit more. "How wonderful that you won a trip to New York, Zoe. Did you enter a contest or something?"

Zoe nodded. "Yes, the magazine *Bridal Fashion* has a contest for designs. I entered a bridal gown design and was chosen one of the top ten winners." She took another sip of tea. "And all ten are invited to attend a fashion show in New York and also speak with a designer."

"Wow, Zoe, that's wonderful," Kelly enthused. "And it's quite a coup for your bridal business."

A small smile tugged at Zoe's mouth. "Thanks, Kelly. I was really excited when I got the phone call last week." The smile disappeared. "But now, I don't know if I'll be able to go. I mean . . . everything's turned upside down . . . I don't know."

"Don't you worry about that now, Zoe. The trip isn't until next month, October, right? Your life will settle down before then. Thanks to the women's shelter, you'll be able to stay in a safe environment." Mimi sipped her creamy tea.

"But . . . what about during the day?" Zoe said, the anxious look claiming her face again. "What if Oscar leaves work early or something and . . . and comes over to the shop? That's where my workshop is. I *have* to go to the shop."

Zoe's voice traveled up the scale again, clearly fearful. Kelly adopted Mimi's technique and reached across the table, placing her hand on Zoe's. "Don't even think about that, Zoe. There are ways to keep you safe. You could always come over here and work if you had to. I mean, there's some space in the storage room behind Mimi's office. I bet she wouldn't mind if you set up shop there for a while."

Mimi's eyes lit up. "That's an excellent idea, Kelly! I wouldn't mind at all. In fact, it would be exciting for our stitchery folks to have you there."

Zoe looked doubtful. "Are you sure, Mimi?"

"Absolutely," Mimi enthused. "We would love to have you at Lambspun. Now you see why I like having Kelly working on her accounts here. She's just a font of good ideas."

Kelly laughed softly. "Well, I'm not sure about that, but I did get another thought right now."

Mimi looked over at Zoe as she gestured toward Kelly. "You see."

"I thought it might be a good idea for Burt to have a little man-to-man talk with Oscar. To remind him that he needs to get control of his temper and suggest some of the counselors here in town that he might call. Kind of giving Oscar a friendly warning. He might also let Oscar know what charges are possible."

Zoe's eyes went wide. "Ohhhh, I don't know . . . that might make Oscar madder. He hates cops. He swears they beat him up when he was younger, and he was arrested in Old Town. He was probably drunk and started cussing them out."

"Well, Burt has experience talking to everybody," Mimi reassured her. "He'll simply have a friendly chat with him. Maybe that will help Oscar straighten out."

Kelly had her doubts, judging from what she'd heard about Oscar. "Zoe, do you want some of us to go with you to get your belongings from your house? Is Oscar working away from home during the day?"

"Yes, thank goodness," Zoe breathed. "Thank you, Kelly. I wanted to go over there today, but I was afraid he might be waiting for me. Or show up while I was there."

"I'll call Lisa and ask if she has time to come with us. Believe me, Oscar won't give you any trouble with the two of us there," Kelly said.

"That's a wonderful idea, Kelly," Mimi said, pushing away from the table. "You can call Lisa right now, then I'll call the shelter contact and the lawyers. Come with me, Zoe, I'll show you that space in the back room."

Zoe looked from Mimi to Kelly and back again. "Thank

you, Mimi, I knew you'd know where to find help. And thank you, Kelly. I . . . I can't tell you how much I appreciate your offering to come with me."

Kelly looked into Zoe's eyes and saw the traces of fear still lurking. "You're welcome, Zoe. You've got friends here. You're not alone."

Zoe turned her head, clearly trying not to tear up, as she pushed back her chair and followed Mimi down the hallway. Kelly drained her cup of coffee, then pulled her smartphone from her jeans pocket.

Kelly lifted the heavy suitcase into the trunk of her sporty car. She had to wedge it in. The trunk wasn't that large. Her backseat was already filled with shoe boxes and a garment bag with Zoe's clothes.

"Okay, I got the other suitcase in my trunk, and the backseat is full, too," Lisa said as she hurried up to Kelly. "We need to take these things to Zoe's shop now; we can't carry any more."

Noticing Zoe rush down the front porch steps, arms full of boxes, Kelly checked her watch. "Mimi said she'd be waiting at Lambspun. Maybe we should take Zoe over there first. My antennae are starting to buzz."

"You're right. Let's get Zoe away from here before that guy shows up."

Kelly glanced around the suburban neighborhood. Neat two-stories and ranch houses lined both sides of the street. Yards and flower beds, children playing in the yards. Clearly a family neighborhood.

Kelly hurried up to Zoe and took a box. "I think we need

to leave now, Zoe. Let's shove these in your passenger seat and get you away from here." Kelly opened the passenger door of Zoe's sedan and held it wide.

Zoe glanced apprehensively over both shoulders, then dumped the boxes into the front seat. "Okay, I guess I've got most everything," she said, hurrying around the car. Zoe opened the driver's door as she dug into her jacket pocket. "Where are my keys?" Her voice rose, clearly agitated.

"Here they are," Kelly said, withdrawing the keys from her own pocket. "I took them for safekeeping when we got here. Don't worry, Zoe, we'll be away from here in a minute. Now start your car and follow after Lisa. She'll head straight for Lambspun."

"Follow me, Zoe," Lisa said over her shoulder as she headed toward her own car.

"I'll be right behind you, Zoe," Kelly said and slammed Zoe's car door shut.

Zoe nodded then glanced over her shoulder and started her car.

Kelly hurried to her own car, Zoe's nervousness starting to make her jumpy. Revving the engine, she watched Zoe pull away from the curb and follow after Lisa, who'd already reached the corner. Kelly pulled into the street, but not before seeing a gray truck speeding around the corner behind them.

Something told Kelly it was Oscar, and she quickly sped up to close the distance between Zoe's car and hers. Sure enough, the gray truck pulled up right behind her. The driver started to blow his horn. Kelly closed all her windows and flipped the door locks closed. Then she grabbed her phone from the center pocket between the seats and pressed Lisa's number.

"Hey, Lisa, this has gotta be Oscar behind me, leaning on his horn. It's a good thing we're going straight to Lambspun. There are more people there. I don't know what this idiot is going to do."

"Good Lord, I can hear him all the way up here with my windows closed. I'm speeding up now. Better call Zoe. I'll call the shop and see who's there."

"Got it," Kelly said, then clicked off.

Fortunately, an intersection was straight ahead with a red light, so Kelly could search her call log for Zoe's number. Finding it, she was about to punch it in, when she felt a bump. Her car jerked forward a bit.

"Son of a . . . sailor!" Kelly said out loud. One of her dad's old Navy curses in cleaned-up form. She checked her rear-view mirror and saw the scowling visage of a dark-haired man, clearly mouthing curses of his own. "Bastard, you better not scratch my car."

Kelly turned around and glared at him. Then pressed Zoe's number. Zoe's frightened voice came on quickly.

"Kelly! That's Oscar! He's following us! What—what are we gonna do?"

"We're going to Lambspun, Zoe. There are more people there. Oscar won't be able to hurt you. We won't let him get near you. And if he tries something, we'll call the cops," Kelly promised as the light turned green again.

"Oh, my God! Oscar will jump out of his car as soon as we get to Lambspun! He'll grab me."

Kelly let Zoe's car move ahead, then nosed in behind her.

Once again, Oscar started blaring his horn as they drove along the busy street, faster now, Kelly noticed. Lisa had picked up the pace, just above the speed limit.

"I promise we won't let Oscar get to you, Zoe," Kelly said, not exactly sure how she would guarantee that. From what she could see in the rearview mirror, Oscar looked kind of beefy. Beefy and mad as hell. "Listen, we'd better hang up and drive. We'll be at Lambspun in a few minutes. Just be ready to run inside. Grab your purse and that's all, okay?"

"O-okay," Zoe said, clearly frightened by her husband's angry, threatening behavior.

Oscar's horn blared, and Kelly punched the buttons on the car's radio. Switching to a rock-and-roll station, she turned the volume up. This way she could drown out Oscar's belligerent tactics.

Finally, the little caravan neared the intersection with the Big Box discount store that dominated the shopping center across the street from the pie-shaped corner that held the Lambspun knit shop. Lisa merged into the left turn lane as she neared the corner. Zoe followed suit, and so did Kelly. Oscar brought up the rear.

At least he didn't blow his horn right away, Kelly thought, watching the left turn light change to green. Lisa sped around the corner, with Zoe right behind her. Kelly, however, stayed put at the intersection, deliberately letting the left turn arrow disappear while she stayed parked in front of Oscar's car.

True to form, Oscar leaned on his horn again, letting it blare even longer. Kelly glimpsed him in the rearview mirror, and the sight was chilling. Oscar's face was bright red and he was clearly shouting his curses this time.

"Sorry, Oscar, but this is the only way I can make sure Zoe gets inside the shop to safety before you get there," Kelly said out loud as the left turn light finally switched to green again. A good three minutes had passed, and Kelly had seen both Lisa's and Zoe's cars turn into the driveway behind Lambspun. Safe, she hoped.

Speeding around the corner, Kelly headed for the familiar driveway and quickly turned into it. She'd gotten ahead of Oscar, who probably was expecting her to delay again. Kelly nosed her car into a space between two other cars and switched off her engine. Oscar's truck rumbled into the driveway and pulled to a stop.

Thankful for her daily running and athlete's speed, Kelly sprinted down the sidewalk bordering the shop and up the front steps. Oscar jumped out of the truck but moved considerably slower, due to what Kelly surmised were at least fifty extra pounds around his belly.

Kelly stood in front of Lambspun's door, her cell phone in her hand, bracing herself for the confrontation.

"Who the hell do you think you are!" Oscar yelled as he came up the steps. "Where's Zoe? Is she in there?" He moved toward Kelly.

"Back up, Oscar," Kelly ordered. "This isn't your house. You can't—"

"I'll do what the hell I want, bitch!" Oscar swore, giving Kelly a push.

She swayed but held her ground. "Oscar, I'm gonna call the cops if you don't back off—"

Lambspun's front door opened then, and Lisa stepped beside Kelly. "Cops are on their way, Oscar. I just called them. I saw you push Kelly. That's assault."

"What the hell? I barely touched her." Oscar scowled at the two of them, the red fading from his face, Kelly noticed.

"That's not the way it looked to me," Lisa said. "We're not Zoe, so you don't scare us."

Kelly couldn't have put it better herself, and she watched Oscar struggle with his anger, sputtering obscenities.

"Better get out of here, Oscar, unless you want me to press charges when the cop comes. They'll find you at your work." Kelly stared right into his angry, bloodshot eyes.

Oscar's expression turned ugly. "*Bitch!* You can't keep a man from his wife!"

"We can if she wants to leave you," Lisa added. "Now you'd better stay away from Zoe, or we'll go to the police. We're all watching over her. She's not alone."

Oscar muttered more curses, looking from Kelly to Lisa. Then he started to back up.

At last, Kelly thought, feeling a glimmer of relief.

"*Zoe!* I know you're in there! You can't just walk away from me, *you hear?*" Oscar bellowed at the top of his voice. "You're my wife, *dammit*! You can't leave unless I say so!"

Kelly took a deep breath. "*You* can leave, Oscar. And you'd better before the police get here."

Oscar scowled at Kelly again and muttered another curse, then backed down the steps.

Kelly waited for him to climb into his truck and actually drive away before she turned to Lisa. They both exchanged a worried look.

"I'm afraid we haven't seen the last of Oscar," Lisa said.

"I'm afraid you're right."

Four

Kelly paused at one of the flower beds near the sidewalk that bordered the knitting shop and the inviting garden nestled behind. Pete's Porch Café at the back of Lambspun took advantage of Fort Connor's early springs, long summers, and extended fall seasons to expand their dining area to the part-shady, part-sunny garden. The tables were usually all taken. Few could resist enjoying breakfast or lunch or even coffee surrounded by lush greenery.

A Spanish-style stucco wall wrapped around one side, separating the entire garden area from the traffic noise along the busy avenue that bordered the property.

Walking along the flagstone path that wound through the garden, Kelly stopped to admire a particularly lovely shade of purple. Cheerful yellow sunflowers stood next to salmon-colored tea roses and spiky bright red salvia.

Everything was still blooming, thanks to the brilliant

Colorado sunshine and the forbearance of the chillier temperatures of autumn.

Glancing toward the golf course, Kelly observed the sun shining brightly, still high in the sky. That would change noticeably this month as the seasons marched inexorably toward the autumnal equinox. September twentieth or twenty-first. Kelly always noted that day because it marked the last day of summerlike daylight. Twelve hours of daylight and twelve hours of darkness. From that point on, there would be less and less daylight, as winter approached. Inescapable.

Kelly heard Carl's bark of recognition and spotted Burt walking from the driveway to the garden pathway. "Hey, I was hoping to see you," Kelly called to him as he neared. "Do you have time for coffee? I'm taking a well-deserved break after wrestling accounts through lunch."

Retired Fort Connor police detective Burt Parker gave Kelly a warm smile when he drew closer. "Perfect timing, Kelly. I wanted to update you regarding that encounter you and Lisa had last Friday."

"Oh, good, I was hoping you would," she said as they walked past wrought iron tables crowded with people lingering over lunches. They continued along the pathway as it curved around to the café entrance on the other side of the building, then up the wooden steps to the glass door. Inside, the tempting aromas of lunch floated on the air, and Kelly was glad she'd already eaten.

Most of the tables were already taken in the main part of the café except one small one beside the window. She pointed to it. "Let's grab that one," she said. "There's so much lunch noise, no one will overhear our conversation."

Burt waved at Jennifer, who was taking care of her customers. Both experienced waitresses, Jennifer and Julie managed the entire café. "Join me in a late lunch, Kelly? We can share one of Pete's wicked burgers."

Kelly pulled out a chair and dumped her briefcase at her feet. Temptation had reared its ugly head. "I'd better not, Burt. I had some leftover grilled salmon filet and a salad an hour ago. I'll watch you enjoy a wicked burger." She gave him a sly smile. "I promise I won't rat on you to Mimi."

Burt chuckled as he settled across the table from her. "Good girl. I try to stay away from those things, but sometimes they just call my name. Like now."

Jennifer approached their table, trusty waitress pad in hand. She brushed her dark auburn hair behind one ear. "Hey, you two, what can I get you for lunch?"

"Well, Kelly here is being good, but I feel like having one of Pete's wicked burgers. How about the Philly cheese with onions."

Kelly groaned, counting up the calories. "Whoa, Burt, that's not slipping off your diet, that's jumping feet first down the hill."

"I know, I know . . ." Burt gave a good-natured smile.

"Don't let her give you a hard time, Burt. Everybody needs a bad burger break every now and then," Jennifer said, grinning, brown eyes alight.

"You're gonna have to run an extra ten miles to mitigate the damage." Kelly couldn't resist teasing her fatherly mentor and advisor on all her previous forays into investigating criminal behaviors. *Sleuthing*, her friends called it.

"Leave Burt and his burger alone, Kelly," Jennifer chided. "Burt's made excellent progress on his diet. Besides, special people are allowed special privileges." She gave Burt a wink. "Coffee for both of you, I take it."

"You got it, Jennifer, and thanks for the absolution," Burt joked. "Although it won't cut any ice with Mimi."

"Don't worry, we won't tell," Kelly promised. Jennifer returned with a coffeepot and cups and poured a black stream of Eduardo's strong brew for both of them. "You and Pete are probably booked with catering jobs all this weekend, aren't you? We haven't seen much of you guys," Kelly said.

"We miss you, too." Jennifer smiled. "But we need to take advantage of all these bookings while we can. We do have that Friday and Saturday later in the month saved for the Megan-Marty nuptials."

"Fall is a busy time on college campuses," Burt said, then sipped his coffee. "Oooo, hot, hot."

"Just right, you mean," Kelly replied and took a deep drink, feeling the harsh burn and rich flavor as it went down her throat. "Ahhhh," she exclaimed in her customary fashion.

Burt shook his head, watching her. "I still don't know how you do that, Kelly. Your throat must be scalded by now."

Jennifer laughed low in her throat. "She's grown an asbestos coating over the years."

Kelly joined her friends' laughter. "Listen, I'll try to stop by tomorrow morning so we can catch up when you're on break."

"That'll work." Jennifer glanced over her shoulder. "I'd better give this order to Eduardo and get back to my other customers. Talk with you later." Off she went, coffeepot in hand.

Kelly watched her good friend move about the cozy café. Pete had started the café shortly after Mimi opened the knitting shop, and both establishments had prospered together over the years. Jennifer had been working at the café for years before she and Pete began seeing each other. Good friends for years, their relationship evolved naturally, to the delight and relief of all of Kelly's friends. Everyone had watched Pete pining away in silence for Jennifer for ages before she paid attention.

"About time," Megan had said, but Kelly knew that there was more reason below the surface. Jennifer had some thinking to do before she could commit to a steady, dependable guy like Pete.

"Did you notice how Jennifer said 'we need to take advantage' of those catering bookings?" Kelly gave Burt a knowing smile.

"Ohhhh, yeah," Burt replied. "Watching those two together warms my old dad's heart." Glancing over at Kelly, he added, "Now all we need is for another particular twosome to get back together. And all will be well."

Kelly rolled her eyes. "Not you, too, Burt. Boy, I have to listen to a steady stream from Megan. Jeeeez!"

"We all simply want to see you two happy again."

Kelly threw back her head. "Arrrrgh! I *am* happy! I'm doing work that I love, and I'm surrounded by all my friends. *Including* Steve! Do you want me to dance around or something?"

Burt took another sip of coffee, smiling his fatherly smile. For some reason, Kelly found that annoying. "No, you two are doing enough dancing around each other. I'm simply waiting for you two to stop dancing and start waltzing *together*. Like you used to." He gave her a sly wink.

Kelly understood his meaning, but decided to pretend she didn't. "Waltzing, you want, huh? I'm not sure I even know how to waltz. Steve probably doesn't, either. But for what it's worth, he and I are going out to the Jazz Bistro for dinner tonight. Who knows? Maybe the jazz group will play a waltz."

Burt grinned. "Well, it's a start. Is he still traveling a lot?"

Kelly nodded, then sipped her coffee. "He was traveling every week for four weeks. And he's got another couple of trips scheduled this month. He squeezed them in to leave time off for the nuptials, as Jennifer would say."

"That's good. He's been working way too much. But it looks like it's paying off. Kaufman's company has been a good fit for Steve."

"Yes, it has," Kelly said, leaning out of the way for Jennifer to serve Burt his wicked burger platter.

"Enjoy," Jennifer advised, placing ketchup and mustard on the table before hurrying off.

The aroma of melted cheese and yummy burger and grilled onions assailed Kelly's nostrils—and her willpower. "Whoa, Burt, that looks seriously delicious. I might steal a bite. Just to help my salmon and greens make it through the afternoon, that is."

"Dig in whenever you want, Kelly. I know I can't finish all of this. Or shouldn't, at least. So it'll go to waste." Burt forked some of the grilled onions and dropped them onto Kelly's saucer.

Since she was drinking her coffee at the time, there was ample saucer space to pile onions. "Oh, brother, they smell good." She felt herself succumbing already.

"Enjoy," Burt echoed Jennifer, then cut his burger in half and took a big bite. "Ummmm," he decreed after a moment of savoring. "This is worth the guilt."

Kelly laughed, then savored a forkful of onions. "Yummy,"

she proclaimed. "Now that we're kind of alone, why don't you update me on what you've learned about old Oscar."

Burt took another bite and lingered over it before speaking. "I was really disturbed listening to Zoe's account of what happened last Friday. And even more so after hearing Lisa's version of the confrontation you two had with Oscar outside the shop front door." He shook his head. "I just wish I had been here. I guarantee Oscar wouldn't have gone over the line like that with me. But it sounds like you and Lisa handled it really well. I'm sure hearing that Lisa called the police calmed him down real fast."

"Yeah, it did. And the fact that Lisa was threatening to press assault charges certainly got his attention."

"Tell me about that drive from Zoe's house. Neither Zoe nor Lisa could really see what he was doing, other than following you closely and blowing his horn."

"Oscar was right on my tail, blaring his horn the entire way from east Fort Connor to Lambspun. He also deliberately bumped my car at a traffic stop. I checked, and there's a little bit of paint scratched off. Bastard." Kelly scowled.

Burt's bushy gray eyebrows knitted together in his worried expression. "That's pretty threatening. You could tell Dan about it if you want, Kelly."

"Let's see how Oscar behaves. I can threaten him with it if he starts showing up around Zoe." She took another forkful of onions while Burt enjoyed his burger. "I called over here to the shop and spoke with Zoe this morning, and she said he hasn't been around at all. Thank goodness. She said she doesn't sleep very well at the shelter, though."

"She'll get used to it," Burt said. "She needs to stay there. The shelter staff will bring her to and from Lambspun every day. But we're all going to take turns with driving Zoe other places. I even went with her to a lawyer's office this morning and then went over to her shop and stayed while she was working on some woman's suit she was altering. No sign of Oscar, either. I made it a point of sitting right by the front window while I read. Just in case he drove by, hoping to find Zoe alone."

"Good man," Kelly praised as Burt returned to his burger. "Is she working here now?"

"She should be. I dropped her here over an hour ago, then I went on an errand."

Kelly spotted Mimi entering the café from the shop hallway. "Uh-oh, Burt. You're busted. Here comes Mimi."

Burt glanced over his shoulder and swallowed a burger bite. "Serves me right. Crime doesn't pay."

"Quick, push that plate over to me. I'll say it's mine," Kelly offered.

"You're a doll, Kelly, but Mimi will smell it on my breath," he said with a contrite smile.

"Ahhhh, yes, burger breath. Well, then I'll be forced to take a bite, won't I? That way it'll be me that's got Philly cheese on my face. Better wipe that left cheek." Burt laughed, but did as she advised as Mimi approached their table.

"Well, well," Mimi said, eyes twinkling. "It looks like you two are enjoying a delicious and fattening burger. What does Jennifer call them?"

"Wicked burger, and you're right. But Burt's been good. He only had a bite," Kelly lied obligingly.

Mimi's eyes danced. "Or two, or . . ."

"Or three . . ." Burt chimed in, then laughed. "Kelly's trying to cover up my sins."

"Oh, don't worry about it, Burt," Mimi said with a dismissive wave of her hand. "Listen, I wanted to tell you that Zoe has to teach a design class at the Westside Presbyterian Church tonight. She went over early because several of the women wanted private lessons, and she had to take supplies over and set up. Zoe said she'd call the shelter contact and let them know what time to show up at the church so they could drive along with her back to the shelter."

"She drove herself?" Burt asked, clearly worried.

"Yes, she did. I wanted to take her, but Connie and Rosa were gone, and I couldn't leave the shop. Zoe convinced me it would be okay because Oscar would be at work. He can't afford to lose his job. Besides, the church wasn't very far away, and there were plenty of church staffers around."

Burt's bushy eyebrows worried each other again. "I guess that's all right. I haven't seen a sign of a gray truck these past few days, so I think he's staying away." Burt smiled. "Or maybe having my old partner Dan drive by Oscar's house with one of the cruisers the other night might have helped cool him down."

Mimi's eyes went wide. "Oh, thank you, Burt. And thank you, Dan."

"Quick thinking," Kelly said, unable to resist taking a wicked bite of the Philly cheese and meat. It was in her hand after all.

"I simply asked him if he could drive by Oscar's house when he had a chance, and he saw a gray truck outside. Thanks to Kelly, we've got the license plate number. Dan drove by on his way home, of course," Burt said innocently.

"Well, good job, Kelly, and good job, Burt." Mimi beamed. "You two deserve that burger after all.

Kelly laughed with her friends, then took another wicked bite.

Kelly relaxed into the comfy armchair in the Lambspun front room, beside the windows and tiled fireplace. The main knitting room was empty, but Kelly wanted to be in the midst of the busy late afternoon shop flow. A customer was at the front counter, where Mimi was ringing up her purchases. Completing another row in her bridesmaid shawl, Kelly started another.

The customer browsed near the counter, examining buttons and needles. Kelly noticed a couple of women browsing in the adjoining room. One of them she'd seen before. "Who's that tall, thin woman with gray hair looking at the cones of thread?" she asked Mimi.

Mimi looked up. "Oh, that's Vera Wilcott, Zoe's sister. She helps Zoe in her sewing business. She works most days at a copy shop on College Avenue."

The name rang a bell inside Kelly's head. That was the woman Zoe was talking to on the phone. Kelly recalled the angry phone conversation she'd overheard last week. Remembered the ugly, demanding tone in Zoe's voice. So Vera was Zoe's sister. Interesting. Evidently sewing ran in Zoe's family.

"I thought I'd seen her here before. That makes sense if she's a seamstress, too."

Mimi lowered her voice. "Yes, Vera is an excellent seamstress. Vera has worked full-time for Zoe in addition to her regular copy shop job. She's definitely helped grow that business over the years." Mimi broke into a bright smile. "Well, hello, Vera. Are you gathering supplies for the latest project?"

Vera walked toward the counter and handed Mimi a cone of thread. "I need about four yards of this one, Mimi." Noticing Kelly, she backed up a little. "Oh, are you helping someone, Mimi? I didn't mean to interrupt."

"No, no, Kelly's simply taking a break from her accounting. She has her home office across the driveway," Mimi said as she took the cone of lavender thread.

"Oh, yes, I remember hearing about you. We haven't had a chance to meet because I don't get in here that often. I work at Quik Copy Shop during most days," Vera said, accompanying her words with a little nod.

"Nice to meet you, Vera." Kelly gave her a bright smile. "Mimi says you're a seamstress, too, and you help out Zoe a lot in her shop."

Vera's face flushed with obvious pleasure at the recognition. "Yes, yes, I do. I sew nights and weekends. It's a lot of hours, but I need the money. The copy shop doesn't pay much."

"Well, that sounds like an ideal situation," Kelly went on. "Did you and Zoe grow up sewing? Sounds like it."

Vera shrugged. "Yes. Mama taught me. I was the older one, so I taught Zoe. We've been sewing for a lifetime, it seems."

Vera appeared to be in her sixties, Kelly guessed. Her hair was mostly gray, and her face was lined. It was hard to tell ages. Some women stayed younger-looking longer. Others aged quickly.

"Here you go, Vera," Mimi said, placing the measured thread into a plastic bag. "I'll put this on Zoe's account."

Vera took the package from Mimi. "Thank you, Mimi. I'd love to sit and chat with both of you," she said, glancing to Kelly, then back to Mimi, "but I'm right in the middle of altering a formal gown. Some woman is going to a charity dance in Denver next week. I worked straight through lunch so I could leave the copy shop early." She stuffed the bag into her voluminous fiber purse.

"Take care, Vera. We'll have coffee in the café next time," Mimi promised. "My treat. In fact, why don't you buy a coffee on your way out? Tell Pete to put it on my account. You look like you could use the caffeine."

Vera flushed and smiled. "Why, thank you, Mimi. That's sweet of you."

"You can take my shortcut to the back of the café," Mimi said, pointing behind her to the passageway hiding beside a file cabinet.

"I'll look forward to seeing you again when I have more time," Vera said as she scooted around the corner.

"Sounds like a busy woman," Kelly observed when Vera had disappeared.

"She certainly is. I don't know how she works full-time at the copy shop, then sews at night for Zoe."

The front-door bell tinkled, and a few seconds later, a pretty middle-aged woman rushed into the front room.

Mimi looked up and smiled warmly. "Well, hello, Leann, it's so good to see—"

"Mimi! I just saw a copy of *Bridal Fashions*," Leann cried as she ran up to the counter. "Zoe was one of the winners in the wedding gown category . . . with *my gown*!"

Mimi drew back, clearly shocked. "*No!* That can't be. Zoe wouldn't steal one of your designs!"

"Yes, she *did*! I've been making that design for bridal clients for years. She must have stolen it when she was working for me six years ago. Dammit! It was bad enough when she copied one of my bridesmaid gowns. I didn't even know

52

about it until I saw someone wearing a dress exactly like the one I designed."

Mimi stared at Leann, obviously perturbed by her accusations. "Leann, I know you've lost some of your dressmaking clients, but to accuse Zoe of stealing . . ."

Kelly observed the scene. Leann was slender and looked to be in her late forties or mid-fifties with short, curly brown hair. She wore a short-sleeve sweater over capri pants, which accented her good figure. She and Mimi obviously were friends. But Kelly didn't know what to make of Leann's accusations. Stealing a style? Could someone even do that?

"But it's true!" Leann said in an angry voice. "Here, I'll show you." She reached inside her purse and withdrew a magazine. The cover showed a beautiful bride staring demurely at a bouquet of flowers.

Leann began paging through the magazine. Mimi and Kelly exchanged a concerned look. "Why don't I get us a cup of tea, Leann? Would you like that?"

"*No!*" Leann exclaimed. "I want to show you this gown. Here it is." She spread the magazine open on the nearby counter. "There it is. The only difference is she's got satin for the bodice. I always used lace by itself. It's a much more delicate look."

"Kelly, why don't you come over and look at this, too. We could use another set of eyes." Mimi beckoned anxiously to Kelly. "Kelly is an accountant, so she has a fine eye for detail."

Kelly had to squelch her smile at Mimi's exaggeration. A fine eye for numbers detail did not translate into a fine eye for fashion design. Nevertheless, she obliged and approached the counter.

"Hi, Leann, I'm Kelly," she said, offering her hand, hoping to calm Leann a bit.

Leann glanced into Kelly's eyes for a second, then grasped her hand for a quick shake. "Hello, Kelly. You take a look at these two gowns and tell me. They're identical. Here's my gown." Leann withdrew a folded page printout of a photo. A bride or model wearing a lacy wedding gown.

Mimi stared at the magazine, then the photo, and so did Kelly. Over and over again. Several times. Mimi's worried expression increased. "Oh, my," was all Mimi said, but Kelly recognized her worried tone.

Kelly stared at the two gowns again. She had to admit they did have the same design. The only difference was the bodice on Leann's was lacy, and the bodice on Zoe's was solid fabric. Kelly tried to find some difference between the two, but it wasn't there. She had to admit that Leann had a good point. Zoe's gown was an exact replica of Leann's.

"You see what I mean!" Leann said again, voice rising. "That's *my* design! She stole it from *me*, and now she's won a bridal gown contest with it! It's not fair! *I* should be the one going to New York! It should be *me!*"

"There, now, Leann," Mimi soothed, patting Leann on the arm. "Yes, it does look like your design, but . . . but maybe Zoe came up with the same idea."

"No, she *didn't*! She stole that pattern from me when she was helping me sew for some of my customers years ago. She must have made a copy of it one night when she was working late and I wasn't there. She and Vera both worked for me when they first came to town and started dressmaking. And she stole some of my customers, too! I know she did."

That statement bothered Kelly, because it would put Zoe

in the vicinity where she could copy Leann's patterns as well as customer records. She didn't know what to say. In the business world, stealing was a little more cut and dried. Embezzlement, draining bank accounts.

"They do look alike, Leann," Kelly said, deciding to take another approach to calm her down. "But there is really no way for you to prove that Zoe stole your design."

Leann's face flushed with obvious anger and frustration as she scowled. "That's what's so unfair. Everyone who looks at the two gowns sees that they're the same. Maybe I should send a photo of my gown to the magazine. They deserve to know they awarded a *cheater*!" She bit off the words.

"Why don't you do that, Leann?" Mimi offered, patting her hand again. "That sounds like a good idea. Even if the magazine doesn't change the winners, you will at least get some recognition for your design."

Leann pressed her lips together, clearly trying to keep her emotions in check. "You bet I will," she said, refolding the photo and shoving it inside the magazine as she closed it. "Meanwhile, I'm going to make sure I tell everybody what Zoe did. She entered *my* design in that contest. I'm telling all my customers, and I've heard she's teaching a class tonight. I think I'll go over there and warn those students to keep their ideas to themselves around Zoe."

With that, Leann turned and rushed from the shop as fast as she'd come in. Kelly looked over at Mimi and saw her friend's face crease with worry.

"Oh, no. I don't think that's a good idea, Kelly," Mimi said.

"I agree, Mimi." Kelly nodded her head. "That is definitely a bad idea."

Five

"**Hey,** perfect timing," Lisa's voice called across the driveway separating the Lambspun shop from Kelly's cottage. Kelly was walking down the concrete walkway that led from her front steps past the planters filled with shade-loving purple and white violas mixed with lavender impatiens.

"Are you coming or going?" Kelly asked as she crossed the driveway. "I'm substituting a knitting break for a coffee break between client accounts. Tomorrow I have to be in Denver all day."

"I finished with my physical therapy clients for the day and had some free time, so I headed here," Lisa said, standing on the sidewalk leading to Lambspun's front door. "Also I'm curious how your date with Steve went last night."

Kelly couldn't keep from smiling. Her friends were so funny as they tried to keep their curiosity in check these past few months. Every time she and Steve had lunch or dinner together, one of her friends would call and ask "how it went." Like clockwork.

Jennifer, Megan, and Lisa took turns checking on what Kelly referred to as the "Kelly-Steve Project." She had no doubt that after they received an update from her, they would share it with the others. And whenever Kelly joined the gang for a Friday night get-together, there were more questions. Subtly phrased, of course. Everyone was cautious so as not to appear to be pushing. Everyone except Megan, that is. Megan left no doubt what her agenda was: getting Kelly and Steve back together as a couple. She was a more dramatic version of Burt. Kelly simply smiled through all attempts.

"We're going tonight. Steve had to reschedule his flight due to a late meeting," Kelly said as they headed toward the front steps.

"Jazz Bistro, right?" Lisa asked.

"That's right. I called and rescheduled us—"

Just then, Mimi rushed out the front door, her face ashen. "Kelly! Lisa! Come inside, quickly! There's someone here from the women's shelter. Zoe is *dead*! She was found in her car in the church parking lot last night."

Kelly halted on the steps, held in place by the shocking news. "*What?*"

Lisa gasped beside her. "What happened? Did that brute Oscar get to her?"

Mimi raised both hands in a helpless gesture. "I don't know! The woman doesn't know, either. It's so awful! She got here a few minutes ago to tell me because the shelter had my name as the place where Zoe was working during the day. Quick, come inside." Mimi beckoned, then hurried through the door again.

Kelly and Lisa rushed inside the knitting shop after Mimi. Customers were still browsing the yarn bins and tables, wandering about the inviting rooms. Any other time Kelly would be tempted to pay attention to the sensuous fibers that spilled from the baskets and bins along the wall. But not now. She followed after Mimi, who was weaving a path through the central yarn room, then around the corner to the hallway which led to Pete's Café. The café would be empty of customers and staff this late in the afternoon. A perfect place for a private conversation.

Mimi approached a table at the back of the café, where a tall, slender woman stood in tee shirt, jeans, and sneakers. She looked to be in her forties.

"I'm sorry to keep you waiting, but I wanted to bring in two of Zoe's friends to hear all this. They helped Zoe move out of her house and escorted her safely here to the shop. She could never have gotten away from Oscar without them!"

The woman gave Kelly and Lisa a wan smile. "That was good of you two. I'm Rhonda, and I help out at the shelter in the late evenings."

Both Kelly and Lisa extended their hands to the woman and introduced themselves.

"How did this happen, Rhonda?" Kelly asked. "Zoe was supposed to be safe at the church teaching a class that night."

"Was it Oscar?" Lisa demanded. "Did he kill her? That *bastard*!"

Rhonda shook her head. "We don't know what happened.

I was the one who was supposed to pick up Zoe after her class last night. But when I arrived at the church, I saw the parking lot filled with police cars and an ambulance. I'd never met Zoe, but I spotted a woman inside her car, so I drove into the lot. I thought she might be sick or something."

Rhonda paused and took a deep breath. "A police officer came up and told me they were blocking access to the parking lot, and I would have to leave. I explained to him that I was there to pick up Zoe Yeager and take her to the women's shelter. He looked kind of surprised, then told me to wait right there. Then he went to talk to another man, not in uniform, and that man came over to see me."

Kelly pictured the imposing Detective Morrison. She and Lieutenant Morrison had squared off with each other several times over the years. Morrison had frowned at Kelly's sleuthing at first. "Was he tall with bushy gray eyebrows?"

Rhonda looked surprised. "Why, yes . . . yes, he was. Do you know him?"

"That's the chief homicide detective, Lieutenant Morrison, and he's very thorough. Tell me, what did he ask you, Rhonda?"

"He wanted to know exactly who I was and wrote down my name and what hours I worked for the women's shelter every week. He also wanted to know why Zoe was staying at the shelter."

"Because of that brute of a husband, Oscar!" Mimi blurted out. "He chased the three of them all the way from Zoe's house here to the shop when she was bringing her things. He was following Kelly's car, blaring his horn. He . . . he even threatened Kelly! She stood in front of the door after Zoe had escaped inside!"

Rhonda looked down. "I asked the detective if Zoe was sick or something, and that's when he told me she was dead."

"What else did Detective Morrison ask you, Rhonda?" Kelly prodded.

"He wanted to know how long Zoe had been at the shelter, and if she had any children or other family members. I told him I thought she had a sister, but I didn't have any phone numbers with me. I gave him the shelter contact phone so they could fill him in on the rest of the details."

"Well, if Zoe had her purse with her, the police would know her name and address. And her car registration would probably be in the glove compartment," Lisa said.

"Oscar's name would also be on that car registration, I hope," Kelly added.

Mimi shook her head. "Poor Zoe. To be killed like that just when she was starting over."

"We don't know if Zoe was killed or if she killed herself," Rhonda said quietly.

Mimi drew back, aghast. "Zoe would never do that! She was starting a whole new life! Free from that brutish Oscar. She'd even gone to talk to a divorce attorney. Burt took her over the other day."

Rhonda gave another wan smile. "I know how you feel. But I have seen it happen. Some women are so frightened by the idea of being alone on their own, they panic. Even with all the help they receive at the shelter, some women close down. If there are no children or other family members who need them, well . . . a few will fall into despair and take their own lives." She shook her head. "It's tragic, but we can help most of the women who come to us. That's what keeps us going." Mimi reached out and squeezed her arm. "Bless you,

Rhonda. All of you at the shelter are saving women's lives. I'm sure you know that."

This time a smile brightened Rhonda's face. "Thank you, Mimi. We do our part." Glancing to her watch, she began to back away. "Listen, I have to get back to the shelter. We've been a little shorthanded today, and they need my help."

"Here, we'll show you out," Kelly offered. "The café doors are already locked, so we have to leave through the shop entrance." She proceeded to lead the foursome from their quiet corner down the hallway into the shop, which was empty now of customers. Rosa was straightening the knitting table in the main room, and Connie had started vacuuming the carpet in the front.

Mimi hurried over to the front door, opening it for Rhonda. "Thank you so much for coming over and telling us. We appreciate it."

"You're more than welcome. Nice to meet all of you," Rhonda said, giving them a good-bye wave before she hurried out the door.

"Suicide my ass," Lisa said, hands on hips.

"Excuse me, girls, but I need to help Connie and Rosa close up," Mimi said, hurrying to the front of the shop.

"I agree, Lisa," Kelly said as they walked out onto the covered front porch of the shop.

"When I stopped in here yesterday morning, Zoe didn't look depressed at all. She was worried about her customers and getting her sewing done, but when I asked her about the trip, she acted excited and happy." Lisa shook her head again. "Man, I wish Burt was here so he could find out details from the cops."

"Yeah, I wondered where he was. Surely Mimi would have

told him. I mean . . . I had lunch with him yesterday and he had been hovering over Zoe like a mother hen all morning. Taking her to the lawyer, then to her shop—"

Kelly stopped her sentence when she spotted Burt's car drive around the corner of the driveway and pull into a parking place.

"Speak of the devil," Lisa joked. "Or in Burt's case, an angel."

"You got that right." Kelly smiled, anxious to begin her interrogation of Burt. Maybe he'd already contacted his old partner in the Fort Connor Police Department and learned something about Zoe's death.

Watching Burt get out of the driver's seat, Kelly expected to see him approach the sidewalk. Instead, Burt walked to the other side of his car and opened the passenger door. *Who's that with him?* Kelly wondered at first. Then she got a look at the woman exiting the car. *Vera.* Burt placed his arm around Vera's shoulders as they approached on the sidewalk.

"Who's that woman?" Lisa asked quietly.

"That's Zoe's older sister, Vera. She's gotta be taking this hard. Mimi said she's a spinster who's only had Zoe and Oscar for family all these years. She helps Zoe with the seamstress work, too."

"Hey, that's nice of you girls to welcome us," Burt said as he helped Vera up the steps. She walked very slowly next to Burt.

Kelly noticed the tears streaking Vera's thin pale face. "Vera, I'm so very sorry to hear about Zoe," she said, reaching out and squeezing Vera's arm through her light sweater.

Kelly didn't feel much meat covering the bone. A skinny little arm.

"I am, too, Vera," Lisa said, stepping up and touching Vera's hand. "I think I remember seeing you at Zoe's workshop one night while she was making my bridesmaid dress last month."

Vera looked up, and blinked her wet blue eyes. A spark of recognition seemed to appear. "Oh, yes, Lisa. Blonde. Yours was daisy yellow."

Lisa smiled brightly. "Yes, that's mine."

"I made that one," Vera said softly. Glancing to Kelly, she added, "Zoe made yours." Vera's lower lip began to tremble.

"Come on in, Vera. Mimi can make you a nice cup of tea," Burt said, shepherding Vera through the front door into the shop.

Kelly and Lisa followed after them, pausing in the foyer. Mimi noticed their entrance and raced over to Vera.

"Vera, dear, my heart aches for you." Mimi grabbed Vera in a big motherly hug, wrapping both arms around Vera's thin frame. Vera responded quickly and buried her face in Mimi's shoulder. "You're coming home with Burt and me tonight. We're having dinner, and you'll stay the night. We don't want you alone."

Kelly felt like she and Lisa were unnecessary presences now. Mother Mimi and fatherly Burt would take good care of Vera. She began to edge away. But first . . .

"Burt, do you have a minute?" she whispered as she pushed the front door open and beckoned Burt and Lisa outside.

"You don't have to ask, Kelly. Yes, I've already spoken with my old partner Dan this afternoon," Burt said. "The shelter called Mimi a couple of hours ago when I was out doing errands. She called me immediately, right after the woman arrived and told her what happened." He wagged his head, a sorrowful expression creasing his features. "It's so tragic. Zoe was trying to start over. And now, she won't get the chance."

"How was she killed?" Kelly probed.

"Dan said she was shot."

"Was it Oscar?" Lisa demanded. "It had to be! Who else would kill Zoe?"

"They don't know," Burt replied. "They're just beginning the investigation. But they did find the gun inside a Dumpster on the other side of the church parking lot."

"Ha!" Lisa crowed triumphantly. "I *knew* it wasn't suicide."

"That was a pretty stupid place to dispose of the gun," Kelly added. "Obviously the killer wasn't thinking."

"Maybe the killer was scared, and simply wanted to get rid of the gun," Burt observed sagely.

"Well, it won't take police long to figure this one out. Kelly and I already met Oscar. And I'd say he meets the 'stupid and not thinking' category to a tee," Lisa proclaimed at her most judgmental.

Burt simply smiled. Kelly, however, couldn't resist repeating what he'd said earlier. "Well, the police have only started their investigation, Lisa. We'll have to wait and see what they find."

"I couldn't have said it better," Burt replied.

Kelly swirled the crisp sauvignon blanc in her glass and took a sip. Delicious. Not too tart. Just right. Glancing across the lounge of the Jazz Bistro, Kelly watched other couples enjoying drinks and food and each other. Laughing together.

From the cozy curved booth where she and Steve sat, Kelly spotted the jazz pianist, Mark, who was playing a jazzed version of a familiar standard. He looked up and caught her eye, gave her a smile, then winked. Kelly smiled back and lifted her glass in recognition.

The effusive café owner and his wife looked ecstatic to see Steve and Kelly walk in together. Kelly had come to the café alone a couple of times and had been asked no questions. It was a great spot to sit and relax at the curved polished wood bar, enjoy a yummy appetizer, maybe a steak, a glass of wine, and listen to great music. A trio always played, sometimes a foursome. Jazz singers joined them frequently, adding their own interpretations.

Kelly was glad she and Steve had gone out tonight. After today's tragic news, she didn't feel like being home alone. Here, she was surrounded by warmth, music, great food and wine, made even better by sharing with a close friend. A very close friend.

Steve set down his wineglass and leaned over the table toward Kelly. "I'm sorry you and the others lost your friend, Kelly. Zoe sounded like a wonderful person." He placed his hand over hers.

His hand felt warm and brought back memories. Good memories. "Thanks. Zoe wasn't a close friend by any means. She was more of an acquaintance. Mimi had known her for several years, but the rest of us only met her when she was making our bridesmaid dresses. Each of us went to her shop for fittings several times." She took a sip of wine. "But I admired her creativity and professionalism. She'd built up her business over several years. That takes a lot of effort."

Steve gave her a rueful smile. "Yeah, it does. I say that calls for a toast. To small business owners, past and present."

Kelly joined his toast as another thought came forward. Leann's accusations that Zoe stole her designs. Maybe Zoe didn't build her business entirely on her own.

Letting that thought slide away, Kelly switched subjects slightly. "You're getting back there, Steve. Working with Sam Kaufman, you're getting back into the game." She gave him a warm smile. "The game you love."

Steve returned her smile. "Yeah, I'm back in the game at last. Thanks to Sam." He took another sip of his wine. "And maybe, just maybe, this new deal with that custom home will help me bring something to the firm Sam has never had before."

"You bet. You're an architect, Sam's not. You can turn all those design innovations that guy wants into reality."

"Well, I hope so. I got a lot of new ideas from that last conference in Oregon."

"I'm sure you did. But you've been incorporating creative touches into all the homes you've built, Steve. I watched you do it."

Steve's gaze warmed even more, and he took her hand in both of his. "This is what I missed the most, Kelly. Those first six months we were apart. Not being able to be with you. Talk with you. Hell, just having you in the same room makes me feel good."

Kelly met his warm gaze and placed her other hand on top of his. "I know. I felt the same way, Steve. I missed talking with you about . . . well, about everything. I missed *being* with you."

Kelly glimpsed a waiter's movement at the corner of her eye. Steve released her hand as he moved out of the server's way.

"Medium rare," the young man proudly announced as he placed the delectable-looking filet mignon before Kelly.

Leaning back into the curved seat, Kelly met Steve's amused gaze as the young man placed another filet in front of Steve.

"We're going to have to work on your timing, friend," Steve said with a smile, glancing at the server.

Six

"All right, Carl, you can go out," Kelly said to her dog as she slid the glass patio door open. "Squirrels are in the trees, just waiting to torment you." The big black Rottweiler charged through the doorway and dashed across the cottage backyard, barking his arrival lest any squirrel be unaware.

"They already know you're there, Carl. They have scouts posted on the upper tree limbs." She pointed to the huge cottonwood shading the backyard, then leaned against the doorjamb to watch Carl begin his surveillance while she finished her first mug of coffee. Carl sniffed every inch of ground that bordered the fence in case renegade squirrels had dared trespass while he was inside having his kibbles breakfast.

"What do you smell, Carl? A cat maybe?" Carl's head jerked up at the "magic word." *Cat*. Oh, yes. Devoutly to be wished. Kelly laughed. "Give it up, Carl. No self-respecting cat would dare come into this yard while you're here." Carl stared at her again as if protesting: *Say it isn't so!*

Kelly had no doubt that cats as well as other furry animals trespassed in her yard during the night. Carl would suddenly bark in the middle of the night as if he sensed their paws treading his turf. After all, the cottage backed up onto a city golf course. Green grass stretched all the way from the back of the fence to the edge of Fort Connor's Old Town. The Cache La Poudre River ran along the southern edge of the greens. So all manner of wildlife were roaming about at night and the early morn hours. Not only cats, but raccoons, foxes, even deer were drawn by the water and the abundance of nearby greenery. Carl did not lack for tempting smells to discover in his early morning investigations.

Kelly's phone jangled. She'd changed the ring tone to a more melodious tune after her phone went off in the middle of a Warner Development meeting.

Burt's name and number flashed on the screen. "Hey, Burt, what's up?" she asked as she answered.

"I'm off doing errands, Kelly. Getting an early start. So I thought I'd let you know what I learned from Dan yesterday evening. He said he and a uniformed officer went to Oscar's house late the night of Zoe's murder to let him know that his wife was dead. Oscar's truck was in the driveway, so they pounded on the door until a sleepy Oscar finally opened it. He reeked of liquor, according to Dan."

"Oh, brother." Kelly could almost picture belligerent Oscar out on a drunk.

"Well, they told him they found Zoe dead in her car earlier that night and asked him where he'd been during those hours."

"I can't wait to hear what he said."

"According to Dan, Oscar didn't even believe them at first. He said they were lying. So Dan described her, and Oscar just stared at them and said they were wrong. It couldn't be Zoe. Then Dan showed him Zoe's wallet and purse, and Oscar started to cry."

"Oh, please." Kelly had trouble believing abusive Oscar would shed tears for his wife.

Burt chuckled at her comment. "Dan asked Oscar again where he'd been that night, and Oscar told them he'd been at the Stop On Inn bar down East Mulberry. Of course, Dan asked how long he was there and where did he go after that, you know, standard questions. Oscar couldn't exactly remember when he'd left, but he said he came straight home."

Kelly snorted in disgust. "I'm sure he did, after he'd gone to that church parking lot and shot Zoe."

"Judge and jury, eh, Kelly?" Burt said, laughing now. "No mercy, right?"

"Not for Oscar. I've been up close and personal with that scumbag. With his track record of abusing Zoe, I'd say he's the number one suspect." Kelly drained her coffee mug, then grabbed her knitting bag and walked out of the cottage.

"Well, he's certainly right up there," Burt agreed. "But there weren't any fingerprints on the gun, so whoever used it either wiped it clean or used gloves. So it's not cut and dried. We all know how easy it is to buy a gun. Who knows? Oscar may have an alibi. Maybe he was at the bar while Zoe was shot. Dan said he'd let me know once they'd interviewed employees at the bar and also some of Oscar's neighbors and coworkers. They need to get a clearer picture."

Kelly headed across the driveway, early morning sunshine bright in her face. She should have brought her sunglasses. "Good. You'll keep me updated, I trust."

"Don't I always?" Burt teased.

She walked down the flagstone pathway into the garden behind the shop. Café tables were already filled with customers enjoying Pete's and Eduardo's hearty breakfast specials. "By the way, exactly where was Zoe shot? In the chest? In the head?"

"In the head. Right in the middle of her forehead. She died quickly, I'm sure." Burt's voice had lost its jovial tone.

"At least she didn't suffer," Kelly said as she walked up the steps to the café's back door.

"Gotta go, Kelly. Talk to you later."

"Later, Burt." Kelly clicked off her phone as she pulled open the door. Stepping into the back of the café, Kelly was close to the prep area and waved to Jennifer, who was loading plates onto a tray.

"Hey, great timing. I was about to take a mini break," Jennifer said as she passed Kelly. "Why don't you grab one of those empty tables in the alcove. I won't have time to go into the shop."

"Will do," Kelly promised and wove her way through the front section of the café, which was filled with breakfast diners. The enticing scent of bacon and eggs and pancakes and Pete's homemade sausage floated on the air, teasing Kelly's nostrils and worst of all—that susceptible breakfast lobe of her brain.

Kelly rounded the corner and waved to Julie, one of the other waitresses, and the new college girl who was trying out as hostess that week. Giving Eduardo the grill cook a big grin, Kelly deliberately didn't look at the plates of breakfast omelets and other temptations lined up on the counter for the waitresses.

Finding the alcove less crowded, Kelly settled at a smaller table. She'd barely sat down when Julie walked up, coffeepot in hand. "I could tell your mug was empty. I figured I'd better bring a refill before you went into lack-of-caffeine shock."

"Thanks, Julie. That would be too scary." Kelly smiled and held out her mug.

Julie poured a black ribbon of coffee into Kelly's open mug. "Yeah, I don't think we want to go there. Are you having any breakfast?"

Kelly sniffed the black nectar. "No, simply catching up with Jen on her mini break. I'll be out of this table and into the shop before you know it."

"Don't rush. It's starting to slow down. See ya." Julie hurried off. Waitresses were always hurrying, it seemed to Kelly. Demanding hungry customers made them that way.

Kelly sniffed the black nectar again, then took a sip and felt that harsh burn. Delicious as always. She caught Eduardo's eye and lifted her mug in salute. Eduardo grinned, flashing his gold front tooth, just as Jennifer came racing around the corner into the alcove.

She plopped into a chair across the table. "Hey, how're you doing? I heard all about the confrontation with Zoe's husband from Lisa and Mimi. And then Zoe winds up dead!" Jennifer's eyes grew huge. "That is *awful*! Zoe was so nice and so talented. I cannot believe someone would kill her."

"My money's on Oscar," Kelly said, then drank deeply.

Jennifer sipped from a takeout cup. "I've heard a lot about him from Mimi. None of it good. He sounds like a classic abuser."

Kelly nodded. "He sure fits the profile, listening to Mimi. And now that I've been face-to-face with him, I can attest that he's physically aggressive. And he was clearly furious Zoe moved out of the house. Enraged even. That's what I saw in his eyes when he was in my face. *Rage.*"

Jennifer closed her eyes and shivered. "Tragic, simply tragic. To think he would wait for Zoe to come out of a class, then shoot her. Do the cops consider Oscar a suspect? Has Burt found out anything? I know he'd tell you if he did."

Kelly took another sip. "It seems old Oscar may not have an alibi. Police went to his house late that night to tell him about Zoe. They found him asleep, in a drunken stupor. Apparently, Oscar said he was at a bar that night, but he couldn't remember when he left to go home."

Jennifer grimaced. "Oooo, drunken stupor, not good. And not remembering, even worse. Of course, the bar will do that." She gave an experienced nod.

"As I said, my money's on Oscar." Kelly took another deep drink. "But there were no prints on the gun, so there will be a full investigation."

"Well, surely someone at the bar that night was sober enough to recall when Oscar was there. And I'll bet the bartender will remember. Sounds like Oscar is a regular, so the bartender probably knows his habits better than Oscar himself." Jennifer glanced at her watch. "Darn, I wish I could hear more, but we're one waitress short on this morning shift and our hostess is a newbie."

"Where are you and Pete catering this weekend?"

"Football luncheon on Saturday, then a family reunion on Sunday." Jennifer started to turn away, but stopped. "By the way, didn't you say you and Steve were going out this week? Where'd you go, Denver?"

"Nope, we had dinner at the Jazz Bistro. Good food, good wines, and good jazz." Kelly smiled, then gave Jennifer a wink.

Jennifer laughed softly, her eyes lighting up. "Hey, your old favorite. I'm sure you two had a great time. Steve really needs a break from all that traveling."

"It was nice." Kelly smiled. "*Really* nice."

"Well, you two deserve it. Are you working in Denver this week?"

"Yeah, Saturday. Warner is bringing in several consultants for an apartment complex he's planning, and that was the only time everyone could meet together."

"Don Warner is always planning something. Sounds interesting. Take care and stop in when you have time again and say hello." Jennifer gave a wave and hurried back to the front of the café.

Kelly slipped her knitting bag over her shoulder and left the table, walking toward the back hallway that led to Lambspun. Entering the loom room, Kelly glanced at the neatly stacked triangular-shaped cones of yarn and thread on the floor-to-ceiling shelves lining two walls. Every color and texture of threads, fibers, and trims imaginable.

Vera hurried into the room from the foyer, carrying what looked like two of the beribboned bridesmaids' headbands. She headed toward the front, where customers lined up at the counter and register.

"How are you doing, Vera?" Kelly called out as the older woman rushed past.

Vera literally jumped, clearly startled, and turned to Kelly. "Oh, Kelly, I didn't see you."

"Sorry I came up behind you like that. Didn't mean to scare you, Vera. I simply wanted to see how you were doing." Kelly gave her a warm smile.

"I'm . . . I'm doing better, Kelly. Thank you for asking," Vera replied. "Having to pick up where Zoe left off with all the customers keeps me from thinking too much." Her thin face pinched. "It's better if I don't think. That's when I get angry."

Kelly reached out and squeezed Vera's arm. Vera didn't have to explain whom she was angry at. Kelly could fill in the unspoken name. *Oscar.* "I agree, Vera. It'll be better for you if you concentrate on picking up where Zoe left off. Zoe wouldn't want the customers to be forgotten."

"Vera! I'm so glad you stopped in," Mimi said as she walked into the room. "Do you have time for a cup of tea?"

"I wish I did, Mimi, but I don't have the time today." The anxious look reclaimed Vera's face. "I had to take today off from my regular job to try and finish some of the dresses Zoe was making for customers. And today won't be enough time to catch up. There are two suits halfway finished. I don't know if the copy shop will let me take another day off."

"Oh, my." Mimi's kind face furrowed with concern. "It sounds like you need help, Vera. You cannot possibly finish all of Zoe's customers plus yours *and* work your full-time job at the same time."

"I thought I might ask Leann to help me," Vera ventured,

"but I wasn't sure how she would take it. She and Zoe didn't get along too well." Vera glanced over her shoulder toward the front of the shop and the customers who formed a line in front of the registers. Rosa was at the counter.

Mimi reached over and gave Vera's arm a motherly pat. "I think Leann would appreciate the extra business, Vera. And we both know what an accomplished seamstress she is."

"I agree," Kelly added. "I bet Leann would be grateful you thought of her."

Vera's thin face relaxed a little, losing the pinched expression, Kelly noticed. "You may be right. I hadn't really thought of it that way. I'd tried to help her over the years when I could by sewing a few things for her clients without telling Zoe. I didn't want to cause any more problems between the two of them."

"Don't you worry about that," Mimi reassured her, escorting Vera toward the central yarn room.

"Oh, let me give you these two bridesmaid headbands. That's what I came in for." Vera offered them to Mimi. "I don't want them to get lost in all the upheaval in the workshop. The yellow one is for Lisa Gerrard, and the green one is for Jennifer Stroud. They've already paid. I checked."

"Thank you, Vera, I'll hold them here safely until the girls can pick them up," she said, accepting the delicate headbands. "Would you like me to have Jennifer bring you a cup of tea to carry with you?"

"No, no, thank you, Mimi," Vera said. A quick smile formed, then was gone. Kelly was surprised at how much the smile softened Vera's face. "I must hurry back to the workshop now and try to finish one of the suits if I can."

"Promise me you'll call Leann on the way over, all right?" Mimi directed when Vera headed toward the foyer.

"I plan to, thank you, Mimi," Vera called over her shoulder. She gave a fluttery little wave, then was out the door.

"Goodness, Vera's got a lot on her plate. I don't see how she can juggle all that work by herself," Kelly said as she walked into the main room and dropped her knitting bag on the table. "I wonder if Leann will decide to help."

Mimi followed after her. "I imagine Leann will leap at the chance to increase her business. She's been struggling these last few years, ever since Zoe started her own specialty designs shop."

"I'm not so sure, Mimi. I mean, judging from the animosity she held for Zoe, I would find it hard to believe Leann would come riding to Zoe Yeager's rescue. But that's exactly what Vera is asking her to do. Rescue Zoe's reputation by finishing her customer orders. Would Leann really do that?"

"I think she would, Kelly. As I said, Leann needs the money. Hopefully, some of her old customers who left her for Zoe will return." Mimi pulled out a chair at the end of the table.

"You know, I have to confess I'm curious about that," Kelly said, settling into a chair at the long library table. "Do you really think Zoe stole some of Leann's designs when she was working there a few years ago? That one gown Leann showed us is definitely a duplicate design."

Mimi pulled a large white plastic bag filled with creamy fleece from the nearby corner. "I'm almost afraid to hazard a guess, Kelly. Maybe I don't want to know. I have always liked Leann, and I liked Zoe. I don't want to picture Zoe deliberately stealing Leann's design. Yet, I must admit, those gowns are identical in style."

Kelly pulled out her bridesmaid shawl from the knitting bag and picked up her stitches where she left off on the circular needles. Soft royal blue wool with mohair. "You know, I overheard Zoe talking to her sister on the phone when I was at her shop a week or so ago. I was surprised at her harsh tone. She said she didn't care if Vera had to work all night on some project. Zoe wanted it finished by the next day. She even told Vera she wouldn't be paid if she didn't finish it on time. You know, that really surprised me, Mimi. I'd only seen Zoe's cheerful, friendly side."

Mimi winced visibly. "Oh, dear. I'm so sorry to hear that. I've overheard Zoe berating Vera once or twice, but I'd hoped it was an uncharacteristic outburst. Vera didn't talk about it. And . . . I suppose I didn't want to think that Zoe would treat her sister like that."

Kelly glanced at Mimi's furrowed brow and worried expression. Clearly, Mimi was concerned about what Kelly had told her. Mimi never liked to think ill of her friends. Kelly knew that, so she left the subject and returned to her knitting.

She was nearly finished. This project had taken Kelly even longer than usual because of her frequent business trips to Denver. Travel ate up the extra blocks of time that might be free. Frequently those odd bits and pieces of time were spent driving, so there was no time left for leisurely knitting. By the time Kelly reached her luxurious hotel suite in Denver, she relaxed by sinking into the hot tub with Jacuzzi, then went to bed.

Like so many others, Kelly found something else slipping in and stealing the stray bits of time she could be knitting:

e-mail and online computer work. Sometimes it was a deluge waiting in her in-box. Time was eaten away by online activities that had become a necessary part of life.

Thankfully, her work schedule had settled into a regular routine these last couple of months. She was enjoying the quieter pace. Don Warner, her hard-driving, dynamic Denver developer boss, was presently immersed in managing his current projects. And the Thornton redevelopment project that had occupied so much of Kelly's time last winter and spring was nearing completion six months later. There were no more mini–mob scene mass meetings in Thornton. Kelly didn't miss those at all. Of course, those mass meetings had provided an opportunity six months ago for Kelly and Steve to meet and slowly renew their friendship, then explore the "new territory" they found themselves in. And explore what came next.

Kelly came to the end of a long row near the top of the triangular shawl. She paused to sip her coffee, then started the next row. After another few rows, she would begin the edging rows which would become the border for the top of the shawl.

"That's coming along nicely, Kelly," Mimi said as she drafted some fleece into her lap.

"Thanks, Mimi. I have only been able to knit in short spurts because of my schedule. If only there was a way to knit and be on the computer at the same time, then I'd be set." Kelly laughed.

"I have no doubt someone will invent it soon," Mimi predicted. "In fact—"

Her next comment was cut off when a Megan hurricane blew right into the knitting room. Kelly looked up in surprise. She hadn't seen one of those windstorms in months. Megan had nailed down all the details of her wedding by last June. Peace and calm had reigned . . . until now.

Megan stared at them, wide-eyed, looking like the frazzled, harried wedding-prep Megan of months ago. "I can't believe this!" She shook a white plastic bag at them. "Eighteen days before the wedding, and she's *pregnant*!"

Kelly blinked. Mimi's mouth dropped open. Drafted fleece and knitting dropped to laps.

"*Who's* pregnant?"

"My *sister, Janet*!" Megan snapped.

"Oh, my . . ."

"How could she do that so close to the wedding?" Megan shook the plastic bag again, clearly indignant. "Now she can't fit into the *dress*!"

"Ahhhh . . ." Kelly and Mimi chorused together.

Megan dropped the plastic bag onto the knitting table and sank into a chair between Mimi and Kelly. *Despair.* Kelly swore she could see a black cloud forming over Megan's head.

Mimi reached over and gave Megan one of her motherly pats. "Don't worry, Megan. There's enough time to make alterations. I'm sure of it. I take it your sister has already tried on the dress, and . . . and . . ."

"And it doesn't *fit*!" Megan complained. "She called me early this morning." Black cloud dropping lower, almost to Megan's forehead. *Gloom.*

Kelly had to wipe away the smile that wanted to appear at Megan's melodramatic mood. She sensed Megan was completely unprepared for this sudden wrench that was thrown into her well-oiled Megan and Marty Wedding Machine. Everything had been clicking along nicely. Caterers, on schedule. Wedding cake, scheduled. Servers, scheduled. Everything was proceeding according to plan. Megan's Master Plan. And now this. There was no room in the Master Plan for last-minute matron of honor screwups.

"She says she'll need a couple of inches more in the waistline!" Megan exclaimed, voice moving up the register. "I've checked the seams and there's not enough material there for two inches! *Arrrrgh!*" Megan threw both hands up to the heavens. Perhaps divine intervention would help. Heavenly seamstresses? Megan sank her head onto her arms on the table. "I can't believe this. Only eighteen days, and Janet does this. How *could* she?"

Kelly sent Mimi a quick grin over Megan's head. "I doubt your sister planned it, Megan."

"It doesn't matter," Megan bemoaned. "How will I find someone to fix this dress in such a short time? Zoe is dead. I don't know anyone else to call." *Deeper gloom.*

"I know someone who might be able to do it," Mimi said as she rose. "Let me give her a call."

"Are you thinking of Leann?" Kelly asked as Mimi walked into the central yarn room.

"Yes, I am. She's wonderful with alterations."

Megan's head popped up. "Tell her I'll pay double!" she called after Mimi.

"There, now. You see? There's a solution," Kelly reassured her friend. Crisis seemingly averted, Kelly returned to her shawl. Thankfully, she was coming into the home stretch. At least, she thought she was. Several long rows with the stitches increasing row by row remained. Then she would began the even rows of border stitches which would provide the edge of the shawl. Long rows took a long time to knit.

"Hopefully," Megan said, leaning back into the chair. "Oh, please, please, have this seamstress be able to make the alterations. *Please!*"

"Are you praying to the Wedding Gods or Heavenly Seamstresses?" Kelly teased.

"Both. Whatever works."

Kelly couldn't resist. "I swear, I haven't seen a Megan Black Cloud of Wedding Despair in several months. You had everything nailed down."

A smile escaped. "You bet I did. After all that effort and searching, I nailed down everything! And I've been checking with them every week this last month, just to make sure they're ready."

Kelly grinned as she continued her stitches. *Slip, wrap, slide. Slip, wrap, slide.* The regular movements of creating each stitch and moving it from the left needle to the right. It was rhythmic and natural by now.

"Woe to any vendor who is unprepared. The Wrath of Megan will descend upon him or her," Kelly intoned in a theatrical voice, hoping to elicit a genuine laugh from Megan.

It worked. Megan laughed. "Okay, okay, I can be a little intense at times—"

"A *little*!"

"Okay, a lot. But you don't have any room to talk, Kelly."

"*Me?*"

"Yeah, you. When you're out sleuthing around, you are just as intense."

"Oh, puh-leeeez . . ."

"Good news," Mimi announced as she bustled into the main room. "I just spoke with Leann O'Hara and explained your situation, and she said she would be glad to help you out, Megan. She has a shop here in Fort Connor, too."

Megan stared at Mimi for a second. "Really? I can't believe it. Is she as good a seamstress as Zoe? I mean . . . do you think she'll do a good job?"

Mimi smiled benevolently and patted Megan on the arm. "Oh, yes. In fact, Zoe was sewing in Leann's shop before she started her own business. Leann is more than qualified to handle your sister's alterations."

Megan closed her eyes, obvious relief flooding her face. "Oh, thank you, thank you, Mimi," she said. "You're a lifesaver."

"Nonsense, dear. I'm just glad I could help," Mimi said with a smile as she settled in her chair and returned to the drafted fleece.

"Mother Mimi strikes again," Kelly teased and joined her friends' laughter as it bounced around the table.

Seven

Kelly clicked her car door open and slipped inside. Her meeting with client Arthur Housemann had gone longer than she'd planned. She'd noticed that Housemann always found time to find out what was happening in her life—after all the business was done, of course. So they'd spent a pleasant half hour over coffee talking about how *her* business was going.

Kelly often thought Arthur Housemann was a lot like her. Focused and targeted. She was sure that was one of the things he appreciated about her work as his financial accountant and CPA. That, and the fact she had played a large part in preventing tragic legal consequences from entangling him and his family a few months ago. Kelly was pleased her sleuthing into the murder of a local real estate investor had uncovered the real perpetrator.

Housemann never forgot that. Kelly sensed he thought of

her almost like a daughter. That always brought a smile. She'd already acquired two fatherly mentors since she'd returned to her childhood home in Fort Connor almost four years ago: Burt Parker and Curt Stackhouse. She could always use a third one. Having lost her own dear father to lung cancer years ago, Kelly appreciated the auxiliary fathers in her life.

She nosed her sporty red car out of the office complex parking lot and into traffic on Fort Connor's busy eastern commercial route. Her cell phone jangled from her briefcase. Kelly slowed her car and moved into the right lane as she retrieved the phone. Burt's name and number flashed on the screen.

"Hey, Burt, how are you?" she asked, coming to a stop at an intersection.

"I'm fine, Kelly. Out doing errands, as usual," Burt's familiar voice came over the line. "Mimi said you have to work in Denver on Saturday."

"Oh, yes. Warner has a special meeting scheduled on a new project. He's bringing in some consultants, so top staff has to gather."

Burt chuckled. "Sounds like a long day. I'm glad he pays you well. Listen, are you dropping by the shop today?"

"I plan to later this afternoon. First, I have to work on client accounts, then I'll earn a knitting break."

"That works. Listen, I called to update you on what I've heard from Dan on the investigation into Zoe's murder."

Kelly maneuvered the car around a corner onto a less busy street. She wanted to concentrate on what Burt was saying without being distracted. "Thanks, Burt. I'm sure the medical examiner didn't find anything out of the ordinary, right?"

"Correct. Zoe died as a result of a gunshot wound to the

head. One shot was fired, Dan said. And it was at close range, which indicates the killer was probably sitting next to Zoe in the car."

Kelly thought about that. "Why on earth would Zoe Yeager allow Oscar to get into her car when she was so afraid of him? Do you think he forced his way into her car?"

"I have no idea, Kelly. But Dan said he went to the bar Oscar frequents. The Stop On Inn. It's east of town on the truck route near the interstate. The bartenders there know Oscar well. He's a regular and comes just about every night. The bartender said Oscar was definitely there the night Zoe was killed. He remembers because Oscar was 'mad as hell,' according to the bartender. And he was drinking more than usual and kept cursing his wife over and over."

Kelly could almost picture the ugly scene. "Wow, that sounds like what I imagined."

"The bartender said he thinks Oscar left around nine o'clock or so but wasn't sure. Zoe's class was over at nine fifteen, so there was plenty of time to get to that church, which is on the east side of town."

"I'd say that should put Oscar right in Dan's bull's-eye. Don't you think so?"

"Well, he's certainly looking guilty. He has no alibi for his whereabouts after he left the bar. He told Dan he went straight home and fell asleep, but he can't prove it."

"I told you I thought he was the killer," Kelly said, slowing for a stop sign.

"I know you did, Kelly, but Dan is still questioning people. There were a couple of guys at the bar that remembered Oscar, and they confirmed he looked 'pretty damn mad,' as one guy put it. But remember, Dan is still questioning people. We don't know what he'll find out."

Kelly heard a tone in Burt's voice she recognized. His skeptical tone. That got her attention. "Did Dan let on that he'd learned something new? I hear that skeptical tone in your voice."

Burt chuckled again. "Boy, I can't hide anything from you anymore, Kelly. You're right. Dan did say that the department was questioning all the women in Zoe's evening class at the church. Maybe those women saw something suspicious. Who knows? Dan isn't saying yet, which means he's still asking questions."

Kelly thought about that as she edged her car back onto a larger thoroughfare, heading toward her cottage. "That makes me curious, too. I wonder what those women had to say. It's a safe bet they didn't see Oscar waiting for Zoe outside. They never would have left Zoe alone with him."

"I agree with you, Kelly. But I sense those women in class saw something, and it was enough to arouse Dan's interest. Listen, I'm pulling into the shopping center parking lot. I'll talk to you later."

"Thanks, Burt," Kelly said as she clicked off and dropped the phone back into her briefcase.

Turning the corner near Lambspun, Kelly next turned into the driveway between the shop and her cottage. Meanwhile, she wondered what those women could possibly have seen that would arouse Dan's interest.

It certainly wouldn't be Oscar. Even Oscar wasn't stupid enough to hang around Zoe's car with a gun in his jacket. Maybe Oscar was hiding near a bush or behind some trees.

Were there any bushes or trees at that parking lot? She ought to drive over there and take a look for herself. Maybe one of them did spot Oscar hiding behind a corner or something.

That idea didn't make sense to Kelly. Then another thought came out of the back of her mind, darting around until it sat right in front of her eyes where she couldn't miss it. Something someone had said.

Leann. Leann O'Hara. The pretty seamstress who was about to rescue Megan's sister's dress. Kelly remembered sitting in the shop when Leann came storming in with a photo of the dress she claimed Zoe stole. Leann was furious. And the last thing that Leann said before she left the shop was she was going to confront Zoe Yeager at her class that night. Leann wanted to warn the students not to trust Zoe.

Kelly pulled her car to a stop in front of her cottage, while a cold sensation rippled through her.

"**Hey,** Kelly, I'm glad I caught you," Megan said as Kelly stepped into Lambspun's foyer later that afternoon.

"Are you coming or going?" Kelly asked as they both moved away from the front door. Two women were walking into the shop right behind them.

"Going. I came in a while ago to give Leann my sister's dress, so she can start the alterations. She promised it would only take a few days." Megan placed her hand on her chest and closed her eyes. "Thank goodness. I was so worried there wouldn't be enough time, but Leann assured me there was."

"I'll bet that was a load off your mind." Kelly smiled at her friend. In her jeans and tee shirt, Megan looked considerably more relaxed now than she did two days ago. "You're lucky that Leann was able to schedule those alterations right now."

"Don't I know it. Leann was so nice and reassuring on the phone when I first spoke to her. Mimi must have told her I was upset because Leann kept telling me not to worry. She promised that she'd be able to make those alterations on time. She couldn't start until today, though, because she had another customer's suit to finish."

"Boy, if she's doing suits, then she's certainly qualified to handle your sister's expanding seams problem." Kelly couldn't keep her grin away, remembering Megan shaking the plastic bag while complaining about her sister's predicament.

Megan smiled. "Now I feel bad I carried on so, but I simply lost it. I'd worked so hard to make sure everything was scheduled. I didn't want any loose ends to cause problems at the last minute." She shook her head. "And then my sister called. Thank goodness I didn't yell at her on the phone. I could tell she felt awful."

"Megan, we all watched you knock yourself out tying down everything wedding related you could think of. If something had to happen, at least it was easily solved. Thanks to Leann." Kelly paused for a second. "You know, I don't really know Leann. I only saw her briefly when she came to talk to Mimi about something. What's she like?"

"Oh, she's really nice and easy to talk to. And Mimi was right when she said she's had a lot of experience. That made me feel a whole lot better. She's in the main room right now, working on my sister's dress." Megan checked her watch and moved toward the door. "I've gotta run. Don't forget we've got a game this evening at Rolland Moore fields."

"It's on my daytimer. We've only got a couple left," Kelly

said, then headed to the main room. Leann O'Hara was sitting at the knitting table, a fire engine red garment spread on her lap.

"Hello, Leann, Megan said you were here," Kelly greeted her as she dropped her knitting bag on the table and settled into a chair.

Leann looked up from the red dress and stared at Kelly for a second, then smiled in recognition. "Hi, there, Kelly. It's Kelly, isn't it? I'm not good with names."

"Kelly, it is," she said, removing the nearly finished wool and mohair shawl from her bag. "I take it that's Megan's sister's dress. I was here with Mimi the other day when Megan came in and told us what happened." Kelly couldn't keep from smiling. "Thank goodness you rode to the rescue. Megan was losing it."

Leann laughed lightly. "Well, I understand how nervous brides are about their big day. Everything has to be simply perfect. But it's inevitable that something goes awry. Some glitch. Luckily, this glitch is easily solved."

Kelly checked the shawl gathered in a soft bunch in her lap. Everything looked okay. Her stitches would never be as perfect as Jennifer's or Lisa's or Megan's, but they looked all right to her. *Good enough*, she thought, and picked up her knitting where she'd left off. After a few stitches she glanced up to see exactly what Leann was doing.

Watching Leann's smooth, spare movements for a few seconds, Kelly asked, "What are you doing exactly, Leann? It doesn't look like you're sewing."

"No sewing yet, Kelly. I'm ripping out the seams of the dress, so I can actually begin alterations."

"What's that you're using? A little knife?"

Leann looked up with a smile and held the little gadget for Kelly to see. "It's a seam ripper. And it's a seamstress's best friend. It makes shorter work of alterations."

Kelly scrutinized the slender piece of metal. Fatter than a pencil with a curved hook at the end. "That looks like a little fishhook."

Leann laughed. "I'm afraid a fishhook would rip out more than the seams, it would probably rip my fingers, too. This metal isn't that sharp, but sharp enough to slice through the thread of each stitch as I move it along. Watch."

Leann inserted the seam ripper into the seam she was working on and started moving it deftly. Each stitch gave way quickly as her hand moved along.

"Wow, I see what you mean," Kelly said, watching her. "Without that little ripper, I can't imagine how long it would take to remove those little stitches."

"Believe me, I don't even want to think about it. Dresses and suits would take forever to finish." She kept moving the seam ripper until she reached the end of the side seam.

"Is that the side of the dress I'm looking at?" Kelly asked, peering at the red fabric.

"Yes, it is." Leann held up the dress. "See, here's the bust. I'll be letting out both side seams and adding the extra material there. Megan's sister Janet and I talked this morning as she took her measurements. That way I'll know exactly how much fabric I need to add. I'm hoping there will be enough left over. I won't know until I can get the extra fabric from Vera. She's working until late tonight, so it'll be tomorrow before she can check the leftover fabric back at . . . at Zoe's workshop." Leann's voice grew softer.

Now that Leann had mentioned Zoe, Kelly decided to

continue. "That was simply awful, wasn't it?" she ventured in a quiet voice so browsing customers in the adjoining rooms wouldn't overhear.

Leann didn't look up, but kept focusing on the red dress as her fingers moved along the seam line. "It was horrible. I cannot believe someone would do that. Who would want to kill Zoe? Do you think someone tried to rob her?"

"I don't know, Leann," Kelly agreed. "I was shocked when I heard. And Mimi was . . . well, you know Mimi. She's had a lot of loss in her life."

Leann glanced up. "Yes, I heard she'd lost her son in a tragic accident when he was at the university years ago."

Kelly tried to think of a circuitous way to ask the question that was bedeviling her, but couldn't figure out how to obscure her curiosity. So she resorted to her usual manner: forthright and straight to the point.

"You know, Leann, I wondered if you really did go to see Zoe at her class that night."

Leann quickly looked up, and a flush spread across her cheeks. "Yes, yes, I did . . . and . . . and I feel awful about it." She ducked her head and focused on the red dress again. "It was a stupid thing to do, I know that now. But I was just so angry at her." Leann's voice had dropped almost to a whisper. "I wish I hadn't gone."

Kelly could feel Leann's regret. "We all have done things we regret, Leann. I know I have."

"I feel so awful that I yelled at her like that."

The sound of a cell phone's music sounded then, and Leann reached into her large fabric purse on the table. She glanced at the phone's screen. "Excuse me, Kelly. I have to take this call. Leann O'Hara," she said crisply into the phone as she rose and walked away.

Kelly returned to her own stitches. Knitting stitches, but stitches nonetheless. She was glad her stitches were large compared to those small stitches that Leann was ripping out. Sewing had always looked difficult to Kelly. Now that she could see the effort involved in simply removing stitches, Kelly decided she would stay with yarn forever. Unraveling knitting stitches, or frogging as knitters called it, was infinitely easier and faster than Leann's work.

"Hi, Kelly," Mimi said as she walked into the main room, both hands full of magazines. Knitting magazines, crocheting magazines, spinning magazines, weaving magazines . . . and many more subjects than Kelly could keep track of. It always amazed her how many fiber-related topics there were. And how many people were involved with them.

"Leann was here when I came, so we got to chat for a few minutes. She's already started on Megan's sister's matron of honor dress."

"I'm so glad Leann could find the time." Mimi started removing some magazines and replacing them with the ones she brought. "I think she did it as a favor for me. She could tell we had a very excitable bride-to-be on our hands."

Kelly laughed, picturing Megan in the midst of one of her melodramatic moments. "Did we ever. I'll bet Marty was glad he was out of town at a conference. This way, he got the melodrama over the phone. Much easier to deal with."

"Well, Leann understood the situation and was kind enough to push a couple of other projects down the calendar so she could focus on this dress. That was awfully nice of her, especially since she's been helping Vera catch up with Zoe's projects. Leann told me some of her old customers have called to get back on her schedule. I'm so glad."

Kelly wondered if those people had been Zoe's customers, but decided not to mention it. Instead, Kelly ventured, "It was nice to talk to Leann when she was . . . you know, acting normal. I'd only seen her when she came storming into the shop the other day, convinced that Zoe stole her dress design."

"Yes, that was . . . well, it wasn't one of Leann's better moments," Mimi said, giving a row of magazines a final pat. "I'm glad to hear that you got to meet Leann as she really is. Good-natured and competent, considerate of others. That's the Leann I know."

Kelly toyed with her next comment, then decided simply to put it out there. First, she looked around, checking to make sure no browsing customers were standing within earshot. "You know, I asked Leann if she really did go to see Zoe at her class that night."

Mimi turned quickly and stared at Kelly, wide-eyed. "You didn't!"

"Yes, I did. I was curious if she followed through on her threat to confront Zoe. Leann admitted she did go to Zoe's class, and in her words she 'yelled at her.' Then she admitted she's very sorry she went. She said she felt awful now."

Mimi frowned in concern. "I'm sure she does. Oh, dear. I was so hoping that Leann had thought better of confronting Zoe, especially at her class in front of all those students."

"The only reason I'm telling you, Mimi, is because Burt updated me earlier today." Kelly leaned forward and dropped her voice. Mimi approached closer and leaned toward Kelly.

"What on earth did he say?"

"Dan told him they were questioning the women in Zoe's class. That made me curious. If police are questioning those students, then there's a good chance one of them would remember Leann barging into their class that night."

"Oh, no, they couldn't possibly think that Leann . . ." Mimi didn't finish the sentence.

"Those students probably don't know Leann. They don't know that she's a really nice person at heart. They don't know what she's really like. All they know is the Leann who accused Zoe of stealing her design. And how angry Leann was."

Mimi drew back, face blanched with concern. "Oh, no . . ."

Kelly turned the corner of the shady residential street. She liked traveling on Fort Connor's older residential streets when she had the time. Many of the homes were built in the early 1900s. There were so many different styles built in those early years and even more built in the 1940s. Gracious designs Kelly was especially attracted to, especially the houses with wraparound porches. They always looked so inviting. Kelly drove slower through the early evening.

There was enough time to enjoy the scenery while she drove to the ball fields. A sweatshirt lay on the seat beside her. Her trusty first baseman's glove was in the trunk with an assortment of bats. Most were wooden. But there was an old metal one she brought out for younger kids when she was coaching softball leagues in the summer. Now that it was September and the kids were back in school, they were involved in their schools' ball teams. Here in Fort Connor, girls softball was a fall sport along with football and volleyball.

Kelly had always been annoyed when different schools had conflicting sports schedules. She'd enjoyed playing volleyball in school, too, but she was better at softball. Plus, softball was played outside in the fresh air and sunshine. You couldn't beat that, in Kelly's eyes. There might be cloudy, chilly days, too, but Kelly forgot those.

Her cell phone jangled, and she dug it from her bag on the seat beside her. Steve's name and number flashed on the smartphone screen. *Was he back from his Arizona trip?* She thought he wasn't returning to Denver until tomorrow.

"Hey, there, are you back in Denver or still in Arizona?" Kelly answered as she nosed the car around another corner.

"Landed in Denver a little while ago. I'm going to grab my bags and head to the office. I want to drop off a ton of materials I picked up at that conference."

"I imagine. You'll have to tell me all about it when we get together next."

"That's another reason I called. I wanted to see if we could have dinner tomorrow night. I thought I'd drive up to Fort Connor to check on Wellesley and Baker Street."

Steve's last building project was in Wellesley, a subdivision north of Fort Connor that Steve had completed over a year ago, and there were still some houses left unsold. Add to that a couple of houses were working their way through bank foreclosure, their owners long since gone. Because of that, Steve had given recent buyers some very sweet deals, and investors made out like bandits. Steve had put a lot of detail work into those moderate-income homes. Marty and Megan had already bought one of the houses, thanks to Steve's generous wedding present of a discounted price. Greg and Lisa were actually renting one of the houses, and were now planning to buy that house from Steve, too.

"Oh, darn. I promised Jayleen and Curt I'd join them for dinner tomorrow night. She's making her famous chili. Why don't you come, too? I'm sure they'd love to see you."

Steve laughed softly, the sound bringing back lots of memories as it came over the phone. "No offense to Curt and Jayleen, but I'd rather have dinner with you. Just the two of us, so I'll hold out for that. When will you be in Denver next?"

Kelly paused, remembering how Steve had once gotten angry and demanding if she wasn't there when he made a sudden visit. That was a year ago, when Steve was in the midst of a career meltdown. A lot had changed since then. Steve had regained his footing in his career, starting over with Sam Kaufman's company. Even more important, Steve had regained himself. The "old" Steve was back. The Steve Kelly knew. The Steve she fell in love with.

Now their relationship was changing. It was familiar, yet different . . . and she liked it. Kelly sensed they were both moving to some new "center point." And they were drawing closer. Almost there.

"As a matter of fact, I'll be in Denver this Saturday. Warner's scheduled a special planning meeting with these new consultants."

This time, Steve laughed out loud. "That sounds like him. Man, I'm glad we're finished with our part of that Thornton project. Those huge meetings sucked the life out of you."

"Tell me about it," Kelly said with a laugh.

"Well, that's perfect timing. I don't have to leave again until Monday. So why don't I make reservations for us on

Saturday night. There's a restaurant I want you to try. I was there a couple of weeks ago with some others."

"Sounds good. I'll look forward to it." She turned her car into the entrance drive leading to the ball fields.

"Me, too." Steve's deep voice dropped lower. "I've missed you, Kelly."

Kelly barely hesitated as she answered. "I've missed you, too. I'll say hi to Megan and Lisa. I'm driving into the ball fields now."

"Hit it out of the park for me, will ya?"

"You betcha," Kelly promised before she clicked off.

Eight

Kelly walked across the driveway separating the cottage and the shop, laptop in her briefcase and empty coffee mug dangling. She didn't feel like working at home this morning. It was a cloudy day with the threat of an afternoon shower. A perfect day to work inside Lambspun. Surrounded by rich colors and luscious fibers, she could work on her accounts at the knitting table. She'd learned how to block out strangers' conversations years ago. As long as they weren't talking to her, Kelly didn't even hear them.

Living in Colorado for over three years, Kelly had become addicted to almost daily sunshine. Bright, sunny days were the norm. Consequently, cloudy days were a surprise. Sometimes they were a welcome break, other times, an unwanted interruption.

Running up the steps to Lambspun's entrance, Kelly was

about to reach for the handle when the door suddenly opened. She jumped out of the way to keep from bumping into Vera.

"Ohhh!" Vera exclaimed, startled.

"Sorry, Vera. I've got to remember not to move so fast."

"That's all right, Kelly. I'm hurrying, too. I only stopped by to leave the extra fabric for Megan's sister's dress."

"Are you hurrying to the copy shop or hurrying back to the workshop?"

"Actually, I'm returning to the workshop. My boss at the copy shop was kind enough to let me reduce my hours so I could catch up with customer projects."

Kelly noticed Vera didn't look as stressed as she had the last few times Kelly had seen her. "How's that going? Mimi said Leann was helping you catch up with all the customer projects. That's good. I know that was a huge burden hanging over you."

Vera's pale blue eyes widened. "Yes, it was. Even so, I got very little sleep earlier in the week, trying to work at the copy shop and keep up with the customer sewing. I'm so glad Leann was good enough to help me. Considering her . . . well, her past history with Zoe, I thought that was kind of Leann."

"Yes, it was. I finally had a chance to talk with Leann the other day. She was here starting the alterations for Megan's sister's matron of honor dress. Megan was frantic when she found out from her sister that the dress no longer fit." Kelly felt compelled to explain why Megan had not asked Vera. "Mimi knew you were swamped with the other sewing so she told Megan to call Leann."

"Yes, I heard all about the dress drama." A little smile tweaked the edges of Vera's mouth. "I've never had children, but I've had to alter several bridesmaids' dresses over the years for the same reason. And sometimes . . . the bridal gown as well. I'm glad Leann was able to fill in, because you're right, I was much too busy with the new garments to handle that." Vera glanced at her watch. "Which reminds me, a customer will be at the shop in half an hour. It was nice chatting with you, Kelly."

Kelly started to open the door until she heard Vera's voice again.

"Oh, yes. There will be a visitation for Zoe at Highland Funeral Home this Saturday at noon. I've had to arrange everything because Oscar is positively useless. He simply sits in front of his television and drinks." Vera scowled. "I can't stand to even talk to him on the phone, let alone go over there. But someone had to step in and take care of arrangements. And he wouldn't even answer the phone when the medical examiner's office called him. That's when they called me. I told them that I would be the responsible party, because Oscar surely was not. He was barely sober when he was at home." She gave a disgusted sniff.

"Thank goodness you were there to take care of the necessary details," Kelly said, surprised by this competent, decisive Vera. Previously, Vera had always appeared hesitant and shy, not one to take charge. Clearly Vera was a lot more competent than she'd appeared. She'd taken charge of an emotionally wrenching situation and had become the responsible party. Oscar was useless.

Kelly gave Vera a good-bye wave before entering the shop. Stepping inside the foyer, Kelly paused to drink in the fall colors. Mimi and the shop elves had been busy. New autumn colors spilled from baskets and bins.

Kelly indulged herself and sank her hands into the chest on the floor that overflowed with fat skeins of large twist yarns. BABY ALPACA, the wrapper said. Unbelievably soft. Pale pink, turquoise, lavender, and deep rose. This was exactly what she needed this morning. A fiber break. Revel in the sensuous feel of the yarns. She trailed her fingers across the various yarns spread out on tables and shelves as she walked through the central yarn room. Drawn to several bins on the wall with grays and pinks, she found kid mohair, baby kid, and super kid mohair mixed with silk. Even baby cashmere. Softer than soft.

Jennifer rounded the corner into the room. "Hey, are you coming or going?"

"Coming. I thought I'd escape looking at the cloudy day by working here. Are you on break?"

"For about ten minutes. C'mon, let's catch up." Jennifer headed toward the main room, where she deposited her bag and sank into a chair.

"You and Pete working tonight?" Kelly asked, settling into the chair beside her.

"No, thankfully. We're booked Friday, Saturday, and Sunday nights. So tonight we can kick back and relax." She withdrew a bundle of maroon yarn and needles from her bag. It looked to Kelly like the beginning of a sweater.

"Wow, I hope Pete is stashing away all those catering revenues," Kelly said as she pulled her laptop from her briefcase.

"Yes, he is, Miss Accountant. Pete's been building his savings slowly and carefully, bless his heart." Jennifer's fast fingers worked the knitting needles, stitches forming quickly. "He's a good influence for someone like me. Watching him squirrel away little bits of cash at a time convinced me to start."

Kelly had to smile. Jennifer was right. Pete *was* a good influence on her . . . in more ways than simply saving money. Jennifer was more relaxed than Kelly had ever seen her. And happier. Much happier. Pete had been able to give Jennifer something all those other "hot" guys and one-night stands had not. *Contentment.* Kelly and her friends marveled at the changes that occurred once Jennifer finally responded to Pete's quiet courtship.

"Are you doing anything tonight?" Jennifer asked, looking up. "We haven't been able to get together with you guys for a while because of the busy season."

"I'd love to, but I've already accepted an invitation from Jayleen and Curt to come up to her ranch tonight for dinner. She's making her chili. I haven't seen the two of them for nearly a month."

"Well, next time. Tell them hello for Pete and me." More knitting rows appeared.

"You should call up Megan and Marty, Greg and Lisa and see if they're busy. Steve called after he returned from an Arizona builders' conference yesterday. He wanted to go to dinner since he was coming into town tonight to check on Wellesley and Baker Street."

Jennifer's head popped up. "Really? Hey, maybe he could stop over at Greg and Lisa's before he drives back. I've got some good news about Wellesley."

"Another sale? That would be wonderful news!" Kelly exclaimed.

"Well, it's looking good so far." Jennifer held up two crossed fingers. "This is an investor, so he's putting a large percentage of cash down. Forty percent. So his loan should go through. Regular buyers . . . it's another story. Lenders have tightened up even more and are requiring at least twenty percent down payment."

"That's extremely hard for most people."

"Tell me about it."

"You should give Steve a call. He might be able to drop by Greg and Lisa's," Kelly suggested as she fired up her laptop and watched the icons pop into place on the screen.

Jennifer glanced at Kelly with a smile. "Were you two able to reschedule your dinner?"

"Yep. I'll be in Denver all day Saturday, so we can meet for dinner that evening. There's a new restaurant Steve wants me to try." She clicked on her worksheet files, and the screen filled with columns of figures.

"I heard about Megan's meltdown the other day." Jennifer grinned. "I'm sorry I missed it. I'd already left for the real estate office. The nerve of her sister, getting pregnant without consulting Megan."

Both Kelly and Jennifer laughed out loud. Megan's meltdowns were few, but they were always memorable.

"Well, well, this sounds jovial. I see that I've returned at the right time," a familiar voice sounded from the archway leading to the central yarn room and the rest of the shop.

Kelly jerked around in her chair the moment she heard that distinctive voice. *Hilda*. Hilda von Steuben. A Lambspun regular and one of the two best knitters at Lambspun. The other being Hilda's sister Lizzie. There Hilda stood, as tall and imposing as always with her silver hair swept up into a bun. Kelly did notice Hilda was using a cane now. Mimi had told them Hilda was suffering from acute arthritis pain in her knees, which had kept her from coming to the shop the last few months.

"*Hilda!*" Kelly cried out in delight as she sprang from her chair. "How wonderful to see you!" She embraced the older woman in a big hug.

"Oh, Hilda, I've missed seeing you," Jennifer said, hugging Hilda when Kelly let go. "We've all missed you. It's so good to see you in the shop."

"Goodness, girls, you must let me catch my breath," Hilda said as she steadied herself. "I have missed all of you more than I can say."

"How are your knees?" Kelly asked, noticing that Hilda looked a little frailer than before. Even her face was thinner. Hilda's cheeks were rosy, though, just like her sister Lizzie's. Both ladies were devotees of blush, or "rouge" as Hilda called it.

"My knees are better, dear," Hilda said, slowly making her way toward the table. Jennifer quickly pulled out a chair and offered it. Hilda grasped Jennifer's outstretched hand and lowered herself into the chair. "Ahhhh, there we go. Thank you, Jennifer. It seems I need a lot more help nowadays."

"Don't you worry, Hilda," Jennifer said, patting her on the shoulder. "We're glad to help. It's so *good* to see you again."

Kelly and Jennifer both settled on either side of Hilda. "Lizzie told us how much trouble the arthritis was giving you. Was the doctor able to give you a shot or something that would help?"

Hilda gave a dismissive wave of the hand. "*Bah!* Those shots only last for a month, and they can't give them that often. My regular doctor discovered a new prescription cream especially for arthritic knees, and it's worked wonders! I've been amazed at the difference it makes. I've been using it for a month now, and every week I found that I could move a little more." She raised one hand. "I am so thankful that our scientists are discovering new medicines like this one. It's given me my life again. Or at least this small part of it." She gave them both a warm smile.

"That's fantastic news, Hilda. Now maybe you'll be able to come here regularly," Kelly said. "I've missed your acerbic wit around the table."

Hilda's papery thin cheeks spread with a wide smile. "My, my, it sounds like the quality of the conversation has deteriorated around here since I've been gone."

"Oh, it has, Hilda," Jennifer said as she stuffed the maroon sweater back into her bag. "I have to return to the café, but I'll stop by again before I leave for the real estate office. Meanwhile, can I get you a cup of tea?"

"That would be lovely, dear. Thank you."

"And give me your mug, Kelly. I noticed it was dangling empty. I'll fill it up for you."

"You are a lifesaver, Jen. Thanks." Kelly handed her the mug.

Kelly leaned against the table, forgetting about her open laptop and the waiting spreadsheets. "Did Lizzie bring you this morning? I imagine driving would be too difficult now."

"You imagine correctly, my dear," Hilda said, placing a smaller than usual knitting bag on the table. "I'm afraid my driving days are over. Yes, Lizzie brought me over. She planned to visit Eustace at the Detention Center down the way."

Hilda withdrew a delicate bundle of lavender froth. Maybe a baby blanket? Spinster sisters, Hilda and Lizzie von Steuben were both retired career secondary school teachers.

They did, however, have a large extended family and scores of grandnieces and grandnephews, ranging in age from infancy to teenagers. Consequently they were always knitting something.

The mention of Lizzie and her late-in-life true love, Eustace Freemont, brought a sad memory. An unscrupulous real estate investor had cheated Eustace's mother out of cherished family property last year. Consequently, mild-mannered historical researcher Eustace had exercised what he called "frontier justice." Unfortunately, the legal system took a dim view of Eustace's actions. Hence, Lizzie's frequent visits to the County Detention Center.

"How is Lizzie doing?" Kelly asked, picturing the round rosy-cheeked little knitter. "And Eustace. How is he holding up?"

Hilda's fingers worked the yarn. "Lizzie is fine, and Eustace is doing quite well, considering. We're all hoping that the Colorado Department of Corrections in Denver will consider Eustace's age and his lifetime of scholarly work before they assign him to a penal facility. Perhaps he could work in a prison library or something."

"Well, that would certainly make more sense than putting an accomplished historical writer like Eustace into the general prison population." Kelly glanced toward the central yarn room and the two women browsing the yarn bins there. "I'll have to remember to ask Marty how that process is going."

"Well, never mind that," Hilda said, glancing up at Kelly. "Right now, I'd much rather hear about you and your young man, Steve. I confess, Kelly, I was most unhappy to hear that you two had stopped seeing each other. Most distressing."

She shook her head, fingers moving quickly. Clearly, Hilda had no arthritis in her hands.

Kelly kept her smile in check. "Well, you'll be pleased to hear that Steve and I have been seeing each other occasionally in Denver these last few months. And Steve came up to join all of us for some baseball and softball games whenever he could last summer."

Hilda's thin face flushed with her obvious pleasure. "Oh, my dear . . . I cannot tell you how happy I am to hear that. Excellent news, indeed. You two belong together, in my humble opinion," she decreed with a trace of Hilda's former authoritarian pronouncements.

Kelly couldn't help grinning. "Well, I'm glad you're happy, Hilda. Just seeing you again makes *me* happy." Kelly rose from her chair to give Hilda another hug.

"Goodness me. Such effusive welcomes." Hilda patted Kelly's arm. "Thank you, Kelly. And I'll be glad to share your good news with Lizzie."

"You do that, Hilda," Kelly said as she spied Jennifer walking toward the main room with their tea and coffee.

Kelly leaned back into the comfy kitchen chair at Jayleen's round maple table. "Man, am I stuffed. Excellent as always, Jayleen. We should crown you Chili Queen."

Jayleen hooted with laughter, tossing her graying blond curls over her shoulder as she took Kelly's empty plate. "*Ha!* All those chili cooks down in Texas might take offense at that, Kelly. We don't want a passel of angry Texans storming up here in the canyon."

"Hmmmm. I hadn't thought about that," Kelly teased her alpaca rancher friend.

"Does that mean you're too full to have a piece of blueberry pie?" Curt Stackhouse asked with a twinkle in his eye.

Kelly smiled at her mentor and advisor. Silver-haired, broad-shouldered, Curt was the image of a Colorado rancher, which was exactly how Curt had spent most of his life— raising cattle and sheep and buying land. However, Curt was also Kelly's trusted advisor on mineral rights and royalties. Curt's guidance was invaluable when natural gas was found on Kelly's Wyoming property.

"Don't tell me Megan made you guys one of Ruthie's blueberry pies? Boy, you two really rate." She took a deep sip of Jayleen's strong coffee.

Curt leaned back into his chair. "It's my daughter Becky's pie. She's been practicing Ruthie's recipe for a while now, and I have to admit, she's come pretty damn close. I can't tell the difference."

"That settles it. I have to have some. Of course, I'll need to run an extra mile tomorrow morning, you understand," Kelly teased.

"You're perfect the way you are, Kelly-girl," Jayleen said as she placed the tempting blueberry pie in the middle of the table. "This has been warming in the oven, so it should be just right. And there's vanilla ice cream, too. You can start us off with the first piece, Kelly. Then Curt and I will dive in."

"Brother, make that two miles tomorrow," Kelly said, watching blueberry syrup drip from the slice of pie Jayleen lifted onto her plate.

Curt handed her a clean fork. "Here you go, Kelly. Dig in.

You know, I was sorry to hear about that woman being killed last week. Jayleen told me she was sewing for Megan's wedding. Hard to believe someone would walk up and shoot a woman like that."

Kelly sliced her fork into the blueberry delicacy, saw the flaky pastry give way, juice dribbling onto her plate. "I've asked Burt a few times if the police have any leads, but he says they're still investigating. I've got my money on Zoe's abusive husband, Oscar. Apparently he spent the night drinking and cursing Zoe, and he has no alibi after he left the bar." She lifted a forkful of blueberries and pastry and savored them as they melted in her mouth. Blueberry heaven.

"Whooooeee, that sounds pretty bad," Jayleen decreed, shaking her head. Jayleen was celebrating fourteen years being sober after spending many years drinking in the Colorado Springs bars. Now Jayleen helped other troubled young women make better choices in their lives.

"He sounds like one bad hombre," Curt concurred.

"Zoe had recently left Oscar and was filing for a divorce. He was furious. In fact, he followed Zoe, Lisa, and me back to Lambspun when Zoe moved her things out of the house." Kelly frowned. "I got to see Oscar's rage up close and personal when he got in my face at the front door."

Curt gave a wry smile. "You were blocking his path, I take it."

"Oh, yeah. Zoe was safe inside. He didn't back down until he learned Lisa had called the cops, and they were on their way."

"That'll work," Jayleen said, shaking her head. "You know, that reinforces what one of my friends told me the other day. She's taken a lot of Zoe's sewing classes, and I recall her saying something about Zoe's husband. I think he came into the class drunk one night." Jayleen shook her head. "Liquor can really mess up your mind. Sounds like it messed up Oscar pretty good."

"Damn right."

Kelly dropped a big scoop of vanilla ice cream onto the pie, then stirred the melting ice cream into the blueberry pie syrup on her plate. "As I said, my money's on Oscar. And I hope the cops don't take long to put his butt away where he can't hurt anyone else."

With that, Kelly lifted another delectable morsel to her mouth. *Ohhhh, yes.* Beyond delicious.

"**Hey,** come on in, buddy. Pizza's on the coffee table," Greg said, ushering Steve inside the house.

"Hey, guys. How're you doing?" Steve said as he slipped off his jacket and tossed it onto a nearby chair before settling into an empty spot around the coffee table.

Relaxing with old friends. Steve could feel the tension leave his shoulders the moment he crossed the threshold. *Man, he needed this.* He'd been coming up more often to relax with the gang until the traveling started.

Steve sank back into the chair. "Hey, the gang's all here," he said with a grin, glancing around at Megan and Marty, Jennifer and Pete, and Lisa and Greg. All of them were smiling at him, clearly glad to see him. "Sorry I haven't been up for a while. That travel schedule is kicking my butt." He reached for a slice of pizza and inhaled it. Way good, but it barely made a dent in his hunger pangs. Steve inhaled another slice. *Ahhhh.*

"Here you go," Greg said, offering Steve his favorite Colorado microbrew. "The rest of the pizza is yours. I think even Marty is full."

Steve laughed, then tipped back the golden ale and took a long drink. Oh, yeah. *Good friends, good beer, good pizza.* He reached for another slice.

Marty, meanwhile, placed his hand on his stomach with a puzzled expression. "Wait a minute . . . is that a hunger pang? No, it's okay. I'm full. For the moment."

Steve took another drink. "Did you feel that?" he joked. "I think the earth just moved."

Soft laughter floated around the little circle. Then Megan spoke up. "Not everyone is here. Kelly's off with Jayleen and Curt I heard." She gave a little frown.

"Matchmaker Megan, at it again," redheaded Marty teased his fiancée with a big smile.

"Hey, I can't help it. I want them back together." Megan pouted.

Jennifer settled back into the sofa, Pete's arm around her shoulders. "Poor Megan. Things are not proceeding according to your schedule, are they?" she said with a little laugh. "When have you ever seen Kelly proceed on schedule except with her clients or ball games?"

Steve swallowed another delicious bite while his friends teased Megan. "It's okay, Megan. Kelly and I are having dinner together in Denver tomorrow."

Megan brightened immediately. "That's great! Maybe you guys could, uh . . . move it along a little . . . or a lot," she suggested slyly, eyes dancing.

Jennifer and Pete laughed out loud.

So did Steve. "Did she just say what I thought she said?" He tipped back his ale.

"She sure did," Marty added, leaning his head back on the sofa as he laughed softly.

"Jeez, Megan," Lisa chided.

"This is Kelly we're talking about," Greg said, then took a deep drink of his beer.

"I know, I know," Megan said defensively. "It's just I'm tired of watching these two dancing around each other."

Steve joined his friends' laughter. "Hey, Megan, I'm ready and willing," he said with a big grin as he slouched in the upholstered chair. "But I'm not gonna jump her, if that's what you're suggesting."

This time the laughter bounced off the walls of Lisa and Greg's great room as Megan turned beet red. Steve reached for another slice of pizza, enjoying the racy comments that followed.

He'd waited for Kelly before. He would wait for her again. Kelly could move as slowly as she wanted. He'd still be there. She was worth the wait.

Nine

"I can really use some coffee," Dave Germaine said as he and Kelly approached the coffee urns set up outside Warner Development's meeting room.

"Me, too," Kelly agreed, waiting her turn behind two other caffeine-deprived staffers. "Twenty-plus overhead charts can make your eyes cross."

Dave laughed. "You got that right. After you." He gestured for Kelly to attack the coffee urns first. "Hey, are you staying in Denver tonight? I was hoping you and I might get together for dinner. There's a new Cajun place over in LoDo that I think you'll like."

Kelly took a sip of the not-strong-but-not-too-weak coffee. *Ackkk.* How do people drink this stuff? She glanced back at handsome Dave Germaine. They'd had several enjoyable dinners several months ago, and they'd dined together a few times these last few months. Whenever Steve was out of town traveling. Kelly was amazed at Dave's ability to sense whenever Steve was gone, and he zeroed in to ask her out. Steve had excellent instincts, however. Consequently, Steve zeroed in on Kelly when he'd seen her talking to Dave at the last of the Thornton project follow-up meetings.

Kelly smiled behind her cup. She'd recognized Steve's behavior. He clearly saw Dave Germaine as a "competitor" for Kelly's affections. Dave, for his part, seemed to sense that. They reminded Kelly of two bighorn Colorado mountain rams, squaring off against each other on a mountaintop. Kelly could almost read Steve's mind. He'd like nothing better than to go head down and knock Dave Germaine over a cliff. To Steve's credit, he didn't punch Dave out, even though Kelly could tell Steve wanted to.

Kelly took another sip of weak coffee as she and Dave moved away from the coffee station. "Maybe another time, Dave. I've already got plans for dinner tonight."

"Damn, that's too bad. Are they solid plans or is there some wiggle room?" he tempted.

"They're solid," Kelly replied, smiling at him.

Dave returned her smile. "Anyone I know?"

Kelly laughed softly. "You've met before. Across the volleyball net."

She saw the flash of recognition in Dave's eyes. "Oh, yeah. Your volleyball friend. You two known each other long?"

She nodded. "Yeah, over three years."

"That long, huh?" Dave grinned. "Is he a good friend or a *really* good friend."

Kelly couldn't resist a wicked grin. "A *really* good friend."

"I see," Dave said with a nod. "Okay, I'll consider myself forewarned."

Kelly laughed softly until her cell phone jangled in her shoulder bag. She fished it out and spotted Burt's name and number flashing on the screen. "I've gotta take this, Dave. A Fort Connor call."

"Talk to you later," Dave said. "And Kelly, just for the record, I don't give up easily."

Kelly held the little phone and let it ring. "Just for the record . . . neither does he." She grinned, then clicked on to the call. "Hey, Burt."

"Hey, Kelly, I can tell I got you at that Denver meeting. I can call you later."

"No, no, it's okay, Burt. We're taking a break. What's up?"

"Well, a lot, actually. Leann came running into the shop a little while ago, panic-stricken. I've never seen her like that. Not like herself at all. Two policemen came over to her house early this morning to question her. They asked her where she was the night of Zoe Yeager's death. Leann told them she went to the Presbyterian Church to see someone, then came home to continue working on her customers' garments."

Kelly felt a cold spot settle in her gut. *Oh, no.* One of those women in Zoe's class probably told the cops about Leann's confrontation with Zoe earlier that evening.

Burt took a deep breath. "Next, the detective asked Leann if she had a gun, and she said no. Then the detective, who must have been Dan from the way Leann described him, asked her if she was sure she didn't have a gun or maybe a gun collection. That's when Leann said she remembered her father's collection in the family room. Apparently, she had her father's pistols and revolvers in a glass case on the wall."

"Uh-oh . . ." Kelly drew in her breath and deliberately edged away from the crowded area outside the meeting room.

"Yeah, you know where I'm going with this, I'm sure. Anyway, Leann told them about the gun collection, and they asked to see it, naturally."

"Why have I got a bad feeling about what you're about to say?"

"Probably because you've already read my mind, Kelly. Leann said she took them into the family room and went over to the glass case, only to find one gun missing."

The cold in Kelly's gut spread. "Oh, no . . ."

Burt sighed again. "Oh, yes. Leann said she was shocked to see it gone and told the detectives, but you can understand how bad that looked."

"Heck, yes."

"It gets worse."

"What?" Kelly stopped walking, her hand pressed to her other ear.

"Leann said the detectives showed her a gun inside a plastic bag and asked if it resembled the gun she was missing. Leann said she was stunned. It looked exactly like it, and she told the detective so. She said her father bought the gun over twenty years ago."

"Oh, brother . . . of course that was the gun used in the murder, no doubt."

"Right, you are, Sherlock. Dan told me they questioned the five women who were in Zoe's evening class, and each of them had recounted Leann's angry confrontation with Zoe earlier that evening. So you can understand why they showed up at Leann's door."

"I understand, Burt, but it doesn't make me feel any better," she said. "I simply cannot picture Leann being angry enough with Zoe to hang around after class and shoot her."

"I know, I know . . ." Burt said with a weary sigh. "I have never understood how someone could rationalize murder, but they do. I understand *why* they do it. They're angry, or they're afraid. Usually it's one or the other."

Kelly noticed her fellow Warner Development folk were traipsing back into the meeting room. "How is Leann doing?"

"She's a wreck, Kelly, to be honest. It took Mimi and me several minutes to calm her down enough to get a straight story out of her. I feel so sorry this is happening."

Kelly could hear the tired sound in Burt's voice. Too many years spent investigating ugly crimes. One person killing another. As old as time itself. She was glad Burt had retired from his Fort Connor police detective position the year before she met him, the same year Kelly came to Fort Connor for her aunt Helen's funeral. It had been Burt who had encouraged her to keep asking questions whenever she found things that didn't make sense. Particularly whenever someone she cared about was involved in a murder. Burt had encouraged her "sleuthing."

In fact, he said he enjoyed it. Thanks to Kelly, he'd said he felt like he hadn't really left the department.

"So am I, Burt. I don't know Leann as well as you and Mimi do, but she certainly appears to be a nice woman. Of course, I have to admit, I was present when she came storming into the shop late one afternoon and showed Mimi and me the photo of Zoe's prizewinning gown. Leann produced a photo of one of her early designs, and I have to admit, Burt . . . those two designs were identical."

"Do you think Zoe stole that design from Leann?"

"Well, they are identical in style, and Zoe worked in Leann's shop for a year before she went out on her own. And according to Mimi, Leann's business was much more successful then, too. Ever since Zoe started her shop, Leann's lost customers. And I do recall Leann saying that Zoe had taken a list of her customers when she worked there. Leann was convinced."

"Really. That's very interesting, Kelly. Thanks for mentioning it. I'll pass that information on to Dan."

"You know, I almost wish I didn't know about it, but I can't pretend I didn't hear the conversation. Now I feel even worse for Leann."

"Don't worry, Kelly. You did the right thing, and you know it. It's new information, and Dan will want to hear it. Thanks, Sherlock."

That didn't make Kelly feel any better. "Has Dan talked with Vera?"

"I imagine he has. Why?"

"According to Leann and Mimi, Vera also worked with Zoe at Leann's shop years ago. Maybe she has more information. And Vera told them she was still working whenever she could for Leann to earn extra money. That was until Zoe's death. Now it looks like Vera is hiring Leann to work for *her* while she finishes Zoe's customers' sewing. Strange how things turn around."

"Strange, indeed, Kelly."

"Listen, Burt, I'll talk to you tomorrow. I won't be back into Fort Connor until late tonight."

"I'll call you if I hear anything else."

"Please, do. Take care, Burt." She clicked off and hurried into the meeting room.

• • •

Kelly took a sip of the French chardonnay. *Ummmm, clean and smooth*, she thought as she savored it. No heavy oak weighing down the flavor. Glancing around the dimly lit restaurant, Kelly admired the brass fixtures and dark woods used in the decor. Cozy like an old English pub, yet elegant and sophisticated like the posh private club it had once been more than a hundred years ago.

"This is a beautiful place, Steve. I've never been here before, although I've heard about it. Good choice." She raised her wineglass to him before taking a sip.

"I thought you'd like it," Steve said with a smile. "By the way, I really like this wine more than I thought I would." He took another sip.

"You know how much I like to try new wines. So I couldn't resist trying this one. I like it."

The sound of a clarinet, sending up a rhythmic jazz riff, drew Kelly's attention to the corner of the room, where the jazz pianist was generously letting the clarinet man take the familiar melody wherever he wished.

"Boy, were they smart to remodel this place several years ago," Kelly observed, looking around the room. "These fixtures alone have doubled in price over the years. And this thick walnut paneling is seriously hard to find in that grade. I know because Arthur Housemann has been building that dream house of his in the canyon, and he's using lots of antique fixtures in his den. He swears the prices have doubled on some items."

Steve laughed softly as he leaned on the table and set his glass down. "That's the challenge of dating an accountant. A romantic dinner can turn into a budgetary discussion."

Kelly met his gaze. He was teasing her, she could tell.

"Hey, budgets can be romantic. If you *love* saving money, I mean," she said with a grin.

Steve leaned both arms on the table, moving closer. "You know how much I love being with you, Kelly. We can take this as slowly as you want. I'm in no hurry. I'm not going anywhere."

"Neither am I," she said, leaning closer. "I'm glad you're here . . . with me."

Unfortunately, the server chose that moment to refill their water glasses. Kelly caught Steve's amused gaze and laughed softly.

"Oh, yeah . . . you can also tell Pretty Boy Germaine, if he has any problems with that, I'll be glad to discuss it with him. Anytime." Steve eyed her over his wineglass.

"You know, he asked me out to dinner tonight," she said with a sly smile. "But I told him I already had plans."

"Sonovabitch," Steve muttered, setting his glass down with a thump. "He moves in whenever I'm out of town."

Kelly laughed. "He's just a colleague, Steve."

"I know, but he's always circling you, like a coyote." Steve scowled. "I'm gonna have to have a talk with this guy."

"You just want an excuse to punch him out," Kelly teased.

"Yeah, that, too."

"You can't do that, Steve."

"Sure I can."

"You could, but Dave's the kind of guy who might sue you for assault. Or he'd bad-mouth you to every builder and developer in Denver. You're rebuilding your business, Steve. The last thing you need is an enemy. Dave's not some scumbag in the canyon who's threatening me. He knows *everybody*."

Steve stared into his wineglass and took a drink. Then

he gave Kelly a crooked smile. "You're right. He probably would. *Damn!* I still hate his guts."

Kelly laughed deep in her throat. "Then take it out on the court. Warner's starting a volleyball league for Metro Denver builders. Why don't you and your friend Vic join another team. I heard Overby Brothers is starting one. That way, we can all have some *friendly* competition."

Steve's eyes lit up. "Great idea. I'll give Vic a call. Then I've gotta practice spiking the ball. *Hard*."

They both laughed out loud as the waiter served their salads.

Ten

Kelly trailed her fingers across the multicolored balls of merino wool and silk as she walked from the Lambspun foyer through the central yarn room. Butter yellow, lime green. Small yarn twists that would require extra small knitting needles. Much smaller than Kelly liked working with.

Spotting Mimi seated in the main knitting room, Kelly headed there. "Hi, Mimi, I was hoping I'd find you here," Kelly said as she dropped her knitting bag on the table and pulled out a chair.

Mimi looked up from the soft forest green yarn she was knitting, and her somber expression vanished, replaced by a bright smile. "Kelly, I'm so glad you came in. I was hoping to see you today."

"That's why I came over this morning before I start my client work. I wanted to talk with you. As you know, Burt called me Saturday when I was in Denver and told me all about Leann." Kelly pulled the almost-finished shawl from her knitting bag.

"That was simply dreadful." Mimi's smile disappeared again as she returned her attention to the green yarn. "I cannot believe this is happening to Leann. She's a competent, talented person. She's not capable of shooting Zoe. That's ridiculous!"

Kelly refrained from commenting that anyone was capable of murder if they had enough reason. That's what the police called motive.

"I agree Leann is a lovely person, Mimi," Kelly said as she picked up her knitting stitches where she left off. This was the last row along the top edge of the shawl. After this row she could bind off all her stitches, and she would be finished. *Finally*. "But the gun she owned was used in Zoe's murder. You have to admit that does look very bad."

Mimi's worry frown appeared. "I know it does. And Leann has no idea what happened to it."

Kelly glanced at her dear friend. Mimi hated to think badly of anyone she knew and liked. It was simply against her nature. "Of course, that naturally makes the police suspicious, as you can understand."

"Of course."

Kelly paused for a moment before adding, "Especially when police heard from the women in Zoe's class that Leann had confronted Zoe that night and accused her of stealing. They were all witnesses to the confrontation."

Mimi didn't answer right away, but her stitches picked up speed. Finally she spoke softly. "I was afraid this would happen, Kelly. Ever since you told me police questioned the

124

women in Zoe's class. I wish Leann hadn't done that. I never thought she'd go through with it, Kelly. Actually drive over to Zoe's class, I mean."

"I wish she hadn't, either," Kelly added. "It certainly makes her look suspicious now. Police know she had a reason to be angry at Zoe, and she was in possession of the murder weapon. Not good, Mimi. Definitely not good."

Mimi's head jerked up. "But what if someone stole that gun? Leann said she couldn't remember the last time she'd even noticed the gun case on the wall. She was so used to seeing it. What if someone else stole the gun?"

Kelly sent Mimi a wry smile. "Well, anything's possible, Mimi. But who in the world would steal a gun from someone's private collection hanging on the wall? You have to admit that sounds a bit far-fetched."

Mimi frowned, clearly trying to conjure a believable scenario for her friend. "Who knows? Maybe . . . maybe some thief came in looking for money or jewelry or something valuable. Maybe he stole it! Then . . . then he sold it on the black market!"

Kelly deliberately kept her smile in check. Mimi's scenario was certainly inventive. "That's entirely possible, Mimi. But then, that would mean some anonymous person who wanted to kill Zoe bought the same gun on the black market. Burt has told us guns are readily available, but the main point is why would this anonymous person want to kill Zoe?"

Mimi's worry frown reappeared, claiming her face. "You're right, Kelly. I know you're right. Why would some criminal want to kill a seamstress in Fort Connor? It makes no sense. *None* of this makes sense."

Deciding to switch subjects slightly, Kelly knitted several stitches along the lengthy top edge of the shawl. "Tell me, how did Leann look Saturday? Burt said she was a wreck."

"Ohhh, she was, Kelly. She was *petrified*," Mimi said, returning to the green afghan. "She was stammering she was so scared. I'd never seen Leann like that. Burt and I took her into the café and poured creamy tea into her until she calmed down, so she could tell us everything that happened."

"Burt says he thinks Dan was the detective who questioned Leann. What did she have to say about him?"

"She was scared to death of him. She thought he was there simply because Zoe had once worked for her. But then he started asking questions about *her*. Leann said that frightened her, especially when he asked about her whereabouts that evening. She said that's when she started to panic."

"Did she mention anything else Dan asked about?" Kelly probed. "Other than her whereabouts that evening and the gun. Did he ask anything about her relationship with Zoe?"

"Let me think," Mimi said, still focusing on the green yarn. "I think she said he asked how long Zoe had worked for her and . . . and if they had parted on good terms. Which they had, of course. Oh, and he asked how well Leann's business was doing, and . . . and . . ." Mimi suddenly looked up at Kelly. "Oh, no . . ."

Kelly watched Mimi's face register the realization of what she'd just said. "Oh, yes, Mimi. Dan deliberately asked those questions about Zoe working for Leann. Some of those women in the class no doubt knew the details of Leann's and Zoe's past history together."

"Oh, no . . ."

"I hope Leann acted calm while she answered Dan's questions," Kelly added, even though she doubted that happened at all.

"Poor Leann . . . who knows what she said. She told us she was so panicked by his questions that she can't even remember what she said." Mimi closed her eyes, knitting dropped to her lap.

Things certainly weren't looking good for Leann, Kelly thought as she focused on her stitches. She did not want to mess up this top row. It would be the most visible because this part of the shawl would be over her shoulders and meet in the front. If she dropped a stitch, the whole world would see. Well . . . the fiber folks at the wedding would see. Most people were oblivious to the mistakes knitters fretted over.

Clearly, Leann did not hold up well under questioning. It sounded as if she wound up looking even more suspicious in Dan's eyes. Kelly would have to ask Burt what Dan actually was thinking. Surely, scores of innocent people have panicked when first questioned by police. It's an intimidating process.

The tinkling of the entry doorbell sounded, and Kelly figured the daily deluge of customers was about to begin. She'd only spied one early shopper in the loom room when she'd first entered. To Kelly's surprise, Leann walked into the main room.

"Hi, Mimi . . . hey, Kelly," Leann said as she approached the table, holding a dress box.

"Leann! I'm so glad you came in," Mimi said, practically leaping from her chair. "How are you doing?"

Kelly barely recognized Leann. Gone was the bright, pretty Leann. Now she looked pale and wan. Leann's eyes were also noticeably redder, the sure signs of weeping. "Mimi told me the police questioned you, Leann. That must have been dreadful," she commiserated. "How are you holding up?"

Leann glanced to Kelly. "Not good, Kelly. That policeman scared me so. My hands were shaking so much, I couldn't sew afterwards. Thank goodness I'd almost finished the matron of honor alteration. Last night, I tried again. I could only sew in short spurts, but I was able to finish it." She set the box on the table.

"That's wonderful, Leann. I'll call Megan," Mimi said, then enveloped Leann in a big hug. Leann returned Mimi's hug.

"I already called," Leann said once she'd released Mimi. "Megan told me to express mail it to her sister so she can try it on and bring it with her when she flies here next week."

"Here, sit down and relax with us for a few minutes," Mimi urged, patting the table. "Would you like some tea?"

Leann gave a small smile as she settled into a chair between Kelly and Mimi. "No, thank you. I've been using your cream tea recipe all yesterday, and I'm kinda overdosing on it."

Kelly reached out and offered some comfort of her own by placing her hand on Leann's arm. "Remember, Leann, you're not alone in all of this. We're here for you. Please tell me if there's anything you need."

Leann looked back at Kelly, gratitude in her eyes. "Thank you, Kelly," she said softly. "I admit I've felt so alone since yesterday. I have no family left. My parents both died a few years ago, and I had no children with my ex-husband. He's way off somewhere on the East Coast. We haven't been in touch for years."

"Well, you can count on your friends, Leann," Mimi declared, giving a motherly pat to Leann's other arm.

Leann glanced down into her lap, her hands clasped tightly together. "Thank you, Mimi . . . you, too, Kelly. I can't tell you how much that means to me."

Kelly sensed that Leann might want to talk with Mimi alone. After all, they'd known each other for years. Kelly decided to remove herself and allow for some private time between the old friends.

She picked up her almost-finished coffee mug. "I need a refill," she exaggerated. "I'm sure you two will excuse me. I hope to see you later, Leann." Leaving her chair, Kelly added, "And don't be dismayed by that detective's questions. Burt tells me that everybody is questioned like that. Try not to worry about it."

"Thanks, Kelly, I'll . . . try not to worry," Leann said, not sounding at all positive to Kelly.

Leaving them, Kelly sped through the adjoining yarn rooms and down the hallway to the café. Spotting Jennifer loading breakfast plates onto her tray, Kelly gave her a wave. "Hey, there. I'm taking a coffee break."

Jennifer lifted the tray expertly to her shoulder and smiled at Kelly. "I thought you were on perpetual coffee break, Kelly."

"Oh, good one," Eduardo teased from beside the grill.

Kelly smelled bacon sizzling on the grill and watched Eduardo place a flat iron on top of the hunk of slices to keep them straight. "Just ignore me, Eduardo," she said, leaning against the counter. "I'm going to stand here and inhale the aromas. I'll gain less weight that way."

The grill cook grinned. "You're fine, Kelly. I swear, you young girls are always worrying about your weight. A little bacon never hurt anybody."

Words to live by, Kelly thought, inhaling the delectable scent. Jennifer approached then, coffeepot in hand.

"Here you go," she said, pouring the dark rich brew into Kelly's mug. "Catch me up while I've got a minute. You and Steve went out Saturday night in Denver, right? How was it?"

Kelly took a deep drink and savored. *Ahhhh*. "It was great. We went to that old private gentlemen's club that was turned into a restaurant several years ago. They did a beautiful job of refurbishing it. Everything is done in that turn-of-the-century period. Gorgeous woods and brass everywhere. The food was delicious, and so were the wines. Even the jazz group was good."

"I was hoping you'd say it was a romantic evening. Sounds like you two were discussing architectural details instead of gazing into each other's eyes," Jennifer teased.

"Well, it was still romantic." Kelly played along. "Steve and I love talking about all those things. Hey, one of my clients is a developer, and Steve's an architect. Plus, he's been to all those construction conferences lately. He's gotten all sorts of new ideas about that house he'll be designing for Sam's friend."

"Oh, wow . . ." Jennifer said with a wicked smile. "Pardon me if I yawn. You two are hopeless."

"Hey, we had a great time," Kelly replied, then sent her friend a sly smile. "And we still managed to gaze into each other's eyes once or twice." She started to walk away.

"Okay, I guess there's hope for you two yet," Jennifer said. Kelly simply raised her mug in salute as she headed for the hallway. Oh, there was hope, all right. Lots and lots of it.

"Hey, you've returned," Burt greeted Kelly when she walked into the Lambspun foyer. "Mimi said you were here this morning, then you had to run back to your office." He set a lacquered box on the edge of the foyer table, which held a guest book and flyers describing the shop and available classes.

"That's about it," Kelly said. "I was all set to finally finish that little bridesmaid shawl. Then Don Warner called me from Denver and asked that I e-mail some additional reports to him right away. After that, I finished the rest of my client work, so I'm free as a bird until the guys' last baseball game tonight. Lisa, Megan, and I are going." She checked her watch. "That gives me a little over an hour."

"Do you have time for a quick coffee break first?"

Kelly recognized Burt's serious voice. "I'll bet you've heard from Dan, right?"

"You'll bet right. C'mon, let's go over to the café," Burt said, beckoning Kelly.

Kelly followed Burt past two browsing customers in the central yarn room, past another woman admiring the Mother Loom, then down the hallway to the café. The café would be empty now, since it was late afternoon. No one to overhear their conversation. Burt chose a small table at the rear of the café, one of their favorite spots.

Kelly plopped her bag on an adjoining chair and settled

across from Burt. Thank goodness she'd already refilled her coffee at home. New information always required a lot of concentration.

"Okay, Burt, you've barely cracked a smile since I came in. That means you heard something that concerned you. What was it?" She took a deep drink of hot brew to fortify herself before he spoke.

Burt let out a deep sigh and leaned forward over the table, folding both of his bear-paw hands. "Dan told me that Leann O'Hara has officially moved onto the suspect list."

Kelly screwed up her face. "I was afraid that would happen. I guess they finished interviewing all those women in Zoe's class, right?"

"Oh, yeah," Burt said with a nod. "And each one of them recalled Leann coming into Zoe's class that night and angrily accusing Zoe of stealing her design."

"Did any of them actually say that Zoe acted like she was scared of Leann?"

"I asked Dan that same question myself, and he told me the women all said Zoe looked a 'little frightened,' in their words."

"Did any of them know about Oscar? Or that Zoe had just escaped an abusive husband?"

"Oh, yes." Burt nodded vigorously. "Dan said all of them made it a point to tell him they knew about Oscar, and that Zoe was filing for divorce. And this is interesting . . . apparently Zoe took a few minutes at the beginning of class to tell everyone about her new situation. So they all knew that Oscar had flown into a rage when Zoe left him."

"Okay, that's more like it," Kelly said, straightening in her chair. "Surely some of those women voiced an opinion about Oscar. I cannot believe they would accuse Leann and ignore Oscar."

"Well, I don't think they accused anyone of anything, Kelly." Burt gave her a fatherly smile. "Dan said each of the women mentioned Leann's confrontation and Zoe's comments about Oscar at the beginning of class. Dan also learned that Oscar had barged into one of Zoe's sewing classes last year. Three of the women were in that class as well, so they saw Oscar at his finest, apparently. Dan said they all reported he obviously had been drinking, because they smelled it on him. He demanded Zoe give him some money, then he left."

"Well, all right, then. They got to see old Oscar at his best. I'm sure they remembered that scene clearly."

"They sure did, and they made a point of saying Zoe looked scared when Oscar showed up that night."

"Okay, at least Dan heard several accounts of how threatening Oscar could be." Kelly glanced into the empty café. "But we still come back to Leann having the murder weapon. *Damn*. We can't get away from that, can we?"

"No, we can't, I'm sorry to say." Burt let out a tired sigh. Too many murders in his lifetime.

"I wish some of Mimi's inventive scenarios were more plausible," Kelly said with a little smile. "I'd like to believe that someone came into Leann's house and stole the gun."

"Well, that's always possible, but that still leads back to who would have—"

"A reason to kill Zoe," Kelly finished for him. "The all-important motive. I know. In reality, anybody who might be tempted to steal a gun would probably use it to rob a convenience store, not plot to kill a seamstress."

"My thoughts exactly."

Kelly released a breath. "Well, if Dan is suspicious of Leann, I suppose we should be, too. Right?"

"You're right, Kelly, even though we may not be happy about it." He glanced at his watch. "I'd better get a move on. There are a few errands left on Mimi's list." He pushed back his chair.

Grabbing her mug and knitting bag, Kelly did the same, and joined Burt as he walked slowly down the hallway. "You know, I'm curious what Vera had to say about Zoe and Leann. She probably knows things no one else does. After all, she worked with Zoe in Leann's shop. She's known both of them and Oscar for years."

"I asked him, and Dan said Vera was the second person they questioned after Oscar. He added that Vera was most helpful. I'll talk to you later, Kelly. Say hi to everyone tonight." Burt gave her a parting smile and hurried for the shop front door. Errands beckoned.

Kelly headed for the knitting table and dropped her stuff, then settled into a chair. No one else was at the table. The shop would be closing in an hour. Plenty of time to finish that shawl. She pulled the royal blue bundle from her knitting bag.

Picking up her stitches where she'd left off, Kelly settled into the relaxing rhythm of knitting. *Slip, wrap, slide. Slip, wrap, slide.* Again and again. Halfway around the top row of the shawl.

"Oh, Kelly, I'm glad you haven't left yet," Mimi said, rushing into the room. "I saw you and Burt go into the café. He told you about his conversation with Dan today, right?"

"I'm afraid so, Mimi." She gave her a wan smile. "It wasn't good news, but you and I had already talked about it earlier.

I wish the facts were different, but they aren't. Leann is definitely a suspect."

Mimi sat in a chair beside Kelly and leaned forward. "Kelly, could I ask you a favor?"

Kelly looked up from her knitting. "Sure, Mimi. What do you need?"

Mimi leaned closer. "Could you please help Leann? You're so good at digging out information, I thought maybe there was something you could find out that would help her."

Kelly let her knitting drop to her lap. She stared into Mimi's wide blue gaze, imploring her. Kelly felt her heart squeeze. "Mimi . . . I . . . I don't think there's anything I could do. I mean . . . the police have got witnesses and the murder weapon—"

"But no fingerprints!" Mimi whispered after glancing over her shoulder at a browsing customer in an adjoining room.

"That's true, but that means either the killer wore gloves or wiped off the gun before throwing it into the Dumpster."

Mimi's expression turned pleading. "I know that, but I simply cannot believe that Leann could kill Zoe. It has to be Oscar. He's a drunkard, and he beat Zoe! Maybe there's someone who knows something but the police don't know about them. You're so cleaver at finding clues, I . . . I thought maybe you could discover something that would help Leann prove she's not guilty."

Kelly felt Mimi's desperation to help her friend reach out. *How could she refuse?* She couldn't. "All right, Mimi. I promise I'll ask some questions and see what I can learn. But that's really all I can do."

Mimi's relief was immediate. "Oh, thank you, Kelly! I

can't tell you how much I appreciate it. I simply could not sit by and allow circumstances to put Leann directly in the police crosshairs."

"I'll do what I can, Mimi," Kelly promised. "But I'm afraid Leann has already put herself right in the middle of police crosshairs."

Rosa rushed up to the archway separating the main room from the center of the shop. "Mimi, that California weaver is on the line. You called her earlier, remember?"

"Oh, yes, yes. I'm coming right now," Mimi said, springing from her chair. Mimi never seemed to sit but merely light on a branch, ready to fly away on a moment's notice. "Thank you so much, Kelly," she said as she rushed from the room.

Kelly picked up her shawl again. No wonder she'd taken so long to finish it. She was always interrupting her knitting. Now, however, Kelly allowed herself to ponder Mimi's request.

Could she find something that the police had not? She'd done it several times before, while sleuthing around previous murders. But this time, there didn't seem to be any loose ends. Dan was a very thorough detective. She knew that. Kelly doubted he would miss something. But then, Kelly had always managed to find details that the police missed. Ferret out information they didn't know. And she always started by asking questions. Lots and lots of questions. And those questions always led to more questions. That's how Kelly found her answers.

She knitted several more stitches. If she was going to start asking questions, where would she start? According to Burt, Dan and the detectives had questioned friends of Zoe's, customers, Oscar's drinking buddies at the bar, the bartender, neighbors, and the women in Zoe's evening class. They'd covered all the bases, it seemed to Kelly.

A hint of something tugged at Kelly's memory. Something said in conversation not long ago. What was it? Who was talking?

The memory moved closer, clearer, until Kelly remembered. *Jayleen.* Jayleen had said she had a friend who was taking Zoe's evening sewing class. And that friend remembered Zoe talking about her husband Oscar.

Once again, Kelly let the shawl drop to her lap. Maybe she could start by asking Jayleen's friend what she remembered about that evening. It was as good a place to start as any. In fact, it was the only place Kelly could think of to begin.

Kelly dug into her jeans pocket for her phone. Now if only Jayleen had that woman's phone number. She flipped through her directory and pressed Jayleen's name and number and listened to the rings. Once, twice, Jayleen was probably outside with the alpaca herd. Fifth ring . . . then a familiar voice sounded. Jayleen's voice mail.

Eleven

Kelly tabbed through the spreadsheet columns, entering various expenses from Arthur Housemann's real estate investments. There were more expenses than last month, she noticed, then checked the previous year's spreadsheet for the same month. Yes, definitely more.

Pausing to take a deep drink from her favorite ceramic mug, Kelly leaned back in her desk chair and looked through the patio door screen. The mild high seventies September temperatures kept summer around longer. That was another thing Kelly liked about Colorado. The weather was constantly a surprise. They could have mild temperatures in the middle of February right after a cold front had brought frigid twenties and teens. Then the next day, it would be in the forties, then rise to the fifties, then sixties. It was hard not to love weather like that. Of course, snowy times and cold fronts did take their turn, but in between the necessary winter temps, balmy weather often held sway.

Carl lay stretched out on the grass, sound asleep in the morning sun. Totally oblivious to Brazen Squirrel's trespassing. The clever furry creature had leaped from an overhanging cottonwood branch to the chain-link fence rail, then a hop and a squirrelly skip and down to the ground. Dangerous territory when Big Dog was awake.

Ahhhh . . . but Brazen knew enough to let sleeping dogs lie. That's when Kelly noticed Brazen did some of his best work. Hiding his treasures. Retrieving others. Kelly spied a nut in Brazen's jaws as he hopped closer to the patio. She glanced at Carl. Out like a rock. No problem.

Brazen had a clear path to the flower beds, one of his favorite hiding places. Kelly had forgiven the brave little squirrel his digging in her gardens. She figured if Brazen had enough guts to breach Big Dog's Territory to hide his winter cache of food, then it was okay with her.

Suddenly, her cell phone jangled. Kelly grabbed for it across her desk before it rang again. Brazen had frozen in place behind the plants. Carl raised his head briefly but, not hearing another ring, let it flop to the grass again. Snooze not to be interrupted. *Ahhhh*, the life of a dog.

Jayleen's name and number flashed on the smartphone screen. "Hi, Jayleen," Kelly said in a quiet voice, noticing Carl rouse himself again.

"Hey, Kelly, I'm sorry I didn't get your message last night. My phone had run down. So I didn't see your message until now."

"That's okay, Jayleen," Kelly said, moving away from her

desk in the sunny corner of her living room. "I knew you'd get back to me when you could. Mimi asked me to poke around a little and ask some questions, so I promised I would."

Jayleen chuckled. "A little sleuthing, right? That makes sense to me. You've got a good track record, Kelly-girl."

"Well, I remembered you said your friend was one of Zoe's students in that evening sewing class, and I hoped you had her number. Do you think she'd mind if I gave her a call?"

"Hell, no," Jayleen declared. "In fact, I already gave my friend a call after I heard your message and told her you wanted to talk with her. She said she didn't mind at all. Here's her number. Ready?"

Kelly hurried back to her desk. Carl was up off the ground and stretching. She wondered if Brazen had a chance to bury his treasure. "Ready," she said and grabbed a pen, scribbling the woman's number on the side of a Housemann Properties worksheet.

"Her name's Anna Sibelius, and she keeps children for day care so she's available all morning to talk. After lunch, she likes to keep it quiet for the kids to sleep."

"Got it. Thanks, Jayleen."

"Anytime, Kelly. I hope you learn something important. That Leann sounds like a nice lady. It would be a damn shame if the police suspected her."

"Well, they already do, so I doubt my efforts will turn up much to change that. The cops have already talked to your friend and the rest of the women at the class. But I promised Mimi I'd do what I could."

"Don't count yourself out yet, Kelly. I've seen you come up with stuff that everyone else has ignored. Well, I've gotta run. Talk to you later." She clicked off.

Kelly read the number again and flipped to the dialing screen. She didn't hold out much hope that she'd learn something the police hadn't, but she still had to try.

"Sunny Acres Day Care," a cheerful voice came over the line. "This is Anna."

"Hi, Anna, my name's Kelly Flynn. My friend Jayleen Swinson gave me your name and number. I hope I'm not getting you at a bad time."

"Actually, this is a good time, Kelly. I'm outside supervising the kids on the playground equipment in my backyard. So we may be interrupted a few times, but it'll work. Jayleen said you had some questions about that class I took with Zoe Yeager. The sewing class."

"Yes, well, my questions are not about the class exactly. I'm more interested in hearing everything you remember about that last class with Zoe. I'm . . . I'm asking for a friend of Leann O'Hara's."

"Oh, yes. I'd met Leann O'Hara at a class she was teaching a few years ago. That's when I first got interested in sewing. She's a really good teacher."

Brother, did Zoe steal away Leann's students as well as her customers? "That's good to know. Then you've met Leann before. Tell me, what did you think when she came into Zoe's class that night? I saw Leann at the Lambspun knit shop that afternoon, and she really looked mad. She swore Zoe copied her design."

"You know . . . I didn't know what to think when I heard her accusing Zoe. It was clear she was really upset. I have no idea if what she said was true or not. But it doesn't really matter, because poor Zoe is dead. *Joey!* Don't grab Susie's hair! Let go. Yes, *now*! Sorry . . . as I said, there will be interruptions. Uhhhh, yes . . . Leann. Yeah, she kind of toned it down a bit after a minute. You know, we were all staring at her . . . and Zoe."

"Did Zoe look scared of Leann at all?"

"No, not really. She looked kinda stunned, you know? I mean, someone comes in and accuses you . . . *Joey, no!* Do *not* hit Billy! Put that stick down right *now*! Sorry, Kelly."

Kelly had to smile. Little Joey sounded like a terror. "No, no, take your time. Joey sounds like a handful."

"Ohhhh, yes," Anna said, a smile in her voice. "But I was a primary teacher for years before I started doing day care. So I've seen lots of 'Joeys,' if you know what I mean."

"Tell me, Anna, did Zoe ever mention her husband Oscar?"

"Ohhhh, yes," Anna repeated, but this time there was no smile in her voice. Quite the opposite, Kelly noticed. "In fact, Zoe told us at the beginning of class that she had left Oscar and was filing for divorce. I applauded. Some of us had even seen Oscar in all his glory." A scornful tone crept in now. "I took one of Zoe's classes last year, and one night Oscar charged into our classroom. Drunk . . . from the smell of him. If not, he was close to it. Now, *that's* when Zoe looked scared. Really scared."

"Whoa, that does sound scary," Kelly agreed. "What did he want? Was he mad about something? I've heard he'd lose his temper over lots of things."

"He came in for money." Anna gave a derisive snort. "He swore he wouldn't leave until he got it. So, of course, Zoe gave him some. Bastard."

Clearly Anna did not hold Oscar in high regard. Kelly

decided to probe deeper. "Did Oscar become violent at any time while he was there?"

"No, but you could tell it was right below the surface. Waiting to explode, if you know what I mean. I had seen bruises on Zoe's face and wondered if she was in one of those abusive marriages. I've had other friends who've gotten into those relationships, and it's tragic. And once I saw Oscar in action, then I knew. I remember telling Zoe then, last year, that she should leave him."

"Boy, I wish Zoe had taken your advice," Kelly offered.

"Ohhhh, I wish she had. She'd be alive today," Anna said emphatically. "I have no doubt in the world that he shot Zoe. That Oscar was one nasty piece of work."

Kelly wasn't expecting that. "Did you tell the police that? I'd heard a detective came out to question all of you in Zoe's last class."

"You bet I did. And the other gals all said the same thing."

"Did you call them or something?"

"No, we got together one evening after Zoe's death to . . . well, talk about it. We were simply blown away by what happened. And we all had the same feeling that Oscar shot Zoe."

Since Anna was so convinced of Oscar's guilt, Kelly decided to follow up on that. "Did you see Oscar hanging around that night? Or parked along the street?"

"Oh, no. He wasn't anywhere to be seen. We wouldn't have left Zoe alone in the parking lot if we saw him there. No way!"

Kelly's little buzzer went off. *Zoe was alone after the class that night? Wasn't the women's shelter staff coming to drive along with her to the shelter?*

"Wait a minute . . . Zoe told Mimi that she was taking her own car to the class because she was going early, and there would be plenty of people at the church. And she said that one of the women's shelter staff would be at the church parking lot waiting for her after class. Then they'd drive with her to the shelter. That way she was never alone."

"That's right. She told me the same thing."

"Then why wasn't a shelter staffer waiting in the parking lot after class?"

"I wondered the same thing, Kelly. And I told her so. But Zoe assured me that they were probably delayed. And she'd drive down to the shopping center parking lot and wait for them. There were lots of people there."

Kelly pondered what Anna said. There was something about the scenario that didn't feel right. "You know, that sounds funny. I'd think the shelter staff would be there early, you know. Considering Oscar was off at the bars, drinking."

"I know, Kelly," Anna said with an audible sigh. "I told Zoe that I'd wait with her in her car, but she assured me she'd be fine at the shopping center. She was already in her car, so I told her I'd wait until she drove off, just to be safe. But her cell phone rang then, and she said it was probably the staffer saying she was on the way. So I got into my car and waited for her to pull out of the parking lot into the residential street before I drove off."

"*What?* She drove off? But Zoe was found shot inside her car, which was still parked in the church lot. I know, because Mimi and I spoke with the shelter staffer who arrived at the parking lot while the police were there."

"Please don't remind me, Kelly. I've been thinking that if I had just stayed with her at the parking lot, Zoe would be alive today."

"Don't feel guilty, Anna. You're not responsible. Something made Zoe drive back into that parking lot. Maybe it was the phone call."

"It must have been. I mean . . . I saw her in my rearview mirror, turning onto the residential street."

"Did you see anyone else on the street? Or sitting in a parked car nearby?"

"No, I didn't, and believe me, I looked," Anna said emphatically. "I checked every parked car I passed to make sure that bastard Oscar wasn't sitting there."

Kelly didn't know what to make of Anna's story. It didn't make sense. Was it the phone call that made Zoe turn around and park again? It had to be. Then, *who* was on the phone?

"What time was this, Anna? Do you remember?"

"Ohhhh, it was after nine o'clock. The class ran a little late, as you can understand. So it was after nine when we got out, nine fifteen or so. I remember glancing at my watch as we were walking out."

"Did you tell the police all of this? I mean, about your conversation with Zoe in the parking lot and watching her drive off? Did you tell them that?"

"I sure did, Kelly. And I told the detective how guilty I felt for not staying. But he said the same thing you did, almost."

Kelly's thoughts were racing. *Who called Zoe?* Was it Oscar? It had to be. What did he say? There was no way that Zoe would agree to wait for Oscar in an empty parking lot at night. What could Oscar say that would make Zoe stay? *Was* it Oscar? Was it the shelter staff?

"This makes no sense, Anna. I can't see Zoe waiting for Oscar or anyone in a dark, deserted parking lot."

"I can't, either, Kelly . . . *Joey! No!* Don't walk in front of the swing! *Ohhhh, noooo!*"

Playground Terror Joey had obviously struck again. Himself, this time.

"Gotta go, Kelly. I wish I could have been more help."

"You were a great help, Anna. Now go patch up Joey," Kelly said before Anna's phone clicked off.

Kelly shoved her phone into her jeans pocket and picked up her mug. Empty. *Rats.* She'd drained her coffeepot already. Time for an Eduardo refill. Besides, there were too many thoughts buzzing around her brain right now. She had to let them buzz around before they settled. Then she could return to her accounts.

Her knitting bag sat at the end of her new sofa, which gave her an idea. She needed to "knit on it." That's what Mimi always said when she needed to think about something. Kelly had discovered a few years ago how conducive to problem solving knitting was. Thoughts and ideas that bombarded her whenever she was sleuthing slowed down and became more ordered when she sat and knitted. Maybe it was the orderly process of stitching itself that helped, the *slip, wrap, slide* repetitive motion. Whatever it was, Kelly found it peaceful and soothing. And she'd gotten some of her best ideas while immersed in the process.

That settled it. Kelly grabbed her knitting bag and her mug and left the cottage. Heading across the driveway, she looked around for Burt's car, but didn't see it. She wanted to tell him what she'd just learned. Maybe Dan hadn't shared everything with Burt.

Kelly raced up the café steps, the caffeine lobe of her brain starting to throb in anticipation. Bursting into the crowded café, she wove her way around the customers and tables until she reached the counter and grill. There she spied Jennifer and gave her a wave, then jiggled her empty mug.

Almost *there,* Kelly thought as she approached the end of the top row of her blue shawl. Five more stitches to bind off, four more, three . . . two, one. *Done!* At last! She was finally finished. Megan, Lisa, and Jen had finished their shawls weeks ago.

She reached for some scissors that sat in the tool tray in the middle of the long knitting table and snipped the dangling yarn tail. Now there were only a few inches to weave inside the other stitches, out of sight.

Kelly examined the long top edge of the triangular shawl. Not bad. Not bad at all, she decided. Her stitches had gotten better, more even. And no dropped stitches. At least, she didn't notice any. Of course, she hadn't really scrutinized the lovely open weave design. She'd probably find something if she looked hard enough.

In fact, she hadn't had the time to eyeball the shawl at all because the edge she was working got longer and longer with every row, thus taking longer to finish. Since time was always in short supply for Kelly, she found herself simply pulling the shawl out of the bag to knit for a few minutes, then shoving the shawl inside the bag when she ran out of time.

Kelly held up the soft royal blue shawl by both ends. Glancing across the rows starting from the top, she looked closely at the open weave design, checking for any large or extra holes where there shouldn't be holes. Down, down, everything looked okay. No extra holes yet. Down to the bottom tip of the triangle. So far, so good. *Yay!* No holes.

But Kelly did see something else. She hadn't noticed it at first. The left side of the shawl looked different than the right side. It looked smaller somehow. But that couldn't be. All the stitches were there. It must be her imagination.

She tried to spread the shawl out on the knitting table to get a better look, pushing aside the patterns and books and balls of yarn scattered about. Was one side of that triangle wider than the other? Kelly peered at the lacy blue shawl and frowned.

Okaaaay . . . there's only one way to tell for sure, Kelly decided. Measure each side of the shawl. Searching through the assorted knitting paraphernalia and tools tray in the middle of the table, she found the tape measure. Now . . . exactly where to measure? Since the shawl was a triangle, she should be able to measure the distance from the top edge of the shawl triangle to the bottom of the other two sides. Even though the shawl was a soft fluffy knitted triangle, it was still a triangle. So it had to be geometric, right? Of course it did. Kelly remembered her geometry. Pythagorean theorems.

Now . . . how to do it? Maybe she could fold it in half. That way she could actually compare the two sides against each other. That would work. Convinced that she'd found a logical, geometric answer to this knitting puzzle, Kelly picked up the shawl and carefully folded it in half, with the top edges aligned and the two ends touching. She stared at the folded shawl and the new triangle it had created. The two sides of the shawl were together, and . . .

She couldn't miss it. One edge of the shawl was about

three inches higher than the other edge. Kelly stared in disbelief. *How did that happen?* Everything looked fine while she was knitting. How did the left side shrink? And why hadn't she noticed?

Kelly knew the answer to the second question. She never had the time to examine the shawl. She was knitting in whatever moments she could steal away from other duties. It was all she could manage to knit several stitches at a time. Examining the shawl was out of the question.

She stared at the shawl with a mixture of disappointment and disgust. Just then, Rosa walked into main room.

"Hey, Kelly, how're you doing?" Rosa asked as she shoved a book onto the shelves.

"Arrrrgh!" Kelly replied, eyes closed.

Rosa turned in surprise. "What's the matter?"

"Look at this!" Kelly pointed at the disappointing, disgusting shawl. "I've been working on it for weeks, and it looked fine. And now that I've finally finished the darn thing, I discover one side is way shorter than the other. *Look!*"

Rosa examined the shawl, fingering the two edges, placing them together. "Yeah, that happens sometimes, Kelly."

That was not the response Kelly was hoping for. "That's what you guys always say! Whenever something weird goes wrong with a knitting project, you guys tell me 'it happens sometimes.'" She scowled at the shawl. "That is unacceptable. There has to be a reason."

Rosa smiled a little. "Okay . . . the most likely reason is the shawl has been shoved in and out of your knitting bag for weeks. Believe me, Kelly, it really does happen. To everybody. It's happened to me."

"Hah!" Kelly countered, still aggravated.

"No, really. But don't worry. We can steam it; that will help it stretch. C'mon, I'll show you how." Rosa beckoned Kelly into the adjoining workroom.

Kelly gathered the soft mohair wool and followed Rosa. "Everyone else's shawls are perfect. I saw them. Mine will be the only one *deformed*."

Rosa laughed as she picked up a large corkboard and laid it on the long worktable. "It's not deformed, Kelly. Your stitches look fine. It's simply shorter." She took the soft wool mohair from Kelly's hands and spread it out on the corkboard.

Kelly watched as Rosa shoved pushpins all along the top edge of the shawl. Then she smoothed out the wider side of the shawl and began pinning that in place.

"Hand me that tape measure over on the counter, would you, please?" Rosa pointed to the counter behind her, laden with small portable looms for Mimi's weaving classes.

"Do you think the shorter side will really stretch enough to match the other?" Kelly asked as she retrieved the tape measure and handed it to Rosa.

"Well, let's hope so. The steaming will be key in softening and loosening the wool fiber. I'll show you how to do it after I've gotten it all pinned in place."

Rosa measured the good side, then marked the spots on the corkboard that would match for the other side of the shawl. Then Rosa's quick fingers began deftly stretching the shorter side and pinning it into place, right over the measured lines.

Kelly was heartened to see the wool stretch into place. "Hey, it's stretching on the board. Do we still have to steam it?"

"Oh, yes. The steaming is what loosens the yarn twist.

Why don't you plug in the steamer for me, please? It's right on the counter, and it's ready to go. I've already used it today." She continued stretching and pinning.

Kelly spotted the metallic wand on the counter, its long cord draped beside it. She retrieved it and dutifully plugged in the mysterious appliance. Kelly had never steamed anything before, but she'd seen several people at the shop doing it.

"There now. All pinned into place. You've seen someone steam yarn before, haven't you?" Rosa asked as she picked up the appliance. A soft hiss sounded from the flat head.

"Yeah, I've seen them, I've just never had to do it myself."

Rosa grinned. "You've lucked out. All of us make friends with the steamer sometime or another. It's really simple, Kelly. You start at the top and press the steamer against the wool and move the wand down slowly, pressing the steam button at the same time. Here, watch me do it once, then you can do it."

Kelly watched intently as Rosa placed the steamer wand at the top of Kelly's shawl and slowly moved down to the edge, steamer hissing loudly while it traveled over the wool. As she studied Rosa's movements, Kelly also sent a yarn plea out to the heavens. *Stretch . . . please.*

Twelve

"**Well,** hello, Kelly." Mimi greeted her in a cheerful voice. "It's always good to see you early in the morning." She returned to filling a yarn bin with skeins of black and gray, tweedlike yarn. HAND-DYED ALPACA, the sign proclaimed.

Kelly dropped her briefcase on the Lambspun knitting table. "I thought I'd work here today, Mimi. That way I can check on my shawl during coffee breaks."

"You sound like a mother hen," Mimi said with a light laugh. "The wool needs time to stretch, Kelly. Don't worry about it."

Kelly sank into a chair. "Don't *worry* about it? Are you *kidding*? The wedding is in ten days! Everyone else's shawls are done, and they're all *perfect*! I saw them. How can I not worry about it? I swear, I even dreamed about it last night."

Kelly frowned as she reached for her mug, but even Eduardo's Divine Brew could not wash away Knitting Angst. She was deep in it and burrowing deeper.

Mimi watched her carefully, clearly recognizing the signs. "How much coffee have you had already?"

"Not enough." Kelly pouted as she pulled out her laptop computer.

"Maybe you need a cup of creamy tea instead," Mother Mimi suggested.

Kelly looked up, aghast, then made a face. "*Ackkkk!*" was her only comment.

Mimi laughed softly. "Have you ever tried hot tea?"

Kelly made a different face as she flipped open her laptop. "Once. When I was a little girl, and Aunt Helen gave it to me. It made me sick. I threw up even more."

"It sounds like you were already sick, but okay. No tea. How about if I get you some of Eduardo's coffee with some cream in it?"

"*Eewwuuuu!*" Kelly said, trying to keep her petulant tone, but Mimi was making it hard. "Defile perfection? Don't you dare."

Mimi threw up both hands. "Okay, I give up. No tea. No cream in your coffee. I'll just leave you to wallow in your Knitting Angst."

Kelly had to laugh as she sank back into the wooden chair. "It's so frustrating, Mimi. Every time I think I'm getting better as a knitter, something happens. I do something *stupid*! Like this mistake on the shawl." She gave a dismissive wave toward the adjoining room, where her blue shawl was stretched out on the blocking board.

"Kelly, you are entirely too hard on yourself," Mimi chided

gently. "We *all* make mistakes like that. Even though we're experienced knitters, we still make mistakes. Ask anyone."

Kelly wasn't ready to climb out of the Angst Swamp yet. "Still, it's so close to the wedding. What if the shawl isn't stretched by then?"

"Don't worry, it'll be fine by the wedding," Mimi promised, reaching over to give Kelly's arm one of her encouraging pats.

"You sure?" Kelly asked, still dubious.

"Trust me, okay? Meanwhile, I think you need some time with your shawl. That will make you feel better. Come on, I'll set up the steamer for you." Mimi beckoned Kelly toward the adjoining workroom.

"You're humoring me, aren't you?" Kelly said, recognizing Mimi's soothing tone. She'd heard it many times over the three-plus years she'd been at Lambspun.

"Yes, I am," Mimi said from the doorway. "And I'm allowed to. You girls call me Mother Mimi, so come along and do what Mother says."

Kelly laughed. "Coming, *Mother*," she said as she rose from her chair and followed Mimi. She spotted her blue shawl lying on the blocking board where she'd left it yesterday. From this angle, it looked fine. Both bottom edges of the shawl looked even.

"See? It's waiting for you to steam it again." Mimi gestured to the board. "Let me refill the steamer, and you'll be ready to go." She took the metal wand and walked into the adjoining office area.

"Are you sure I can't hurt it by steaming it again? It looks okay now," Kelly asked Mimi, who was standing beside a sink.

"Not at all. In fact, you need to steam it several times." Mimi walked back into the workroom and plugged the steamer cord into a socket. "There now. Let this heat up, then steam it exactly the way you did yesterday. Rosa told me she showed you."

Kelly nodded. "Start at the top edge of the shawl and move downward gently."

"Good girl." Mimi gave her a smile. "Now do that again, every six hours or so. Check first to see if the wool is still damp. If it is, then wait till it feels drier."

"Yes, ma'am." Kelly played along, taking the metal steamer.

"It'll be ready in a minute," Mimi said, walking toward the hallway. "I have to check up front. Rosa may need help with customers. Now, you start steaming. It'll make you feel better."

Kelly rolled her eyes. "Just don't bring me any creamed tea."

Mimi's light laughter floated behind her as she walked away.

No one else was in the room. She'd come over before the shop was officially open. Kelly stared at the shawl stretched on the corkboard, which lay on a worktable. It looked perfect to Kelly. She stroked the soft blue wool and mohair yarn. The pushpins were clearly holding the shawl in place, and she'd measured each side. Both bottom edges were exactly the same length and the same width. Now . . . if the shawl only held its shape when the pushpins were removed, she'd be happy.

The steamer hissed in her hand, snakelike. She pushed the steamer button and a blast of hot steam shot out of the flat head of the wand. The steamer snake was clearly ready.

"Okay, shawl, time for another session," she said as she bent over the board and started steaming.

She did the correct side first, with lighter pressure, as Rosa had instructed. Then she moved to the side of the shawl that needed to be lengthened. She let the steamer linger over the stitches longer while she exerted more pressure on the yarn.

"Stretch. *Stretch*. You want to stretch," she said to the yarn, then glanced over her shoulder to make sure no customers were approaching. "C'mon, be a good yarn and stretch. Stretching is good."

She moved the wand down, holding it in place over the area that had looked the shortest. Now it was stretched into its proper length.

"Stretch, *strettttch*. You're wool. You come from sheep. The sheep want you to stretch," she commanded.

"Oh, boy, it's worse than I thought," Jennifer's voice sounded as she walked into the room, coffee mug in hand. "Mimi said you were deep in the Knitting Angst Swamp, but it's worse than that. Now you're talking to the yarn."

Kelly looked up at her friend, but kept on steaming. "Don't you talk to your yarn?"

"Actually, no. But then, I'm not cooped up in a cottage all day staring at numbers on a spreadsheet. I'm talking to people constantly in the café." Jennifer settled into a chair at the worktable and pulled out the maroon wool sweater she was knitting.

"I'm not cooped up in the cottage," Kelly corrected. "It's quiet and peaceful there. And when I want conversation, I come over here. Of course, sometimes I get more aggravation than conversation, like now."

"Am I annoying you?" Jennifer asked innocently, looking up from her needles. "Good. You need to be annoyed periodically. It's good for you."

"Believe me, the yarn is annoying me enough." Kelly returned her concentration to steaming the shorter side of the shawl.

"Actually, I think the yarn annoyance is merely a symptom."

"Symptom of what?" Kelly asked absently, focusing her considerable concentration on the shawl's edge.

"Yarn aggravation is just a symptom of the deeper problem," Jennifer said sagely. "Once that's addressed, all will be well." Her fingers moved rapidly, stitches forming on her needles.

Kelly paused over the steamer and glanced at her friend. Jennifer was going somewhere with this, so she might as well play along. At least it was better than arguing with the yarn.

"Deeper problem?" she parroted. "And what, pray tell, would that be?"

"Simple. You and Steve need to get back together. And by 'together' I mean *together* together. Like you used to be. Then all will be well," Jennifer pronounced, as if she were giving the local weather. Cloudy tonight, sunny tomorrow, maybe.

Kelly stopped steaming and turned to her friend, expecting to see a smile. Jennifer was calmly knitting away. "Excuse me?"

Jennifer glanced up and gave her an indulgent smile. "You have questions, Young Skywalker?"

A laugh escaped before Kelly stopped it. *Okaaaay*. Jennifer was obviously in a playful mood. "Uh, yes . . . Obi Wan. I beg to differ. Steve and I have gotten together. Many times. We've gone to dinner countless times. We've been out with you guys, we see each other here in Fort Connor and in Denver—"

"*Hold!*" Jennifer commanded, hand up in stop position.

"I don't recall Obi Wan Kenobi saying that. Or did you just slip from *Star Wars* into *Star Trek*? You sound like a Klingon."

"Obi Wan is on a meditation break, so I'm speaking as the Doctor of Love right now."

"Ahhhh, I remember her. But that was before you were with Pete. You know, *together* together with Pete," Kelly teased with a wicked grin.

Jennifer didn't bat an eye, but Kelly did spot a smile. "Nevertheless, that doctoral certificate is still hanging on my bulletin board. It may be covered over with catering schedules now, but it's still there. So I'm speaking as a trained and seasoned expert."

"Ahhhh . . . I see."

"And as such, it is my professional opinion that you and Steve need to move this dating thing into the fast lane and get serious. It is positively painful to watch you two trying not to let on how much you want each other. Steve wants you. You want Steve. For heaven's sake, get it over with and move back in with each other. Both of you are seriously deprived."

Jennifer returned to her knitting, as if she'd just told Kelly what she needed to buy at the grocery store.

Kelly kept her smile in check, but it was difficult. "Deprived, huh?"

"You're unusually dense today, Young Skywalker. If you're not careful, I'll hand your training over to Yoda. You'll recognize her. Short, dark, curly hair. Quick temper."

Kelly snickered. "*Oh, no!* Not Yoda!"

"Seriously. Megan's blood pressure is rocketing. Lisa's biting her nails. Greg refuses to ride in Steve's truck anymore because all he plays are sad country songs. Marty rode with Steve once and was depressed for days. Mimi and Burt are losing patience. Curt and Jayleen lost it months ago. Steve's own father is still mad at him. Even Pete and I are beginning to get pissed, and we're the patient ones."

Kelly just laughed.

"So for the health and sanity of all your friends, why don't you two just get it over with and jump in bed, okay? Do us all a favor, willya? We'll all feel better. And you and Steve will feel a *whole* lot better. I promise you." Jennifer held up her hand, Scout style.

This time, Kelly bent over the blocking table, she was laughing so hard.

Jennifer glanced at her watch. "Well, that's enough counseling for today. Gotta get back to the café." She gathered her knitting into its bag as she rose.

Kelly tried to catch her breath.

"Heed my words, Young Skywalker, or the Force will leave you flat." Jennifer then gave a combination Klingon and Empire trooper salute, then hurried down the hallway back to the café.

Kelly laughed softly, watching her friend leave. You had

to love friends like that. No one else would talk to her like Jennifer. She turned off the steamer and placed it on the shelf, then patted the shawl. Nice and damp. Perfect for stretching, Mimi said. Now maybe she could get some accounting work done.

Heading back into the main room, Kelly saw Burt setting up his spinning wheel in the corner. She wondered if Burt had overheard Jennifer's Obi Wan–Love Doctor advice. Even if he had, Burt wouldn't let on.

"Hey, Burt, you can keep me company while I'm working on my clients," Kelly said as she returned to her laptop computer at the table.

Burt looked up and gave Kelly a smile. "I'll enjoy your company, Kelly. But first, let's take a minute to talk, shall we?"

"Sure. What's up?" she said, settling into the wooden chair.

Burt pulled out a chair beside her and leaned closer. He glanced over his shoulder, then spoke in a soft voice. "I heard from Dan. They've learned that Leann O'Hara and Oscar Yeager had a brief affair two years ago."

Kelly sat upright in an instant. "*What!*" she exclaimed, louder than she'd intended. She lowered her voice as she leaned toward Burt. "I can't believe that! A nice woman like Leann with *Oscar*! Good Lord! He's a drunk and a brute. What was she *thinking*?"

Burt gave a rueful smile. "I feel the same way, Kelly. I can't understand it, either. Leann must have been really lonely or desperate or something to get together with him."

Kelly frowned. "Okay, what are the police thinking? What connection does this have to Zoe's murder?"

"Well, there are several possibilities, Kelly. Leann owned

the murder weapon and had the gun in a glass case in her home. Oscar, no doubt, saw it there. Dan said that the most obvious way for Oscar to have access to the gun would be if Leann gave it to him. If so, and Oscar used the gun to shoot Zoe, then Leann would be an accomplice."

"But what if she didn't know he was going to kill Zoe?" Kelly protested.

"Even so, Kelly. If she willingly gave Oscar the gun, then she's drawn into it. Whether it's fair or not."

"I'll bet Oscar stole the gun. That sounds like a more plausible scenario. I can attribute Leann's liaison with Oscar to temporary insanity maybe. But I cannot see her helping Oscar murder his wife."

"That's possibility number two. Oscar stole the gun when Leann wasn't looking or . . . or came in while Leann was out. Then he killed Zoe without anyone knowing it was him."

"I'll vote for that one."

"Then, of course, there's the third possibility that we already know about. Perhaps Leann used the gun to kill Zoe. Learning Leann and Oscar have been lovers tends to make other possibilities open up. Who knows? Maybe Leann really loved Oscar and did whatever he asked. Smart people do stupid things all the time, Kelly."

Kelly screwed up her face. "Yeah, but with Oscar? *Yuck!*"

"Believe me, there are a lot worse types out there than Oscar, and they often attract good women to help them. I know, it makes no sense. But sex mixes up people's thinking, and they can make very bad decisions."

Kelly wagged her head. "Boy, this makes it look worse for Leann, doesn't it?"

"I'm afraid so, Kelly."

"Has Dan gone to question Leann again?"

"He's going to see her today. I haven't told Mimi. I know I can trust you to keep information confidential."

She let out a sigh. "You know you can, Burt. This is so sad. Leann has moved front and center in Dan's suspect circle."

"Yeah, you're right, Kelly," Burt said as he returned to his spinning spot in the corner. "I need to spin awhile and let my thoughts settle."

"I wish I had something to knit, Burt, and I'd join you, but I only brought my briefcase this morning. My half-finished projects are back in the bag."

Burt grabbed a handful of cream-colored fleece from a large plastic bag at his feet and began drafting the wool—stretching the fibers into what spinners called batten or roving. That way, it was easier to spin.

"I saw your blue shawl tacked on the blocking board. It looks good, Kelly."

"If only it will hold its shape after those pins are removed. That's why I'm working here today, so I can steam it several times." She glanced over to Burt, whose feet began to work the spinning wheel's treadle. "Mother Mimi's orders."

"Yes, I heard about that," he said, smiling as the roving slid through his parted fingers, joining the yarn twist that wound around the moving wheel.

Kelly fired up her laptop and waited for the icons to blink into life. Meanwhile, the disturbing images of Leann together with Oscar kept intruding. Talk about a lapse of judgment. There was no other way to explain it. Whatever the reason, now the police had even more reason to suspect Leann's involvement in Zoe's death.

Icons blinked into place, and Kelly clicked on the one

labeled HOUSEMANN. The screen obliged and a spreadsheet appeared, with tabs below leading to more spreadsheets. Numbers, numbers everywhere.

Instead of diving into the numbers and eliminating the Oscar-Leann images, another thought popped up. Her conversation yesterday with Jayleen's friend, Anna. The shawl problem had temporarily chased away the memory of Anna's account of Zoe in the parking lot that evening.

"You know, Burt, I had an interesting conversation with a woman yesterday. She was a friend of Jayleen's and had mentioned that she was taking Zoe Yeager's sewing class. Jayleen gave me her number, and I called her yesterday morning. I wanted to tell you, but you and Mimi escaped to the mountains all day." She smiled.

"We sure did, and boy, was it worth it. You should go up there, Kelly. Or better, you and Steve should go up there together." He caught her eye and grinned. "And don't come down until you two are back together again."

Kelly had to laugh. So Burt did overhear Jennifer's Obi Wan advice. She should have known. "Boy, this is the morning for advice. At least you're not hiding behind a *Star Wars* character."

"I would if it would do any good."

"Okay . . . I'll take it under advisement. Boy, you guys are something else. Anyway, I wanted to tell you what this woman, Anna, had to say. First, she mentioned that Zoe told the entire class she'd left Oscar and was filing for divorce. Anna said she applauded because she'd seen Oscar before. And she told me about the time Oscar came into Zoe's class last year and demanded money. Anna said he looked drunk to her."

"Oscar at his finest." Burt didn't look up, simply kept feeding the roving onto the wheel, his feet rhythmically pedaling.

"I agree. But here's where it gets interesting. Anna said they all left class together, and Zoe was surprised that the shelter staffer wasn't already there, waiting for her."

Burt's head popped up at that. "What? That's part of their procedure."

"Well, Anna said Zoe told her she would drive to the nearby shopping center and wait there. She figured they were delayed. Then Zoe's phone rang while she was getting into her car and she told Anna it was probably the staffer calling."

"Still. Zoe's husband was a proven threat to her. They should have been there."

"I thought so, too, and so did Anna. In fact, she waited in her car to make sure Zoe drove out of the parking lot. And get this, Burt. Anna said Zoe was behind her, and she watched Zoe drive out of the lot onto the residential street. Anna figured she was safe then, so she drove off. Of course, now she's feeling majorly guilty because she thinks if she'd stayed, Zoe would still be alive."

Burt stopped spinning and stared at Kelly. "Zoe drove out of the lot? But police found her car in the church parking lot with Zoe dead inside."

"That's exactly what I told Anna. So . . . if Anna saw Zoe drive out of the lot, then something made Zoe turn around and drive back and park her car there. I cannot figure out what would make Zoe do that unless it was the phone call. What do you think, Burt? I wonder who called Zoe. And what did they say? Was it the shelter saying they were running late?

Was Oscar lurking in the bushes waiting for a moment when Zoe was alone? What happened?"

Burt frowned, clearly thinking. "Those are good questions, Kelly. Dan never mentioned that conversation with Anna. And he certainly never mentioned the shelter staff was delayed. As I recall, the staffer assigned to Zoe told both you and Mimi that she arrived at the church parking lot to pick up Zoe and found the police there. Zoe was already dead in her car."

"I remember. So what happened? What made Zoe return to the parking lot?"

"You know, that's bothering me, too, Kelly. Dan has been really busy with another case, so he's only had a few minutes to talk. I'll bet those details slipped his mind. That's understandable, considering he'd learned that rival seamstress Leann owned the murder weapon, and she'd threatened Zoe the same night. And now, the news of Leann and Oscar." Burt shook his head. "I'll send Dan an e-mail and ask him to give me a call when he has a little more time. Let's see what he says. Did that woman Anna tell the police all of this?"

Kelly nodded. "She said she did. She and the other women are all convinced it was Oscar who killed Zoe. They didn't see Leann as a threat, mainly because Zoe didn't act scared of her."

"We've got lots of questions, Kelly. Let's see what Dan can tell us, okay?" Burt returned to his spinning.

Kelly turned her attention back to her waiting spreadsheets. Thank goodness for numbers. You could lose yourself in them. And all bothersome and annoying questions disappeared . . . temporarily.

Thirteen

"**It** sounds like you're having a great time designing that mountain home, Arthur," Kelly said to her client as they walked out of his office. Housemann was dressed in jeans and a denim shirt instead of his usual conservative dark gray business suit.

"Oh, I am, Kelly," Housemann said with a smile. "I've been jotting down ideas for years in case I ever had the chance to build my dream house in the mountains. It took longer to happen than I'd hoped, but it's a reality at last."

Kelly shifted her shoulder briefcase. "I'm going to have to drive up there and see how it's coming. The last time I checked, the builder had only broken ground."

"Oh, yes, I remember he said you'd stopped by. He'd poured the foundation, that's all. You'll be surprised how well it's coming along. He's trying to get under roof before mid-October."

"Ah, yes, mountain snowstorms," Kelly said as they walked across the anteroom of Housemann's office. His elderly secretary was away from her desk.

"We've been lucky so far. Only one storm has dropped a couple of inches, and there have only been light dustings since. But our luck won't hold. October will bring colder temperatures at night, and more storms will sweep through the mountains."

"That's true, even though we've had such mild September weather, and fall seems a long way off." She paused at the entry door and looked at her formerly staid client, now relaxed and happier-looking than she'd ever seen him. "Well, I'm simply glad you chose to build this home now. I'm sure the builder gave you a fantastic price. Home construction has dried up except in these special custom projects."

Housemann nodded. "You're so right, Kelly. Both my architect and the builder gave me steep discounts. I tell you, it's so bad now that builders have had to cut back their crews to next to nothing. They're putting up Sheetrock and hammering nails themselves."

"I can understand that. Everyone says this is the worst housing downturn they've seen since the recession of the eighties."

"It's worse, Kelly. I lived through that one and survived. This one is far deeper," Housemann replied sagely.

"Well, at least you're secure, Arthur," she said before turning to leave. "Even though I can't say the same for that formerly fat cash reserve of yours. Forgive me, but the little CPA lobe of my brain gets a twinge watching those construction bills eat away at it."

Housemann laughed softly. "That's why I never worry

about the accounts, Kelly. I know you're watching over them like a Rottweiler on patrol. Let me know when you've driving up into the canyon, and I'll give you a tour."

"Will do, Arthur, take care," Kelly said with a wave, then turned toward the elevator.

Arthur Housemann's observations matched everything Steve had told her about the continued depressed state of the housing market. Moderate- and low-income housing construction was stalled. And the steady stream of foreclosed houses flooding the market added to the inventory of properties available for sale. Consequently, there was continued downward pressure on prices of existing houses listed for sale. In Denver, prices had plummeted.

Walking into the office complex parking lot, Kelly clicked her car lock, then dumped her briefcase onto the passenger seat before she jumped into her sporty car. Revving the engine, she maneuvered out of the lot and into the surrounding street's traffic.

Her cell phone jangled, and Kelly slipped it from the briefcase pocket. Burt's name and number flashed on the screen.

"Hey, Burt, how're you doing?"

"I'm okay, Kelly. Are you driving? You sound the way you do when you're in your car."

"Good ear, Burt. Yeah, I finished an appointment with Arthur Housemann and am on my way home. With a little luck, I'll have a few minutes to drop by the shop and check on my shawl."

Burt chuckled. "Your shawl is doing well, Kelly. I gave it a pat earlier this morning as I passed by. Listen, I thought I'd give you an update before I disappear into shopping centers and errands the rest of the day."

"Perfect timing. Did you hear from Dan?"

"Yes, I did. He called this morning and told me a lot more about the investigation. I shared what you'd heard from Anna, and Dan confirmed she told them the same thing. He and the guys came up with the same theories we did. Someone called Zoe, and that's why she turned around and drove back into the church parking lot. Who called her is the unanswered question."

"Was there a number on her cell phone log?"

"That's one of the puzzling things about this case. The phone number comes up as 'out of area' network, which could mean the caller used one of those disposable phones. There's no way to trace those."

"You know, that makes me suspicious, Burt," Kelly said, easing her car around a corner. "It sounds like the killer wanted to disguise his identity."

"Could be, Kelly. Or it could simply be that those phones are a cheap way to have cell service. But Zoe's phone does show a call from her to the shelter in the late afternoon. Dan checked with the shelter to see why they were delayed in picking up Zoe that night. You and I had both wondered about that, Kelly."

"You bet we did. What did the shelter folks have to say?"

"They said that Zoe called a second time in the early evening and told them she'd be delayed with her class and not to come until ten thirty." He paused.

"*What!* That doesn't make sense. Zoe's class got out about nine fifteen according to Anna. And Zoe was going to the shopping center to wait. If she'd told the shelter a later time, she would have said something to Anna, right? I mean, Anna was worried about her."

"One would think, Kelly. Dan agrees, it made no sense. Particularly since there's no second call to the shelter listed on Zoe's cell phone log. So Dan naturally questioned them on the calls to make sure they weren't mistaken. The shelter staff checked their call logs, and there definitely were two calls listed as being from Zoe Yeager that evening. One call matches the time on her cell phone. That call message was listed as 'pickup time' for nine fifteen in the evening. Then later after Zoe's class started, there's another call, listed as being from Zoe Yeager. The message line says 'pick up time changed to ten thirty.'"

Kelly's little buzzer went off inside. Something was very wrong about that second call. "Whoa, Burt . . . that makes me even more suspicious. Zoe didn't make that second call. The killer did, so there would be no potential witnesses."

"That's exactly what I'm thinking, Kelly. And Dan is, too. That explains why the shelter staffer wasn't there at nine fifteen waiting for Zoe. There's only one other explanation. Maybe Zoe asked one of the women in her class to make the call."

Kelly's buzzer went off. "My instinct says no on that, Burt."

"Yeah, mine, too."

"Did Dan talk with the person who was on phone duty that night?"

"It's hard to narrow that kind of stuff down, Kelly. These places are using part-time volunteers to handle things like that. Believe me, they're lucky to have someone around who can help out. No one remembers who was answering phones that night. Different people, no doubt."

Kelly pondered what Burt had told her as she merged onto a main thoroughfare. "You know . . . this murder has become more complicated."

Burt laughed softly. "Welcome to Dan's world. And what used to be my world. We seldom found these nice-and-easy, open-and-shut cases. Not where murder is concerned, especially these kinds of cases. Killer and victim knew each other. And it sounds more and more like the killer planned it carefully."

"Yeah, it does. And that kind of messes up my pet theory. You know . . . Oscar, the nasty villain husband, as killer."

"I agree, Kelly. It's hard to picture Oscar as being the sort who would plan how he was going to kill Zoe. Oscar fits the crime of passion category better. Killing Zoe in a rage is easier to imagine. But over the years, I've learned that people are capable of acting out of character if it suits them."

"That's true. And that's why I'm not ready to let go of Oscar yet." Kelly nosed her car around the corner of the street that bordered Lambspun. "By the way, I keep forgetting to ask you who called the cops to the church that evening? I remember the shelter gal, Rhonda, told Mimi and me the cops were already there when she arrived at the parking lot. And there was more than one cop car, plus the ambulance, she said."

"Yeah, I wondered about that as well, Kelly. Dan said the police dispatcher had received a call from a woman about ten o'clock. Apparently she was a neighbor who was out walking her dog. She was concerned there was a car in the parking lot and the church was all dark. She'd never seen a car there so late before. So a cruiser went by to investigate and found Zoe."

"Did Dan talk to the woman? I wonder if she saw anyone lurking around the church grounds."

"No, he couldn't. The dispatcher said the woman hung up when he asked her name, and—"

"Don't you guys capture the phone number of anyone who calls?" Kelly interrupted.

"Yes, we do, and the number showed up as one of the phones in the Super Duper Discount Store. It's located in a mini mall a couple of blocks from the church parking lot."

Kelly's buzzer went off again. "I wonder why that woman would go to the store to make a call. Maybe it was closer than her home."

"I don't know, Kelly. But I thought you'd find that interesting. I sure did. Dan sent an officer to question the staff at the store, but he didn't learn anything. Those discount stores have smaller staffs at night, so there aren't many people walking around. Plus, most of the clerks are stocking shelves."

"Boy, Burt . . . this case is getting curiouser and curiouser, as Alice would say."

Burt chuckled. "Well, I'll tell Dan to be on the lookout for a white rabbit with a pocket watch."

"The phone caller was a woman who called the shelter a second time, and it was a woman who called the cops that night. I hate to say it, Burt, but that points right to Leann."

Burt sighed. "I know it does, Kelly. And I can't tell you how unhappy that makes me."

Kelly steered her car into the driveway between her cottage and Lambspun. "It's still hard to picture Leann shooting Zoe. Even Anna said that Leann had calmed down while she was in their class. It didn't sound like Leann would fall into the crime of passion category. She wasn't enraged."

"Mimi said the same thing. It's hard to picture. However, there is another scenario that is a possibility. Leann and Oscar may have planned this murder together."

That thought did not set well with Kelly. "That doesn't feel right, Burt. I've already chalked up Leann's affair as a moment of temporary insanity."

Burt laughed. "I know, Kelly. But you can't forget the gun. There's no way Leann can escape that connection."

"Yeah, yeah . . . can't get past the gun. Or the fact that she and Oscar had an affair."

"If they did plan it together, then that would explain the two mysterious phone calls. The second call to the shelter, and the call to the police department. Both came from a woman."

Kelly let out an exasperated breath as she parked her car in front of the cottage. "You're right, Burt. I simply don't like to think that Leann and slimy Oscar planned this murder together. It's too depressing." Turning off the ignition, she grabbed her briefcase and pushed open the driver's door.

"I hear you, Kelly. Listen, I'm driving into the shopping center. I'll talk to you later, okay."

Kelly clicked off her phone and hurried inside her cottage. If she changed clothes quickly, then she could check her shawl at Lambspun before settling into her accounts. Then the numbers could chase away the disturbing images in her mind.

• • •

Balancing a full mug of Eduardo's coffee, Kelly rounded the corner from the hallway into Lambspun's center yarn room. She thought she heard Mimi's voice coming from the knitting table in the main room. Since she'd already steamed her shawl, Kelly figured she deserved a quick sit 'n' knit break with Mimi before returning to her accounts.

As she approached the archway, Kelly noticed someone else with Mimi. *Vera.* "Hello, Mimi," she greeted cheerfully as she chose a chair facing both women. "Vera, I haven't seen you in quite a while. How are you doing?"

Vera gave Kelly a warm smile. "I'm doing well, Kelly. Thank you for asking."

Mimi spoke up, her voice assuming the Mother Mimi Has Spoken tone that Kelly recognized. "Vera stopped in for some sewing supplies, but I forced her to slow down for a minute and tell me what's been happening since she last came in here. Goodness, it's been over a week. What have you heard from the police? Have they learned anything more about Zoe's murder?"

Kelly had to give Mimi credit. She looked at Vera with wide-eyed incredulity. Yet Burt had no doubt been keeping Mimi informed.

"Yes, Vera, please tell us if you know something. We're all dying of curiosity here," Kelly joined in. "Have the police learned *anything*?"

Vera straightened her shoulders a bit, Kelly noticed. "Yes, they've been questioning a lot of people from what I've been told. I make it a point of calling that nice detective Morrison every week to see what he's learned. He's been very informative."

Mimi leaned over the table, eyes even wider. "Do they have any information about the killer? Have they found any clues?"

Kelly didn't bother to say a thing. Mimi was playing the role of innocent questioner so well. Clearly, Mimi didn't want to let on that Burt had been keeping them both updated on the investigation. Maybe if Vera could be encouraged to talk in the relaxed shop setting, she might provide more details the police could use.

"Yes, they have, but it was not good news. Police traced the murder weapon to Leann." Vera's worried frown creased her face. "Apparently it was one of the guns her father owned. I guess I never even noticed she had a gun case on her wall."

"Oh, no!" Mimi exclaimed, hand to her face. "I can't believe that!"

Kelly couldn't resist playing along. "You're kidding! Do the police actually believe Leann killed Zoe? That's . . . that's *crazy*!"

Vera nodded, glancing at both women. "I agree. And I told the police that when they questioned me the second time. They asked me if I had occasion to be at Leann's house. Well, of course I did. I sewed for her at night, almost as much as I sewed for Zoe, for heaven's sake. Then, the detective asked if I'd ever noticed the gun case on the wall, and if I'd ever noticed that a gun was missing." Vera puckered up her mouth. "Well, of course, I didn't. I don't notice furniture."

"Did the detective give any indication they suspected Leann?" Kelly asked, adopting Mimi's wide-eyed demeanor.

"No, they didn't, thank goodness," Vera replied. "But just for good measure, I made it a point to tell the detective that Leann leaves her back door open as a convenience for clients during the day. That way, they can leave garments inside on Leann's worktable in the family room."

"Really? That means someone else could have come into Leann's house when she was gone and stolen the gun," Kelly suggested.

Vera arched a thin brow and nodded solemnly. "Precisely. And I also made it a point to tell the detective who I thought must have stolen the gun *and* killed my sister!"

It didn't take a mind reader to figure out who Vera meant. But Kelly played along, as did Mimi. Both of them leaned forward, closer to Vera. "*Oscar*. It has to be him," Kelly said in a deliberately ominous tone.

Vera leaned forward toward them, her face an angry mask. "*Exactly!* The man is a brute. He beat my sister whenever he flew into a rage. I told the police that. When they first came to my apartment and told me about Zoe, I told them it had to be Oscar. He'd *threatened* Zoe! He . . . he was following her. He must have been! He followed her that night . . . and shot her! I *know* he did!"

Mimi leaned forward and patted Vera's hand. "There, there, Vera, don't bring back all those awful memories. They're too disturbing. I'm sure police will find the evidence they need. Don't worry," she said in a comforting voice.

Vera took a deep breath. "I pray they do, Mimi. Oscar has absolutely no explanation for his whereabouts that night, except for being at a barroom." She gave a disdainful sniff.

"I'm sure police will find something," Mimi said, not looking the least bit confident.

An idea came to Kelly. Another piece of information police had learned but Vera hadn't mentioned yet. Leann's affair with Oscar. Perhaps Vera didn't know. Kelly did not think that likely. Vera appeared to be a sharp observer of details. Kelly pondered how best to approach the subject, and decided she would slide into it from another topic. A more subtle approach.

"You mentioned Leann kept her back door unlocked so anyone could have stolen the gun," Kelly ventured.

"That's right," Vera repeated, nodding. "That's how I know Oscar could have gotten the gun."

Kelly deliberately frowned. "But how would Oscar know Leann had a gun collection on her wall? I mean . . . he didn't sew for Leann, so how would he know? Had he been in Leann's house before?"

Vera puckered her mouth again, in what Kelly was recognizing as her expression of distaste. She was about to say something she didn't like. She stared at the library table for a few seconds. "I'm fairly certain that Oscar had been in Leann's house before."

Kelly recognized the door Vera's comment left open. So Kelly walked straight through. Although she didn't charge through in her usual fashion. She meandered slowly, creeping up on the unpleasant topic.

"You know, Vera. That kind of makes me wonder. I had heard some gossip about Leann and Oscar, and . . . and I thought I'd ask you if it was true."

Mimi was watching Kelly closely, she noticed, probably surprised she was venturing into that territory.

"What kind of gossip?" Vera asked, looking at Kelly suspiciously.

Kelly took a deep breath as if hesitating. "Someone told me Leann and Oscar had an affair once. Well . . . it was so outrageous, I didn't want to believe it. But the person told me they'd seen them together once. A few years ago."

Again, Mimi's jaw dropped, hand to her face. "No! I cannot believe that!"

Vera narrowed her gaze on Kelly. "Who told you that?"

"I'm afraid I cannot reveal the person's identity. Someone who comes to the shop regularly. Let's just say I trust the person."

Vera scowled at Kelly, then frowned at the table again. More wrinkles appearing on top of the others. Vera's face had turned into one big wrinkle. "I'm afraid it's true, as awful as it sounds. Yes. Leann did respond to that snake Oscar's advances. He was always cheating on Zoe, usually with some barroom floozy."

"Oh, my . . ." Mimi said, still looking shocked.

"So that would explain how Oscar would have learned about Leann's gun collection," Kelly continued. "Now it makes sense."

"Exactly. That's how I know in my bones Oscar crept into Leann's house and stole a gun," Vera said vehemently.

"Well, it doesn't make sense to me," Mimi spoke, clearly not acting this time. "How could a sensible woman like Leann even think about . . . about getting together with that drunken Oscar?"

Vera nodded. "I know how you feel, Mimi. I feel the same way. Leann is a good woman. But . . . she was going through a difficult time then. So I think Oscar simply got to Leann in a weak moment."

Kelly had to follow up on that. "What was happening in

Leann's life that made her susceptible, do you think? You probably know her better than most, Vera. You worked with her regularly. What was the difficulty she was experiencing? Money issues?"

Vera glanced to the side. "Partly. Her sewing business had fallen off. Zoe had started her own shop and several of Leann's customers began going to Zoe. So, I'm sure Leann wasn't earning as much money. I mean, she had a life insurance annuity that her first husband left her, but she depended on her sewing business to pay most of her bills."

Kelly glanced over to Mimi. Mimi had a worried expression, so Kelly continued gently. "That must have been really hard for her. After all, she gave Zoe her break, didn't she? Zoe learned a lot in Leann's shop, I'll bet."

Vera nodded, still looking down. "Yes, she did. And I did, too. I have always said that Leann made it possible for Zoe to become successful."

Kelly pondered how to broach this next topic. But she had to ask. She'd wondered about it ever since she'd heard Leann accuse Zoe that afternoon in Lambspun.

"You know, Vera, I hate to sound disrespectful, but I have always wondered if there was any truth to Leann's accusations. She came storming into Lambspun late one afternoon, mad as hell. Mimi and I were the only ones here. She swore that Zoe stole her design and submitted it to the magazine contest. She showed us a picture of her gown taken years before and compared it to the photo Zoe sent to the magazine. And, you know, those designs looked identical."

Vera slowly raised her head and stared off into the adjoining yarn room. Her mouth puckered, but she didn't say anything.

"I figured you would know, Vera. You were there with both of them," Kelly prodded.

"Yes," Vera said in a quiet voice. "Yes, it's true. I saw Zoe take the pattern and a photo of Leann's design. I didn't say anything. How could I? Zoe was my sister, and she also paid me to sew for her. I could barely make my monthly bills on my copy shop job. So . . . so I kept quiet."

Mimi didn't say anything, but Kelly could tell she didn't like what she heard.

"Leann also accused Zoe of stealing some of her customers. Was that true, too?" She matched Vera's quiet tone.

Vera closed her eyes and nodded. "Yes, yes, I'm afraid that's true, too. I saw Zoe on Leann's computer, copying files one afternoon. Again . . . I felt bad for Leann, but . . . but how could I say anything?" She gave a helpless shrug.

Kelly paused. "Well, that might explain Leann's weak moment with Oscar. She was clearly under stress. Losing customers and losing income. If she suspected Zoe then, well, maybe the affair was a way to get revenge against Zoe. As twisted as that sounds."

"Poor Leann," Mimi said, shaking her head. "I'm sorry to hear that about Zoe. I hate to speak ill of the dead, but that was wrong."

"Yes, it was," Vera said, glancing to both women. "Believe me, I hated to tell that to the police, but I did. I told them all about what happened with Zoe and Leann. Then I repeated my belief that Oscar Yeager killed Zoe. He stole the gun, and he shot my sister."

Mimi spoke softly. "Let's hope the police can find someone who saw Oscar near the parking lot. Some evidence linking him to the murder."

Kelly didn't say a word. She was afraid police had much more evidence linking Leann to the murder. Meanwhile, she needed to check with Burt to see if he knew how much information Vera had shared with police.

Vera suddenly pushed back her chair and rose. "I'm sorry, but I do need to get back to the shop. I'm working on one of my customer's suits, and I need to stay on schedule." She grabbed her sewing bag.

Mimi rose as well, joining her. "Thank you so much for sharing with us, Vera. Kelly and I were wondering what had been happening. Even though, I confess I'm startled, I appreciate knowing,"

"Yes, Vera, thank you for your honesty," Kelly added.

"You're welcome. By the way, Kelly, you're an accountant. You must know several lawyers. I want to talk to someone about a will. Could you recommend someone?"

"Surely, Vera. You know, Lawrence Chambers has been in practice here in Fort Connor for over forty years. He's very nice. I'm sure he would take good care of you."

"Thank you, Kelly, I appreciate it. Bye, now," she said as she turned to leave, Mimi walking beside her.

Kelly watched them leave. She really needed to work on her accounts. Maybe then she could chase away all the unpleasant images that were dancing inside her head right now.

Fourteen

Kelly turned her car into the driveway beside Leann O'Hara's house and parked behind Leann's car. Kelly had taken a chance and driven to Leann's house this morning, hoping to find her at home. The conversation with Vera yesterday afternoon had continued to bother Kelly.

The idea of Leann conspiring with brutish Oscar to plan Zoe's death would not come into focus in her mind. Something was wrong with that picture, and Kelly intended to find out what it was. Even if it meant having a difficult conversation with Leann.

Kelly slammed the car door behind her and approached Leann's back door. Since Vera had mentioned this was the entrance Leann's customers used, Kelly figured Leann's workroom was close by. It must have been because Leann opened the door before Kelly climbed the steps.

"Kelly, it's good to see you," Leann said, welcoming Kelly

inside. "What brings you here? Did something happen to your bridesmaid gown?"

"No, no, it's still hanging in the garment bag," Kelly said as she entered Leann's family room. She glanced around briefly and spotted a glass case on the wall near the dining room. Sure enough, she glimpsed the dark metal of mounted pistols and revolvers. She turned to Leann and chose her words carefully. *How best to approach this subject?* "I simply wondered how you were doing, Leann. Have you heard anything more about the investigation?"

All traces of Leann's smile disappeared, concern replacing it. "I'm . . . I'm doing all right, I suppose, Kelly," she said, gesturing toward one of the family room chairs as she sat on the edge of a sofa. "I haven't heard much. The police detective called me and asked me again what times I was here at my house the night Zoe was killed." She shrugged. "I told him I couldn't recall exactly what time I returned from the church where Zoe was teaching, but I think it was about eight thirty."

Leann looked down at the gray suit jacket she held in her lap. "Then he asked again if I could recall making any phone calls or seeing anyone in the neighborhood who could confirm I was at my home that night." Her voice dropped. "I told him I didn't make any calls, and I didn't notice any neighbors that night. It was dark by then, so none of my elderly neighbors would be outside." She gave another little shrug, which had an air of hopelessness to Kelly.

Kelly felt so sorry for Leann. She wished the facts that had been unearthed in the investigation were different. But they weren't, and they raised suspicions which pointed directly at Leann. Kelly wanted answers, and she hoped being face-to-face with Leann would help. She wanted to see Leann's reaction. Hopefully, Kelly would pick up on something, a gesture, a look in Leann's eyes, something.

"I'm sorry all this is happening, Leann," Kelly began as she perched on the edge of an upholstered chair. "Believe me, I don't usually intrude in people's private matters, but I heard something recently which disturbed me. I simply wanted to see if it was true or not."

Leann quickly glanced up at Kelly, an apprehensive look in her eyes. "What . . . what was it?"

"I heard you and Oscar Yeager had an affair a few years ago. Is that true, Leann? I confess, I find it hard to believe."

Leann's face flushed crimson, and she broke off her gaze, staring into her lap again. After several seconds she spoke in a soft voice. "Yes, it's true, I'm afraid. It was a mistake that I've regretted over the years. We were only together a few times. It didn't take me long to come to my senses."

Kelly wished Leann would raise her head again so Kelly could look into her eyes. But Leann kept her head down, looking for all the world as if she was ashamed of what Kelly discovered.

"Again, I'm sorry, Leann. But I couldn't believe the gossip was true, and I wanted to ask you," Kelly said gently. "I'm sorry if I poked into a painful memory."

"Who told you?" Leann asked, staring out toward the dining room.

"Someone who comes to the shop regularly, so I can't reveal the name. But it concerned me the moment I heard it. Tell me, have the police asked you about it, Leann?"

She nodded. "Oh, yes, and I got a very bad feeling afterwards. The tone in that detective's voice disturbed me. I could tell he suspected me of being involved in Zoe's death."

Finally Leann looked back at Kelly. "I swear I had nothing to do with Zoe's murder. My father's gun is missing, and that makes me looks guilty. I know that. But . . . but I *swear* I did not kill Zoe!"

Kelly stared into Leann's frightened gaze. She appeared absolutely sincere. Kelly wanted to believe Leann, but she'd met too many expert liars over the past few years. Poking around in murders had brought Kelly up close and personal with several killers. Most had cleverly planned their crimes, leaving trails that pointed to others and away from themselves. Kelly wished she didn't have the suspicious nature she did, but she couldn't help it. She was naturally skeptical.

"Unfortunately, the unlocked back door made it easy for someone to steal the gun. But there's no proof anyone stole it."

Leann's voice dropped to a whisper. "I know. That's what scares me, Kelly. I have no proof I was here that night."

Kelly now regretted coming to see Leann. She had received no clues whatsoever as to whether Leann was telling the truth or lying. None. Instead of finding answers, she'd poked and probed into someone's obviously painful memories.

"Listen, Leann, I'm sorry I even came over," she said as she rose. "My questions have upset you. I shouldn't have come."

"No . . . no . . . I'm glad you did. At least you cared enough. I've been holed up here sewing and barely talking to anyone since the detective came a few days ago," she said as she followed Kelly toward the back door.

Kelly searched for something she could say to Leann and found the only thing that might help her. "Have you spoken to a lawyer, Leann? If not, I think you should. You're going to need someone in your corner if the police come to question you again." Kelly tried not to let all of her concern show.

Leann's eyes grew as wide as teacups. "No . . . no, I don't know any lawyers."

At last. Kelly found something she could do to help Leann. "Well, I know several lawyers, so let me see who is doing pro bono work and might be interested in representing you. You definitely need legal advice, Leann. I'll make some calls and get back to you this afternoon, all right?" Kelly paused, the back door partially open.

Gratitude shimmered in Leann's eyes. "Oh, thank you, Kelly! I can't tell you how much I appreciate your help. Thank you so much!"

Leann stood at the door, clutching the gray jacket to her chest. *It must be a mass of wrinkles by now*, Kelly figured. She'd watched Leann twist the fabric in her lap during their entire conversation.

"It's the least I can do, Leann," Kelly said and meant every word. "I'll call you later." With that, Kelly raced down the porch steps and hurried to her car.

She revved the engine as she checked the directory on her smartphone, then pressed Lisa's number and angled her car down the driveway and onto a residential street.

"Hey, what's up?" Lisa answered.

"I'm about to call Marty and ask a favor, but first tell me how Megan's doing. Calm and collected, I hope. No wedding crises or problems? I haven't seen her since our last game the other night."

Lisa chuckled. "No crises. All's well, so far, Megan says. She's on the phone most of the time, checking every last detail. Making sure all is well before her relatives arrive this weekend. She's so anal."

"Hey, don't make fun. We analytical types can't help ourselves. Detail is where we live."

"Yeah, yeah, yeah. What did you want to ask Marty?"

"I wanted his recommendations for good lawyers who take pro bono cases. Marty has wedding celebrations on his mind, so he can't do it. But Leann O'Hara needs a good lawyer."

Lisa took in her breath on the other end of the phone. "You're kidding! That nasty Oscar is the guilty one. How could the police suspect Leann?"

"Well, a lot of information has come out recently. The murder weapon belonged to Leann, and—"

"Wait, there's a therapy patient walking toward my exam room. You can fill me in at the shop. I was going to drop by later. Bye."

Kelly heard Lisa's phone click off and did the same. Maybe she could work at the shop when she returned. That way she'd be there when Lisa dropped in. And she could always check on her shawl. She hadn't steamed it today. Mimi had said she wanted to remove the pins soon. The shawl had gone through four days of steaming and stretching, steaming and stretching. Surely the rebellious wool would have relented by now and assumed its correct shape. But then again, Kelly was leery of assumptions. Every time she assumed something, the opposite happened.

Meanwhile, Kelly slowed to a stop at an intersection, then searched her phone's directory for Marty Harrington's number.

Kelly tabbed through the spreadsheet as she sipped her coffee. Customers browsed through nearby yarn bins, but she was oblivious. Only the numbers existed at the moment. That was one of the rewards of working with columns and rows of numbers. You could lose yourself in them. Worries vanished. Concerns disappeared. Only the numbers remained. Calming.

The sound of her cell phone penetrated her concentration. Steve's name and number flashed on the screen. Worksheet numbers disappeared, and she eagerly reached for the phone. "Hey, there, are you still up in the high country with that new client or are you back in Denver?"

"Hey, there, yourself," Steve's deep voice sounded, bringing a warm sensation inside her. "I'm back in Denver now so I can print up some new house plans. But I'm going to try to drive into Fort Connor tonight. I wanted to have dinner with you before I head back up to the mountains."

The sound of Steve's voice in her ear brought back a ton of memories, really good memories, and their accompanying sensations. "That sounds like a plan. I'd love to meet for dinner. You can catch me up on what's happening with the house design. When would you get here approximately? I'll make reservations."

"Around seven or so. Hope that's not too late."

Not for you, Kelly thought, and let her smile infuse her voice. "Sounds good to me. You want to meet me here or at the Bistro?"

"Wait for me at the cottage. We'll get more time together." His voice dropped lower. "I missed you, Kelly."

That felt really good inside, and Kelly responded honestly. "I've missed you, too."

"That's really good to hear."

"It's the truth."

"Damn, I wish I had more time but I have to drive back to Denver tonight. I promised both Sam and Baxter I'd meet them early tomorrow morning with the new drawings."

"Hey, you'll have more time next week. Sam knows you're taking a few days off for the wedding, right?"

"Oh, yeah. It's been on the calendar for months. Uh-oh. Got a call from Sam coming in. Gotta go. See you tonight, Kelly."

"You bet," Kelly promised, matching Steve's warm tone before she clicked off.

Jennifer could make all the jokes she wanted, but the nice-and-easy approach she and Steve had taken worked just fine. Whenever they talked, it felt like old times. Comfortable, warm, and satisfying. They were almost back to where they'd left off, but better. The last year they were together had been tense and stressful. But now . . . now Kelly could feel both of them return to the way they had always been. Best friends who loved being with each other . . . then became lovers.

When that next step would come about, Kelly didn't know. Maybe next week when Steve was staying in Fort Connor for Megan and Marty's wedding. There would be no deadlines and no schedules for either of them. Kelly had also carved out some time on her calendar for celebrating with her friends and for relaxing. Maybe she and Steve could relax together.

Kelly stared at her spreadsheet, but her mind was no longer on the numbers. In fact, she almost didn't hear the little voice that sounded from the archway at the entrance to the main room. She glanced up and saw Lizzie von Steuben approach, Hilda's round, plump dumpling of a sister.

"Goodness, you must have been lost in your accounts,

Kelly," Lizzie said with her trademark dimpled smile. She plopped her tapestry knitting bag on the table, then sat across from Kelly. "How are you, dear?"

"Lizzie! How good to see you!" Kelly cried. "I've missed you the other times you've visited the shop. How *are* you?" Kelly pushed her laptop computer aside and leaned over the table.

"I'm fine, dear, just fine," Lizzie said, pulling out a pastel blue knitting project from her bag.

Kelly couldn't tell what Lizzie was knitting. It didn't look like one of Lizzie's usual grandniece or grandnephew baby blankets. It was bigger.

"It was good to see Hilda again," Kelly said. "I'm so glad her doctor found a new medication for her arthritic knees. It sounds like it's made a huge difference in her ability to move around."

"Oh, it has," Lizzie replied, her needles rhythmically moving through the light blue yarn. Picking up stitches, sliding them off one needle onto another.

Kelly wondered if she'd ever knit that fast. But then, Lizzie and Hilda were not only fast, but also accurate. No uneven stitches or empty spaces where they shouldn't be in their finished garments. Kelly decided she'd better stick with her slower speed in order to maintain whatever level of accuracy she possessed, meager though it might be.

"The new anti-inflammatory cream has done wonders for Hilda. Now she can actually come here to Lambspun again, as well as her literary club meeting, which she'd sorely missed. And church is much easier, too." Lizzie nodded, her silver hair swept up in its usual twist complete with a pastel blue bow.

"Please tell me Hilda wasn't trying to kneel in church." Kelly grimaced at the thought.

Lizzie looked up from her yarn, her bright blue eyes earnest. "Goodness, no! I made sure of that. And I still forbid her to kneel even though her knees have improved."

Kelly smiled at the image of younger sister Lizzie bossing around her imposing and bigger older sister.

Another memory intruded then. Lizzie and her beau, Eustace Freemont. Love had come late in life to Lizzie and Eustace. It was obvious that they had found their "soul mates" in each other. The fact that erudite and scholarly Eustace was now residing in the Larimer County Detention Center had definitely provided a challenge to their blossoming relationship. However, during these last six months Lizzie had proved herself quite adept at overcoming challenges.

"How is Eustace doing?" Kelly asked gently.

Lizzie's cheeks grew rosier, and she dimpled as she smiled at Kelly. "Ohhhh, Eustace is doing well. We're both so grateful he was temporarily assigned to Larimer County's facility here in town. It has made visiting much easier."

"Marty explained to us how that works. Colorado Department of Corrections first assigns prisoners to a Regional Diagnostic Center. After that, Eustace would be assigned to a particular prison."

"That's correct, dear. Since there was no bed space available at the Diagnostic Center when Eustace was sentenced, he was temporarily placed in the Larimer County Detention Center. Hopefully, our good fortune will hold when Eustace is permanently placed in a facility somewhere else. I've been praying he could be assigned to a prison library or clerical duties."

Eustace was already in his mid-seventies, and Kelly often worried about his being able to survive in a difficult prison environment. Surely working in the library or a prison office would be a better usage for a man like Eustace than more taxing duties such as cleaning up the highways.

"I sincerely hope so, Lizzie. Maybe he could perform minor administrative tasks. I know that Marty has written to the Regional Diagnostic Center on Eustace's behalf. Maybe that will help."

"We can never thank young Marty enough. He was so committed to helping Eustace. He's a wonderful attorney, and such a good boy."

Kelly had to hide her smile. Crazed Marty was definitely a different person in his legal role. She'd seen him in action defending others before. People who'd been caught up in the legal system and needed help, help they couldn't afford. Marty had been kind enough to provide his services free, or pro bono, to several people Kelly had met while in the midst of her sleuthing.

"How often are you allowed to visit Eustace?"

"Here in town at the County Detention Center, I'm allowed to visit twice a week for thirty minutes each time. Even though we have to see each other through a glass partition and speak on the phone, those visits do a world of good. For me as well as for Eustace. He calls me his returning dove." Her bright eyes twinkled.

Kelly noticed that Lizzie's fingers had picked up speed even though she wasn't looking. *How can someone knit that fast and not watch?* "What are you making, Lizzie? It doesn't look like a baby blanket."

Lizzie's light laugh floated. "Oh, my, no. This is an afghan

I'm knitting for some family at the homeless shelter. So many people have lost their homes and are out of work. I try to help the best way I can."

"It's beautiful, Lizzie," Kelly said, fingering the even rows of perfect stitches. "And that's so kind of you. Is the pattern difficult? Maybe I'll knit one for the shelter this fall before the cold weather sets in."

"That would be wonderful, dear. The pattern isn't difficult at all. I'll be glad to show you." Lizzie's dimpled smile disappeared. "I hope you don't mind if I change the subject, dear, but there's been something I've wanted to ask you. Mimi told me about Zoe Yeager's awful murder. Such a tragedy." She shook her silvery head. "I'd only seen Zoe once, at a church function. She was very pretty and a very talented seamstress, too, from what I hear. Mimi said you were using those sleuthing skills of yours, dear. Have you learned anything?"

Kelly was a bit startled by Lizzie's question. *How many people had Mimi talked to?* "Oh, I'm simply asking a few questions, Lizzie. You know me. Always curious." Kelly gave a nonchalant shrug.

Lizzie sent her a sly little smile. "Oh, yes, dear. I certainly do know you. And once you're intrigued by a murder investigation, you dig in. You've unearthed details that the police didn't even know existed. And you've always been able to contribute to the investigation."

"Thank you, Lizzie." Kelly tried to sound nonchalant. "I was glad I could help."

"Well, your considerable skills may not be needed for this crime," Lizzie said, fingers moving faster. "It sounds like the guilty party is obvious."

"That's a surprising comment," Kelly said, wondering at

Lizzie's uncharacteristically blunt statement. "Did Mimi tell you that?"

Lizzie looked up at Kelly, her blue eyes wide. "Oh, no, dear. Mimi would never be so indiscreet. I spoke with Vera earlier this week. We've known each other for years. We both go to the same church, so we chat together each Sunday after the service. We're nearly the same age, so we've got a lot in common."

"Did Vera or Zoe ever do any sewing for you or Hilda?"

Lizzie smiled. "No, dear. Hilda and I do our own sewing. Anyway, I'd dropped by the shop where Vera works to copy some documents for Eustace. There was no one else in the shop at the time, so Vera filled me in on the investigation. It seems the police have been keeping her informed." Lizzie returned her concentration to her knitting. "That's very kind of them to do so. Vera's convinced Oscar Yeager killed her sister. Why Zoe didn't leave that horrid husband of hers earlier is beyond me."

"Well, I agree with you, Lizzie. He sounds like a violent drunk who was constantly mooching off Zoe's sewing shop earnings."

"Yes, indeed." Lizzie gave a determined nod. "And he gambled away Vera's savings, too. She told me so."

That surprised Kelly. "Really? I never knew that. I hadn't heard Oscar was a gambler."

Lizzie turned her intense blue gaze to Kelly. "He might as well have been. He took all of the money Vera's mother had left her. It was her nest egg, for heaven's sake! He put it in some reckless business scheme and lost every penny! Now the poor woman has *nothing* to support herself in her old age." Lizzie's voice turned judgmental. "Poor thing."

"That's awful!" Kelly exclaimed. Oscar was even worse than she'd thought. He was lower than low. "How did he get her money? Didn't she have it in a bank or something?"

"Vera told me she was getting ready to invest it in an IRA. But then Zoe pleaded with her to allow Oscar to invest the money. Zoe didn't even think about what was good for her sister, just her shiftless husband. He'd started working for a financial consultant and was looking for clients." Lizzie gave an indignant sniff.

Kelly couldn't believe sensible Vera would hand over money to reprobate Oscar. "Why on earth would she do that? It makes no sense."

"I know, dear. I wouldn't have done it, either. But Vera said Zoe kept pushing her, wheedling and pleading, to give Oscar a chance. If you ask me, Zoe treated her sister shamefully. She paid Vera a pittance for sewing hours on end. She'd also promised Vera years ago that she would make Vera a partner in the business, but she never did." Lizzie's voice turned more judgmental. "Anyway, Vera admitted she was scared of Oscar, having seen him hit Zoe many times, and she was afraid not to give him the money. Afraid of what he might do to her." Lizzie gave Kelly an ominous look.

Kelly was surprised by Lizzie's harsh comments. Then once again, she remembered Zoe's phone call weeks before and the ugly, demanding tone in Zoe's voice as she berated her older sister.

"That is awful, simply awful," Kelly said, picturing skinny Vera cowering before beefy Oscar. "I wonder why Mimi or Burt didn't tell me that story."

"Perhaps they didn't know," Lizzie suggested. "Vera's a very private person. Maybe she didn't want many people to know what had happened. She was probably ashamed that her own sister would take advantage of her like that. But Vera and I are friends, so she feels more comfortable with me. That's why she's told me things she wouldn't tell Mimi or Burt." Lizzie leaned closer to Kelly and glanced toward the browsing customers in the next room, then lowered her voice. "Vera even shared that Zoe took the last piece of family jewelry Vera had from her mother. It was the night Zoe ran away from Oscar and stayed at Vera's apartment. Vera saw Zoe reaching into the drawer where the diamond pin was kept. Zoe told her she needed money to support herself now that she'd left Oscar." Lizzie scowled over her knitting at Kelly. "Vera protested, of course, but Zoe begged and wheedled and pleaded and was out the door with the diamond pin before Vera could stop her. How could Zoe do that to her sister? She knew that was the last thing of value Vera possessed. Shameful, I tell you, simply shameful. I hate to speak ill of the dead, but there was no excuse for Zoe's behavior toward her sister."

"Goodness, Lizzie, I had no idea Zoe had taken advantage of Vera like that," Kelly said, completely taken aback by Lizzie's story. "Would you mind if I shared what you told me with Burt? Then he can share it with Mimi, if he chooses."

"Go ahead, dear. Burt knows how to keep confidences."

Just then, Kelly heard her cell phone's familiar ring. Noticing her Denver developer client Don Warner's name on the screen, Kelly forced away the images of Oscar, Zoe, and Vera from her mind. *Back to business*, she thought as she pushed away from the knitting table.

Fifteen

Kelly stood up from her ergonomic computer chair and stretched, arms overhead, then sauntered into the kitchen to refill her coffee mug. The morning had dawned gray and cloudy and slightly chilly. That had been enough to send Carl back inside to snooze on his doggie bed beside the patio door.

Leaning against the kitchen counter, Kelly sipped her coffee and stared out into the gray morning. The hour-and-a-half conference call from Warner Development had taken a good chunk of time. But she'd also gotten a lot done on Arthur Housemann's accounts.

After a quick check of business e-mails, maybe she could escape to the café and grab a salad. Her fridge was empty. She needed to go shopping this evening, after all the errands. The Wedding List errands. Kelly was supposed to pick up all the bridesmaid shoes from the shop where they'd been dyed to match the gowns, and then deliver then to the brides-maids. She'd promised Megan she'd do this last-minute er-rand, because Lisa was in therapy sessions all afternoon and Jen was catering with Pete.

Kelly was walking back to her corner office area when a quick movement through the glass patio door caught her eye. Brazen Squirrel was skittering across the yard and into her flower beds once again. Kelly glanced down at Carl and saw him snoozing away. Big Dog's Territory was unguarded.

Brazen scampered between the tall green tulip leaves, blooms long since gone. Now that Brazen was closer, Kelly glimpsed what looked like a nut in his jaws. *Clever squirrel,* she thought. He was still busy putting up his food stores for the winter. Brazen obviously saw that Big Dog was asleep and grabbed his chance. Kelly wasn't about to snitch on him.

Just then, Kelly's cell phone jangled, and she quickly snatched it, watching Big Dog himself raise his head and blink at her. Brazen had frozen in place amid her flower beds. Luckily for the little furry guy, Carl's head flopped back down on the doggie bed and slumber ensued . . . barely interrupted.

Lawrence Chambers's name and number flashed on her smartphone screen. "Well, hello, Mr. Chambers, how are you? We haven't spoken for a while." Kelly had never been able to bring herself to call the elderly friend of her late aunt Helen by his first name even though Kelly now used Chambers's legal services herself.

"I'm doing well, Kelly, and I know you are," Chambers's mellow voice sounded. "I wondered if we could schedule a time for you to drop by my office so we can discuss those Wyoming properties of yours. I wanted to go over your nat-ural gas leases and their royalties."

"Has something come up? Are there any problems?"

"No, no, nothing like that," Chambers's voice reassured. "I simply like to chat with my business clients face-to-face at least once a year. That way they have a chance to bring up any issues which might concern them."

"Of course, Mr. Chambers, I'll be happy to meet with you, but could we schedule it in a couple of weeks or so, please? My friend Megan is having her wedding this Saturday, and all of us over here at Lambspun are completely absorbed in wedding preparations . . . if you know what I mean," she said with a little laugh.

"Oh, I understand completely, my dear. My niece was married this past June, and our entire family gathered for the event. Relatives showed up from all over Colorado, Wyoming, and points west." He chuckled.

"Thanks, Mr. Chambers. I'll put a note on my daytimer to call you in a couple of weeks, how's that?"

"That's fine, Kelly. And please send my best wishes to your friend on the happy occasion. Oh, by the way . . . I had a call from another of your friends, the other day. Vera Wilcott, an older lady."

"Oh, yes, she's a seamstress and helped make the bridesmaid dresses. She asked if I could recommend a good lawyer because she wanted to make a will. Naturally I gave her your name. Did she make an appointment?"

"No, she didn't, as a matter of fact. She simply asked me questions over the phone, but she never mentioned a will. She wanted to know about Colorado inheritance laws."

"Oh, really?" Kelly said, surprised by his reply.

"Yes, it seems she's concerned about her sister's property. Apparently her sister was that poor unfortunate woman who was shot and killed outside the Presbyterian Church two weeks ago. Such a tragedy."

"Yes, it certainly was tragic. All of us knew Zoe Yeager because she was the seamstress who designed and made our bridesmaid gowns. She was very talented."

"That is such a shame to see someone die so violently. And your friend is convinced Mrs. Yeager's own husband is the one responsible. That is simply dreadful. In my personal opinion, I'm surprised the police haven't arrested the man yet. According to this woman Vera, he's a habitual wife beater and a drunkard as well as a thief. Apparently he stole her savings. I am shocked the man is still roaming about free."

"Well, I have to agree with Vera's assessment of Oscar Yeager, but I'm surprised she revealed so much."

"Oh, I'm used to it, Kelly. As a lawyer, people come into my office with various problems, and we start talking. Then, the next thing you know, they've told me far more about themselves than they'd planned." He laughed softly.

"Well, I'll bear that in mind, Mr. Chambers, the next time I come into your office. I'll make sure not to spill any secrets," she teased.

"Don't worry, Kelly, your secrets will be safe with me," Chambers said, smile still in his voice. "We'll visit in a couple of weeks; meanwhile, you and your friends enjoy the nuptials."

"Thank you, Mr. Chambers, we plan to," Kelly said before clicking off.

She shoved her phone into her jeans pocket, noticing that Carl was finally off his bed and stretching a long doggie stretch. She checked her watch. Nearly noon. She could have an early lunch, then check on her shawl before she returned to the Housemann accounts. By four o'clock she needed to leave on shoe errands.

Carl was beside the door, ready to go out. Kelly saw that Brazen Squirrel had finished burying his nut stash and was scampering across the yard. Carl hadn't even noticed yet.

"Okay, Big Guy, go out and see who's been creeping around your yard," she said as she slid the glass door open. Brazen was already safely on the top rail of the fence, dashing toward the cottonwood tree.

Carl stepped outside, gave another big stretch, and sniffed the air. His head lifted, catching a bit of Brazen's scent drifting by, no doubt. Then straight as an arrow, Carl trotted over to the flower beds and snuffled around.

"Too late, Big Guy," Kelly said before she closed the patio door. *If you snooze, you lose.*

"I can tell you hated Eduardo's chicken salad," Jennifer said as she poured a black stream of coffee into Kelly's carryout mug.

Kelly dropped her napkin on her empty plate and pushed back her chair. "Oh, yes, it was dreadful," she said with a wink. "Where are you and Pete catering this evening?"

Jennifer cleared Kelly's plate and wiped the table. "A local philanthropic sorority is having a fund-raiser tonight for their scholarship fund. It benefits older women students, so that's definitely a worthy cause. Pete's mom went back to school after her kids left for college. So that's a cause that's close to his heart."

Kelly grabbed her shoulder briefcase and mug. "Pete's a

great guy, no doubt about it," she said, walking with Jennifer toward the café counter.

"Got that right," Jennifer said with a grin. "And speaking of great guys, have you heard from yours lately? Is he still in the mountains with that new client?"

"Yes, he is. But last Friday he was back in Denver to draw up more house plans, and he drove up that night so we could go to dinner at the Bistro."

"Well, that was sweet of him," Jennifer said with a big grin. "Back to your favorite place. I'll bet you two had a great time."

Kelly took a deep drink of Eduardo's brew and savored. "It was nice. *Really* nice. And for the record, Steve didn't want to go back to Denver that night, but he had to. Clients were waiting early in the morning." She grinned slyly.

"That's good to hear. I'd say this wedding is coming right on time. Steve is going to be here for the rehearsal Friday, right?" She walked around the counter and placed the dishes in a large plastic tub.

"Absolutely. He's cleared his schedule . . . and so have I." Kelly gave her friend a wink, then headed down the hallway to the knitting shop.

Remembering her shawl, Kelly walked into the classroom area and looked around for the stretching board. It was nowhere to be seen. Glancing into the adjacent office and storage room, Kelly spied the rectangular board leaning against an office file cabinet, her blue shawl still there.

"Hey, Kelly," Rosa said from the corner file cabinet, where she was obviously searching for something. "Coming to check on your shawl, I bet."

"Yeah, Mimi unpinned it over the weekend, so I wanted

to see how it looked. I've steamed and stretched it for several days, exactly like you said to do."

Rosa looked over at her with a younger version of a Mother Mimi smile. "You did good, Kelly. Your shawl stretched a lot."

Kelly walked over and stared at the fuzzy blue triangle hanging on the board. The shawl was tacked only at the top edges. She visually traced the edges of the triangle, comparing the left side to the right side. The right side to the left side . . . wait a minute. Kelly peered at the triangle. The offending left side had stretched, but not enough. It was still more than an inch shorter than the right side.

"*What?* It's still shorter! How could that happen? I steamed and steamed it again and again. And look! It's *still* shorter!" Kelly pointed accusingly at the offending shawl.

"It did stretch, Kelly," Rosa consoled. "Just not enough."

"*Arrrrgh!*"

"I thought I heard your voice, Kelly," Mimi said as she entered the room.

"Look that that!" Kelly waved her finger at the fuzzy blue triangle. "How could that happen, Mimi? I checked those edges just three days ago and they were perfect. Both sides were even. And as soon as those pins were removed, it shrank again!"

"Well, wool will do that sometimes," Mimi said.

"*Bad wool! Bad wool!*" Kelly glared at the shawl. Rosa snickered beside the file cabinet.

"Don't worry, Kelly," Mimi soothed. "I can fix it."

"What? More steaming? It doesn't work. My shawl will be the only one that looks different. That is *so* frustrating." She frowned at the shawl again.

"No, no more steaming. I have some other tricks up my sleeve," Mimi said archly. "I've learned how to outsmart wool over the years." She beckoned Kelly toward the classroom again.

"Are you sure?" Kelly asked, still dubious as she followed Mimi. She cast one last accusatory look over her shoulder.

"Absolutely. I promise I can fix your shawl so the left side will match the right or get so close, you can't tell the difference."

Kelly gave Mimi a skeptical look. "You sure about that?"

Mimi held up her palm. "I swear," she said with a big smile. "Trust me, Kelly. Now you go settle at the table and get into your accounts. In fact, I think there may be a couple of donuts left from this morning's group. Go relax with your numbers." Mimi made a shooing gesture. "Leave the shawl to me."

"Okaaaay," Kelly said as she headed to the main room. "Mother Mimi knows best. I trust you. Put your Mimi Magic to work."

Burt was at his wheel in the corner, spinning away, as Kelly entered. "Hey, Kelly. You can settle in and keep me company, okay?"

"Boy, I'm glad you're spinning, Burt," she said as she plopped her briefcase and mug on the table near the corner. "That will help me relax after my bout of Knitting Angst."

Burt grinned. "I heard. Go on, have a donut. Keep me from eating another."

Kelly settled into a chair and withdrew her laptop and files. Glancing toward the nearby plate, she spied two donuts—one powdered, the other covered with cinnamon and sugar. A favorite. She had no business eating a donut. She'd just had lunch. Normally, Kelly would have been able to ignore the donut's sugary call, but not after a bout of Knitting Angst.

"Don't mind if I do." She snatched up the cinnamon-sugar one and took a bite, following it with a deep drink of coffee.

Coffee and donuts. The downfall of office workers everywhere. One-person offices or corporate high-rises with scores of employees. Donuts were everywhere. Sugary temptations leading people astray. *Bad donuts. Bad donuts.* Who invented donuts anyway?

She polished off the sugary morsel while she watched the familiar icons flash onto her screen, and her worksheets filled the page. Work beckoned.

"Before you get into your accounts, Kelly, I'd better fill you in on what I heard from Dan this morning." Burt's spinning wheel slowed to a stop and Burt leaned back in his chair.

Kelly observed her friend and mentor. "You don't look very happy, Burt. I take it the police still haven't found anything linking Oscar to the church parking lot."

"Well, you're right about that, Kelly. The closest connection they found was a part-time waitress who told them Oscar hit on her after he left the bar. Apparently they'd been together before. Oscar wanted to come over, but she turned him down. She did say that Oscar followed her in his car for several blocks, then turned onto the same main street that runs past the Presbyterian Church on the west side of town."

"Whoa, Burt, that's great!" Kelly exclaimed. "That proves Oscar was near the church that night. Or close by. That's great news."

"Not really. It proves nothing except Oscar was driving

around that night before he went home. There're still no witnesses who saw him or his truck in or around the Presbyterian Church that night."

Kelly scowled. "Darn it!"

"But I do have new information which involves the church parking lot. Dan said he was finally able to talk to the female employee who was cleaning the church that night. She works for a cleaning company in town, and they'd said she was afraid to talk to Dan and the guys at first. Apparently, she's undocumented and was afraid she'd get in trouble if she talked to police."

"So what did Dan do to convince her?"

"Dan told her boss at the company that he was only interested in learning what she'd seen the night of Zoe Yeager's murder. She was working at the church during that time period. So her boss got another worker to translate for her and explained the situation, and she agreed to talk to Dan with the other guy translating."

"Did she see anything?"

"She sure did. She said she noticed the women in Zoe's classroom when they left and went outside to the parking lot. She was cleaning the main entrance hallway at the time. Basically, she confirmed what Anna had told them, Dan said. They all got into their cars and drove away."

Kelly leaned forward eagerly. "Did she see Zoe drive back into the parking lot? Did she see anyone approach the car?"

Burt hunched over the drafted wool in his lap, hands folded. "She didn't see Zoe drive back into the church parking lot because she was cleaning the rooms on the other side of the hallway then. But she said that later on, when she was cleaning the rooms beside the parking lot, she did see Zoe's car outside. And she saw someone standing beside the car, talking to Zoe."

"Was it Oscar, I hope?"

Burt shook his head. "No, Kelly, I'm afraid not. It was a woman. She said it didn't look like any of the women from Zoe's class, but she couldn't tell. It was completely dark outside by then, and the woman standing outside the car wore a hooded jacket, so she couldn't even tell what color hair she had. But she said she's certain it was a woman from the slender body and the bare legs."

Kelly sat back. *Damn!* She had hoped this cleaning woman spotted Oscar Yeager in the parking lot. He'd threatened Zoe repeatedly. And yet there was no trace of Oscar showing up there that night. Instead, a woman was seen standing beside Zoe's car. Kelly looked over at Burt. His expression matched hers.

"That's even more bad news for Leann, isn't it, Burt?"

Burt shook his head sadly. "I'm afraid so, Kelly."

"Oh, brother . . . I feel that noose tightening around Leann's neck," Kelly said. "Did Dan give any indication of what he was thinking?"

"Not yet, but I know him. He's a smart detective. He's got to conclude the woman was Leann. I would in that situation. It doesn't matter if I know and like the person or not. Nice people can kill, too, if they have enough reason. I'm afraid it happens all the time. Leann had the motive, the means, and the opportunity to kill Zoe."

Sadly, Kelly had to agree with him. "Have you told Mimi yet?"

"No, and I don't think I will. She'll find out in time. Especially if Leann's arrested. A lot of the evidence will come out then."

"Boy, I'm glad I gave Leann those lawyers' phone numbers. She didn't know any lawyers. Thank goodness Marty was able to give me names of ones who do pro bono work."

"When did you speak with Leann?"

"I went over there Friday. I simply wanted to ask her about her affair with Oscar." Kelly shrugged. "And I admit, I wanted to watch her face when I asked her about the investigation and what the police were saying."

Burt quirked a brow. "Did you pick up anything?"

"Not a thing, Burt." Kelly shook her head. "Leann swore she didn't kill Zoe. And she had no real explanation for her affair with Oscar, except it didn't last long and she regretted doing it."

"I'm wondering if she helped Oscar. Maybe that's the explanation. I mean, if she really loved the guy, maybe . . . I don't know." Burt shrugged.

"I don't, either, Burt. This is one frustrating case."

Burt gave her a wry smile. "You can say that again, Sherlock." He pushed away from the spinning wheel and rose. "I think I need some coffee. Can I get you some, Kelly?"

"That's okay, Burt. I'm good." Kelly lifted her mug.

"I'm going to stretch my legs outside a bit, too. I need some fresh air," Burt said as he left the room.

Kelly returned to her spreadsheets, hoping the numbers would quickly chase away the thoughts about nice people doing bad things. Things like killing. But her cell phone distracted her first.

Megan's name and number flashed on the screen. "Hey, there, Bride-to-be, how're you doing?"

"Not so good, Kelly. I'm in the bathroom of the La Cre-perie Café, escaping for a few minutes. I'm here with my mom and dad and sister, and they haven't stopped talking since they got up this morning. In fact, they haven't stopped talking since they got here on Saturday. Jeeeez . . ."

Uh-oh. Kelly could feel Megan's stress coming over the phone. Not good. "I guess they're super excited about the wedding—"

"*Excited!*" Megan blurted out. "They are waaaay beyond excited. Excited I can handle. It's the questions that are driv-ing me crazy! I swear, if my mom asks me one more time about the caterer, I'm gonna *scream*. At *her*! And that's not good. She'll start to cry, then I'll feel awful . . ."

Oh, brother . . . Kelly sensed a Megan Meltdown was im-minent. "I bet they simply want to feel involved, that's all. You live pretty far away from them," she ventured.

"You sound like Lisa. You're right. Absolutely right. Ohhhh, now I feel bad."

"Can your sister help? Tell her you need her to help dis-tract them somehow."

"No, she's no help at all. This round of morning sickness is worse than the other two. Janet's either throwing up in the bathroom or asleep with the medicine the doctor gave her."

Think fast, Kelly prodded herself. A Megan Meltdown would not be pretty and could spoil the happy pre-wedding festivities. To be avoided at all costs. *What to do? What to do?* Suddenly, Kelly knew.

"Hey, Megan, I've got an idea. How about if we give you a little break? Let me ask Mimi if she and Burt could take your parents to dinner this evening. That would give you some time alone."

"Ohhhh, Kelly, that . . . that would be *wonderful*! I just called up to complain in private. I wasn't expecting you to solve it. I mean . . ."

"Hey, I like solving problems. It's what I do for a living. Albeit, number problems are a heckuva lot easier to solve than people problems."

"Boy, is that the truth. Do you think Mimi and Burt can do it?"

"I'll bet they would. In fact, they'd probably enjoy it. Plus, you and Marty could spend time together. I'm sure his relatives are driving him nuts, too."

"You don't want to know. They're hordes of them, scattered all over Larimer County and Colorado. He says he never knew there were so many Harringtons and Stackhouses. He swears he's seen people he's never even heard of."

"Okay, hang in there. I'll suggest to Mimi that they go over in the late afternoon. So why don't you take your folks to the mall, where there are lots of other people around. Plus open space." She laughed.

"Good idea. Oooops, someone's knocking on the bathroom door. Gotta go. Thank you, Kelly. You don't know how much I appreciate this!"

"Yeah, I do," Kelly said before Megan clicked off.

Kelly shoved her phone into her jeans pocket and reached for her coffee mug. She took a deep drink of caffeine, then walked toward the front room where Rosa and Mimi were helping customers. It was time to ask Mother Mimi to ride to the rescue once again. This time, it wasn't unruly yarn that needed soothing; it was wild and woolly relatives.

Sixteen

Kelly ran up the steps to Pete's Café and shoved open the front door. Today she wanted one of Eduardo's big breakfasts. She was starving. Those familiar tempting aromas drifted past her nose—eggs, bacon, sausage, pancakes, biscuits. *Yum!* Her stomach growled.

"Hey, Kelly, over here," Lisa's voice beckoned. Kelly spotted her friend waving at her across the crowded café. Kelly headed straight for the empty chair at Lisa's table.

"Perfect, now I can order faster," she said as she pulled out the chair across from Lisa. "I don't know why, but I'm starving this morning. I ran the usual distance, so maybe it's wedding prep anxiety or something."

"I did the same thing," Lisa said, pointing to her nearly empty plate. "I think we're all hyper. Megan Stress is getting to everyone."

"I know. She called me yesterday afternoon from a bathroom at the La Creperie Café." She caught Jennifer's eye and waved.

Lisa swallowed her last bite of biscuit. "Tell me about it. She called me three times yesterday morning. Short one-minute bursts of venting. I swear she has my schedule memorized so she knows exactly when the breaks are between clients."

Kelly had to laugh. "She probably called me, but I was on a conference call most of the morning."

"I could tell what you're talking about even before I walked up." Jennifer poured coffee into Kelly's cup, then Lisa's. "Megan Family Overload, right? She called me twice yesterday; how often did she catch you guys?"

Lisa held up three fingers while she sipped her coffee. Jennifer laughed.

"She only got me once, and I could tell that a Megan Meltdown was approaching, and we want to avoid that at all costs."

"Amen," Lisa interjected, then returned to her coffee.

"So, I decided an intervention was in order. I asked Mimi and Burt if they could ride to Megan's rescue and take her folks to dinner last night. That would give Megan a break and a chance for her to get together with Marty. For some R and R." Kelly smiled slyly.

"Genius, I salute you." Lisa held up her cup. "I can totally understand Megan's reaction. We all know how much she likes her quiet work space. I mean, that's why she and Marty chose one of Steve's four-bedroom houses in our neighborhood. So they could each have their own office. And no one is more devoted to her routine than Megan. Even more than you, Kelly. So you can imagine what a whole week of uninterrupted family time can do to her." Lisa closed her eyes with a shudder.

"Yeah, she admitted yesterday she was ready to scream at someone and that would not be good. A Megan Meltdown is not a pretty sight."

"That's for sure," Jennifer said, taking out her order pad. "That's why I scheduled entertainment for Megan's family today and tomorrow. What are you having, Kelly?"

"The big breakfast and make it biscuits this time," Kelly said, leaning on the table. "What kind of entertainment?"

"Yeah, Jen, spill it," Lisa urged.

Jennifer paused long enough to write Kelly's order. "I thought some outdoor activities would be in order. So I asked Jayleen and Curt if they could help out by giving Megan's relatives an escorted tour for a couple of days. Old Town Fort Connor today, then drive into Poudre Canyon and Bellevue Canyon for tomorrow. They'll love seeing everything, plus it should tire them out. And that would be a good thing in this case."

"Another genius suggestion." Lisa saluted Jennifer with her mug this time. "I know I'm being a slug by not helping out, but I had to front-load my schedule this week. It was the only way I could squeeze my clients' appointments in so I could take a couple of days off."

"Same here," Jennifer said. "That's why I called for help. Curt and Jayleen were glad to do it. They'll be stopping in for coffee soon before they head over to Megan's. I've gotta give this to Eduardo, or Kelly won't have anything to eat. Talk to you guys later."

"See you, Jen," Lisa said as she rose from the table. "I have to head back to the sports clinic. Thanks to Jennifer, we both may have a fairly quiet day free of Megan Stress breaks."

"Two days of sightseeing should definitely mellow out Megan's folks. And Megan. She'll be able to see the finish line at last. Curt and Jayleen are babysitting the relatives today and tomorrow. That leaves Thursday, but Megan should be all relaxed by then. On Friday, everything officially starts. Bridesmaid luncheon at café, wedding rehearsal and dinner at Jayleen's ranch, bachelor party, then wedding on Saturday."

"Not a minute too soon," Lisa said. "I tell you, Greg and I love Marty, but we've gotta get our privacy back. I mean, he's there *every* night. Thankfully, he was out with Megan's family for a few hours the other night. And tonight he'll be having dinner with his relatives." She rolled her eyes.

Kelly simply laughed. "The finish line is in sight. Hang in there."

"How would you know?" Lisa teased. "Has Steve spent the night yet?"

"We've both cleared our schedules the next few days," Kelly said with a sly smile.

Lisa threw her head back and stared at the heavens. "Thank Gawd! *At last!* Now we can all relax this weekend. I'll spread the word." She gave Kelly a wave as she turned to leave.

"And you can stop biting your nails," Kelly called after her. She took a deep drink of coffee, amused that the details of her relationship with Steve had been the subject of such anguished discussion. So much for privacy.

Curt and Jayleen walked into the café then, and Kelly

waved them over. "Hey, I hear you two are taking escort duty today and tomorrow. That's really nice of you. Now Megan can calm down." She grinned.

"Awwww, it's no problem, Kelly-girl," Jayleen said as she took the seat Lisa had vacated.

Curt held out his mug and accepted a coffee refill from waitress Julie before sitting at Kelly's table. "We'll enjoy getting to know her folks," he said.

"Still, that's a big-time commitment right before the wedding," Kelly said as another server placed her breakfast order in front of her.

Jayleen gave a dismissive wave. "Everything's ready. I don't have to do a thing. The house is clean and waiting for the rehearsal dinner Friday night. The rental company is coming Friday morning to put up the tent and canopies. That area was mowed last week so it should be fine for the wedding." She gave Kelly a big grin. "There's nothing left for me to do."

"Don't let all that good food go to waste," Curt advised, pointing toward Kelly's plate. "Dig in."

"Thanks. I'm starving." Kelly took a big bite of scrambled eggs with cheese, followed by bacon.

"I hope Steve plans to come up from Denver for all the celebrations on Friday," Curt said, eyeing her carefully.

Kelly swallowed a mouthful of bacon and biscuit, followed by a sip of coffee. "Yes, indeed, he's cleared his calendar for the next few days." She gave them a sly smile. "And so have I."

"Lordy, Lordy, that's good news," Jayleen crowed, her grin spreading.

Curt snorted. "It's about time. Way past time, if you ask

me. I was about to saddle up, go out, and round you two up like a couple of strays. I'd have done it, too, if I thought it would do any good."

Kelly tried not to laugh while she chewed, but she couldn't help it. Picturing Curt riding with lasso in hand after Kelly and Steve, who were racing through the Colorado foothills. Too funny.

"That wouldn't do a lick of good," Jayleen said with a laugh. "You know people don't have the sense that animals do. Especially when men and women are together. *Whooooeeee!* Now, *that's* ornery!"

This time, Kelly spilled her coffee she was laughing so hard. Jennifer came up, coffeepot in hand. "Hey, guys, do you need more coffee?"

Curt shook his head and pushed back his chair. "No, thanks, Jennifer. We should be heading over to Megan's house. Get an early start on that sightseeing."

Jayleen rose as well. "None for me, Jennifer. I've got a mug in Curt's car."

"You taking that big old Lincoln of yours, Curt?" Kelly teased, now that she'd caught her breath.

"Sure am. It has plenty of room for visiting relatives," Curt said with a smile. "It's come in very handy this week."

"Lord have mercy, you should see Curt's ranch house. It is packed full of family."

"I think everyone will be glad when Megan and Marty are finally married and things can return to normal," Jennifer said.

"Shoot, girl, I'm not sure any of us would recognize normal if it walked right up and bit us," Jayleen said as she and Curt turned to go.

"See you Friday," Curt said.

Kelly and Jennifer were laughing so hard, they simply waved good-bye.

Kelly walked into the front room of Lambspun. Mimi was at the counter helping a customer. "Mimi, is it all right if I knit here in the corner? Connie is teaching a class at the knitting table."

"Sure, Kelly," Mimi said with a smile. "Settle in there with your laptop. It's a great spot with all the windows. Great light."

"Thanks, Mimi. Numbers don't make much noise," she said as she sank into the comfy upholstered armchair. *Soft, soft*, she thought. Maybe she should buy a chair like this for the cottage. It would be great to snooze in.

Kelly popped open her laptop and waited for the icons to appear on the screen so she could return to her spreadsheets. She was almost finished with Housemann's accounts. In order to stay on schedule, she needed to finish Warner Development by Thursday night. Then she would be able to take off a few days. Both Arthur Housemann and Don Warner were aware that she wouldn't be taking business calls on Friday or the weekend.

Mimi approached the winding table that sat nearby, a floppy skein of burnt orange yarn in her hands. "Burt told me that things are looking worse for Leann," Mimi said in a quiet voice as she sat at the table. She loosened the skein and shook out the yarn, which formed into a large circle in her hands. She placed the yarn circle around the holders on the skein winder.

"I know, Mimi. Leann has no alibi for that night, and the murder weapon was hers. Plus, she had a reason to hate Zoe Yeager, as you and I know." It was said that the truth hurts. This time it would hurt Leann O'Hara.

Mimi pulled out a strand of yarn and wound it around the spindle of the ball winder at the other end of the table. "I feel so sorry for Leann. I don't want to see her charged with Zoe's murder, and yet . . ." Mimi's words trailed off as she slowly started turning a handle next to the ball winder. The winder started turning, winding the yarn from the skein winder on the other side of the table. Winding it all into a fat ball of yarn.

Kelly finished for her. "And yet, all the facts police have uncovered so far point to Leann. As Burt said yesterday, Leann had the motive, the means, and the opportunity to kill Zoe. Our feelings about her don't matter at all."

A woman Kelly didn't recognize stepped into the room then. She appeared to be in her fifties or so, Kelly guessed.

"Well, hello, Mimi, it's good to see you. I missed you the last time I was in here," the woman said.

Mimi swiveled around in her chair and gave the woman a huge smile. "Christine! How good to see you. How are you doing?"

"I'm trying to readjust to being back home," Christine said as she walked over to the shelves in front of the counter. "My husband and I just returned from a two-week cruise around the Mediterranean. Italy, Greece, Turkey, Spain, Portugal, even Morocco. It was wonderful!"

Mimi hopped out of her chair. "That sounds fabulous, Christine. I would love to take a European cruise like that. Now if I could only convince Burt."

"Well, my husband Ralph was the one who convinced me. Then I had to ask permission at the pharmacy. Two weeks is long for a vacation, but Super Duper is pretty good about granting permission if we give them enough notice." Christine bent over the shelves and fingered some of the new yarns stacked there.

Kelly looked up over her computer, her attention caught by the mention of the chain discount store near the church where Zoe was killed. The phone call notifying police about Zoe's parked car came from the Super Duper Discount Store. Was there another Super Duper in town? Kelly wasn't sure.

"I'm so glad you had that opportunity," Mimi said. "Are you looking for a new yarn project? Those yarns are really popular. We can barely keep them in stock. They knit up a certain way and the yarn curls up as you knit."

"You know, a woman on the cruise ship had something like that. It really was fascinating. I took several yarns from my own stash collection. Ralph's been threatening to clean out those storage shelves of mine," she said with a light laugh.

"Well, take a look and see if you're interested. The instruction sheet is posted over there." Mimi pointed to the wall beside the counter.

"All right, I'll check it out. Actually, I'm here to meet my old friend Vera Wilcott. I have some slacks to lengthen. She's been doing my alterations ever since she and her sister came to town." Christine's face saddened. "Wasn't that awful what happened to Zoe Yeager? I couldn't believe it when I heard who was killed. We were leaving the very next day for our trip, and the newspaper only mentioned a woman was found dead in the Presbyterian Church parking lot. I didn't learn who it was until we returned. Who in the world would shoot Zoe? She was such a nice woman."

Mimi's smile disappeared. "I know, Christine. It's simply tragic."

"And Vera told me the police haven't found the murderer yet! That's terrible! A killer is on the loose, roaming Fort Connor!" She gave a shudder. "It's too awful to think about."

Just then, a voice called from the adjacent room. "Sorry I'm a little late, Christine." Vera hurried into the front room, face flushed. "I had to finish a fitting for one of my newer clients. Did you bring those slacks with you?"

"Yes, I did." Christine withdrew a plastic bag from her large purse. "First, let me give you a big hug. You've been through a lot while I was gone." She opened her arms wide and beckoned Vera into her embrace.

"Vera has been a trooper," Mimi said as the two friends hugged each other. "She's stepped up and handled everything. Zoe's sewing clients, even all the funeral details."

Vera glanced down as if embarrassed by the praise. Christine patted her on the arm and added, "You can count on Vera."

"I was just doing what needed to be done," Vera said in a quiet voice as she accepted the plastic bag. "Now, when do you need these slacks?"

"It would be great if I could have them by this Friday. We're going to a dinner banquet. But I don't want to cause you a problem with your other clients."

Vera gave a dismissive wave. "It won't be a problem. I can move someone else's project around and get these finished, maybe even tonight."

"That would be great," Christine said. "Do you want me

to pick them up at your shop? It would have to be in the afternoon. I have to return to working the night shift like I did before we left on vacation, you remember? I go in at six o'clock and work until two a.m."

Vera gave a shiver. "I certainly do. I hope you won't have to work those long nights much longer."

"Well, now that my colleagues have taken my shifts while I was gone, I'm filling in for them so they can have some time off. Fair is fair."

"Well, don't you worry. I'll bring these over to you at the pharmacy. Maybe tomorrow night. That way, you won't have to take time driving over to the shop."

"That's sweet of you, Vera. Thanks."

"That's what friends are for," Vera said, then glanced at her watch. "I'd better run. One of my clients is coming in for a fitting in less than an hour. Bye-bye, everyone."

Kelly joined Mimi and Christine in good-byes as Vera raced from the room.

"That's one busy lady," Mimi said. "I'm so happy she's been able to keep Zoe's business going. In fact, Vera said she should be able to quit the copy shop job in a few months."

"That would be wonderful if she could," Christine said, her attention drawn to the loopy yarns again. "She's such a hard worker."

"Take your time, Christine," Mimi said, returning to the winding table. "Let me know when you find the yarn you like."

Kelly stared at her spreadsheets, but her mind wasn't on the numbers. She was curious to know if that Super Duper was the one near the Presbyterian Church where Zoe was killed. Maybe Christine remembered seeing a woman come in looking for a phone that night. However, Kelly knew she had to work up to such a question.

"Tell me, Christine, how long have you been a pharmacist?" she asked.

Christine glanced over at Kelly. "For over twenty years. I started working with a large chain drugstore back in Ohio, then we moved here six years ago. That's how Vera and I met. She and Zoe and I were in a newcomers' club after we arrived. We wanted to meet people and make friends."

"Have you worked at the Super Duper the entire six years you've been here? How do you like it?" Kelly asked. She noticed Mimi glance at her while winding the orange yarn.

"It's a nice place to work," Christine said as she fondled a deep purple yarn. "Super Duper is a smaller drugstore chain, so there's more of a personal approach. I really like the difference between that and the huge chain I worked for earlier."

"How many Super Dupers are here in town?"

"Just the one where I work. You know, the one over on Taft Hill Road in the shopping center. It's near the corner of Western Avenue."

Kelly paused, choosing her next question carefully. "You know, that's the shopping center not far from the church parking lot where Zoe Yeager was killed." She deliberately let her voice become dramatic. Mimi sent her a quizzical look.

"Yes, you're right. Our store is only a couple of blocks away from the Presbyterian Church."

Kelly leaned forward over her laptop and dropped her voice. "Mimi, didn't Burt say the police had a call from a woman that night who saw Zoe's car in the parking lot and was concerned? Didn't police say the woman called them from that Super Duper?"

The light of understanding went off in Mimi's eyes. "Oh, yes, I believe you're right. I do remember Burt saying police told him that."

"Is there a public pay phone in the store, Christine? I can't remember being in Super Duper, but you would know."

Christine glanced over at Kelly. "There's no public pay phone. But we do have a phone near our pharmacy counter. For the convenience of our customers. People often need to check with their doctors' offices about prescriptions."

Kelly felt her little buzzer go off inside. "Did you work that night, Christine?"

"Actually, I did. I wasn't scheduled to work since it was the night before my trip. But the new pharmacist on duty called and begged me to help out in the middle of her shift. She'd cut her hand opening a carton so she had to run to the urgent care for a couple of stitches. She was back in a hour, so I didn't even log in. I didn't want her to get in trouble. She's still in the new employee trial period."

"You know, the woman who called police that night must have used the pharmacy phone," Kelly continued. "Think back, Christine. Do you recall seeing a woman in the store using the phone? Or even asking for a phone?"

Christine stared out the front window for a moment. "No, I don't recall seeing anyone using the phone that night. The only person I remember seeing was Vera. She came in to drop off a dress I'd wanted altered for the trip. She's such a sweetie. I don't recall seeing anyone wandering around asking questions. But then, I was away from the front desk a lot. Most people use the drive-up pharmacy window." Christine turned her attention to the loopy yarns again, fingering a blue and green selection.

Kelly quickly caught Mimi's gaze, which looked as surprised as Kelly felt. Vera had stopped by the Super Duper store that night? The store that was only two blocks from where her sister was murdered. Had she told police that? Kelly didn't remember Burt mentioning it, and he certainly would have.

Somewhere in the back of Kelly's mind a little memory fragment teased. She grasped at it, but it darted away.

"I think I'll go with this deep purple, Mimi. Let me buy it, then I'd better run. I've got two more errands before I have to go home and get ready to report in for work tonight."

"That will make a beautiful scarf, Christine," Mimi said as she headed toward the counter. "Let me get a copy of those instructions for you."

Kelly quickly saved her spreadsheets and shut down her laptop. She needed some quiet time to think. That little memory fragment still nagged her, which indicated it was important. She slid her files and laptop into her briefcase and rose from her cozy corner chair. "Mimi, I'll see you tomorrow. I've got to finish my accounts at home. Christine, it was nice to meet you," she said, giving them both a good-bye wave.

Kelly sped through the central yarn room and out the front door, her mind racing. *What was it she couldn't remember?* Something about Vera. Something Vera told police. What was it Burt said? Kelly hurried across the driveway and into her cottage. There she dumped her briefcase and phone and headed to the kitchen.

Coffee. She needed caffeine. That would spur her memory. She pulled out the coffeemaker and quickly started another pot. Within a minute, the enticing aroma of coffee brewing tickled Kelly's nostrils. *Ahhhh.*

She leaned against the counter, willing her memory to bring that fragment front and center. What was it Burt said? Something about Vera talking to police . . . something about the night Zoe was killed . . . what was it? What was it? The little memory fragment drifted from the back of her mind, circled once more, then came front and center . . . and into focus. *That was it!* She remembered now. Dan told Burt that Vera said she had been at her apartment all night, sewing.

Kelly stole some coffee before it finished brewing, causing a loud hiss of steam when coffee droplets fell on the heating unit. She leaned back against the counter and took a deep drink while she pondered what she'd just heard from Christine.

Was Christine remembering correctly? Had Vera come into her pharmacy the same night that Zoe was killed? If so, then why did she tell police she was at home sewing? Maybe . . . maybe she *did* tell the police, but also told them she'd run an errand first. Maybe Dan left out that part when he told Burt. *Which was true?*

All Kelly knew was that this was important information. The police clearly hadn't questioned Christine, because they didn't even know about her working at Super Duper's pharmacy that night. The pharmacist trainee was scheduled. And she was still there when police came to ask questions later that night after they'd found Zoe's body. No doubt the police dispatcher quickly traced the informant's call to Super Duper's phone. Burt said police had questioned Super Duper employees but no one recalled seeing a woman come in and ask for a phone. If Christine had remained in town, she might have felt compelled to go to the police herself once she started reading the newspaper stories. But Christine and her husband left the very next day for their two-week cruise. The newspaper stories didn't come out until the following day.

Finishing off the smaller cup, Kelly poured herself a mugful. Then she started to pace around her small cottage living room. She needed to talk to Burt. Tell him about pharmacist Christine. Dan would surely want to talk with her. Maybe if Dan and imposing Lieutenant Morrison questioned Christine, she might remember some detail she'd temporarily forgotten.

Kelly grabbed her phone. She had to tell Burt now. That was the only way she could return to her accounts and concentrate. A puzzling murder was too tempting. The desire to unravel it was strong. And this puzzle was way more complicated than her accounts.

Punching in Burt's number, Kelly waited for him to answer. Unfortunately, Burt's number rang and rang, then switched to voice mail. She left a message telling him about pharmacist Christine and asked him to call her when he had a moment. Returning to her corner computer table, Kelly set her mug and her phone alongside her laptop and disappeared once again into the numbers.

Seventeen

Kelly heard her cell phone's familiar ring as she revved her car's engine. Digging the phone out of her jeans pocket, she saw Burt's name and number. "Hey, there, Burt," she said as she angled out of the shopping center parking space. "I was hoping you'd see my message this morning. Did your phone run out of juice last night?"

"Not really. Mimi and I took some free time and escaped into the mountains overnight. Enjoyed some peace and quiet before all the wedding festivities start. We drove up the Big Thompson Canyon into Estes Park and stayed at our favorite inn. It's right on the lake in town and has beautiful views of the Rockies. We just got back into the shop a little while ago."

What a great idea, Kelly thought. *It would be nice to get away . . . after all the wedding celebration ends . . . hmmmm.*

"I don't blame you, Burt. Resting up before all the craziness and festivities begin. Did you have a chance to hear my phone message last night? I was wondering what your thoughts were about pharmacist Christine."

"I have to agree with you, Kelly. Dan will certainly want to question pharmacist Christine. In fact, I've already called and left him a message."

"Oh, good, good," Kelly said, relieved that Burt also thought the pharmacist's information was important. She nosed her car around a corner onto a larger thoroughfare. "I'm curious about something else, Burt. Didn't you say that Vera told police she was at home sewing the night of Zoe's murder?"

"You remember correctly, Kelly. That's exactly what Dan told me. Why do you ask?"

"Yesterday, when I asked Christine if she saw anyone in the Super Duper pharmacy using the phone or asking for one, she said she didn't remember seeing anyone except Vera." Kelly paused. "She said Vera came by the pharmacy that night to bring her some clothes she'd altered for her. I wondered why Vera never mentioned that. Of course, Christine may have the dates mixed up in her mind. Maybe it was the day before. Anyway, I thought it was something Dan would want to know about. Particularly if he questions Christine."

"You bet Dan will want to know that. Good job, Sherlock! In fact, I think it's important enough that I'm going to leave another message for Dan and tell him what you've learned. Great detective work, Kelly. Once again, you've found something police have missed."

It felt good hearing that. It verified her instincts were still spot-on. "I'm glad you feel the same way, Burt. When my instinct starts buzzing, well . . . you know I have to follow up on it."

Burt's chuckle sounded over the phone. "No need to explain those instincts of yours, Sherlock. I've learned to trust them, and between you and me . . . so has Dan. Let's see what he learns."

"Great. Call me when you hear something."

"Always."

Kelly clicked off her phone and was about to toss it on the seat when it rang again in her hand. This time, Lisa's name and number flashed on the screen.

Boy, it must be the morning for phone calls, she thought as she pulled into the right-hand lane and slowed down for a traffic light before answering. "Hey, there, what's up? Has Megan been calling you?"

"No, all is quiet on the Megan front. The Curt and Jayleen Sightseeing Express is working. I only heard from her once yesterday, and she sounded waaaay more relaxed."

"Excellent. Well, the Express should take them into the canyons today. Megan should be all mellowed out by tomorrow. Well, mellowed for Megan, that is." Kelly had to laugh.

"We'll take what we can get. Listen, I have a favor to ask you. Do you have any errands to run today?"

"Actually, I'm out doing errands right now. Can you believe I'd forgotten to buy printer cartridges? I went to print out Housemann's financial statements, and the cartridge gave out halfway through. I have to put a list on the fridge."

"I'm glad I caught you at a good time. Would you be able to drop by the sports clinic parking lot and get the dress box from the backseat of my car? It's my bridesmaid dress. The hem is falling down on one side and needs to be fixed. I'm *totally* swamped all day, so I can't drive it over to Leann. I thought maybe she could fix it by tomorrow or Friday if she got it today."

"Sure thing," Kelly said as traffic moved once more. She made a mental note to turn onto another thoroughfare up ahead that would take her to the sports clinic. "What happened? Did it come loose or something?"

"Uhhhh . . . I was trying it on with the new bridesmaid shoes and caught the heel in the hem . . . and it ripped out."

Kelly's little buzzer went off. There was something about that answer that didn't make sense. Something Lisa wasn't saying. "How in the world did you do that? Why didn't you take the dress off over your head?"

"Ahhhh . . . it's complicated."

Kelly heard the smile in Lisa's voice. "Why do I get the feeling Greg was involved?"

Lisa laughed softly. "Let's just say that I can't run very fast in high heels."

Kelly laughed louder. "Was he chasing you around the house or what?"

"I was trying on the dress with the shoes, and Greg thought I looked so cute, he decided to play 'Catch the Bridesmaid.'"

Kelly snickered. "Where was Marty all this time?"

"Oh, he was having dinner with his relatives. Man . . . this wedding can't come a moment too soon." She laughed softly. "Oooops, here comes my next therapy patient. My car door lock combo is 19658. Thanks, Kelly." She clicked off.

Kelly memorized the numbers as she turned onto the avenue that led to the sports clinic.

• • •

Kelly drove into Leann's driveway and parked beside her car. Taking Lisa's dress box with her, she hurried up the driveway leading to the back porch entrance to Leann's shop. She needed to return to her cottage and dive into Warner Development accounts. Only two days left to finish, today and tomorrow. After that, it was Friday, and the festivities began.

She raced up the steps and onto the porch, heading to the back door. Kelly was about to knock when the door suddenly opened and Leann stepped out.

Leann jumped, clearly startled. "Oh, Kelly! I didn't see you."

Kelly quickly backed up. "Sorry, Leann, I didn't mean to scare you. I was coming to drop off Lisa's bridesmaid dress. She accidentally caught her heel in the hem, and it came loose. Lisa was hoping you'd have time to fix it before the wedding."

"Oh, surely. I'll be glad to," Leann said, setting the box on a table inside her house. Coming out again, she closed the door behind her and said, "Perfect timing, Kelly. Another five minutes, and you would have missed me."

Kelly looked at Leann. She looked different. She was no longer wearing somber gray or navy blue clothing like the last few times Kelly had seen her. Leann was back to wearing bright colors and attractive outfits. Now she looked like she did the first time Kelly saw her—lively and pretty.

Curious, Kelly asked, "Are you going off on errands? That's what I've been doing all morning so far."

"No, I've got something a lot more important than errands to do, Kelly." Leann walked across the back porch and out the door, Kelly following her.

Now her curiosity was really raised. "What's up, Leann? Did the police question you again?" she asked as she and Leann went down the steps.

Leann stopped on the driveway beside her car and turned to Kelly. That was when Kelly saw it. The frightened look that she'd recently seen on Leann's face was gone. Leann looked straight into Kelly's eyes now like she did when Kelly first met her.

"Yes, they did, Kelly, and I can't thank you enough for giving me those lawyers' names. I chose William Shelby, and he is excellent. Believe me, I couldn't have gotten through that third police interrogation without him. He clarified all sorts of information for me."

"That's wonderful, Leann. I'm glad I could help. So how did that third visit with police go?"

"Well, it's obvious the detectives consider me a suspect. In fact, they even asked if I had kept on seeing Oscar Yeager. My lawyer, William, thinks they're exploring the possibility that Oscar and I planned Zoe's murder together! Can you *believe* that?" Real anger shone in Leann's eyes now.

"That's hard for me to believe, Leann," Kelly replied with the truth. She still had trouble picturing that scenario.

"After the meeting, William and I went to his office to talk. And he told me that he had done some checking, and the police had not been able to trace the gun because my father never had it registered. So there were no records. That means there was only one way the police could have known that I had a gun collection. Someone *told* them. And I know who that someone is."

Kelly was totally taken aback by this revelation. "Who was it?"

"Oscar Yeager. That's who. He's the only one who would have a reason to tell police about my father's guns. He's trying to throw suspicion onto *me* and away from him!"

Kelly stared at her. Clearly, Leann was back to her feisty former self. And the fire of conviction flashed in her eyes. "I think you may be right, Leann."

"I know I'm right," Leann replied, her chin lifting. "That's why I'm going over to Oscar's right now and confront him. I want to hear Oscar say it to my face." With that, Leann turned and unlocked her car door, ready to mount up and ride off to battle the dragon.

Kelly gulped. *Oh, no.* "Uhhh, Leann . . . I don't think that's a good idea," she protested, watching Leann get into her car and start the engine. "Oscar is a wife beater. No telling what he'll do if you make him mad."

Leann looked out at Kelly with confidence. "He won't hit me, Kelly. I know he won't."

Good Lord! "Leann . . . I don't think you should do this, I really don't."

"I have to, Kelly. It's important. I'm going to make him admit that he lied to police about me." She put the car into gear.

Kelly sprang into action. "Listen . . . at least let me go along with you. That way you won't be alone with Oscar."

Leann looked up at her and gave a little smile. "Why, thank you, Kelly. I would welcome the company."

Kelly sped around the car and jumped into the passenger seat. Leann pulled out of the driveway and drove into the adjoining residential street. Meanwhile, Kelly tried to think of things she could say to dissuade Leann from this rash action.

"I really think you should reconsider this, Leann. Oscar Yeager is a known wife beater and abuser. He may have been on his best behavior when you two were together, but that was then. If you get in his face now, no telling what he will do. Or try to do."

"I'm not afraid of him, Kelly." Leann's voice was completely calm as she merged onto a busy thoroughfare.

Kelly had to admire Leann's courageous spirit. It would surely help get her through what lay ahead of her in the police investigation of Zoe's murder. But this foolhardy action . . . where had that come from? Kelly decided to try another tack.

"You know, police are questioning people who worked the night of the murder at the big drugstore a few blocks away. They're hoping someone saw something." Maybe that would catch Leann's attention.

"That's good. Maybe someone saw Oscar nearby." She turned from the large thoroughfare into another street.

Kelly watched Leann's profile. Her jaw was set. Clearly, Leann had made up her mind. All Kelly could do was to ride shotgun to Leann's sheriff when she confronted Big Bad Outlaw Oscar. Kelly didn't like that picture at all.

Leann turned her car onto a neighborhood street that looked vaguely familiar. After they turned another corner, Kelly spotted the Yeager house across the street. There in the driveway was the beat-up gray truck that had ridden her bumper three weeks ago.

"Good, Oscar's at home," Leann observed as she pulled her car along the curb in front of the Yeager house.

"Are you sure you want to do this, Leann?" Kelly asked when Leann had turned off the car.

Leann looked directly into Kelly's eyes. "Yes, Kelly. I want to see Oscar's face when I ask him about the gun. I'll be able to tell if he's lying." Leann pushed open the car door and got out.

Kelly didn't say anything else. Leann obviously had her mind made up, and nothing Kelly said had dissuaded her. Kelly followed after Leann as she walked up the narrow concrete walkway to the front stoop. Pausing for a few seconds, Leann rang the doorbell. Kelly stepped forward to stand beside Leann . . . just in case Oscar did not react as mildly as Leann assumed.

The front door opened and Oscar stood on the doorstep in his tee shirt and jeans, barefoot and unshaven. He glanced briefly at Kelly, then stared at Leann. "What do you want?"

"I want to ask you a question, Oscar, and I want you to tell me the truth," Leann said, her voice lower than normal but there was a strength to it Kelly hadn't heard before.

Oscar scowled at her for a second. Suddenly his scowl turned to a leer. "What's the matter, Leann? You miss me? You wanna come over and see me again?"

Kelly caught the scent of alcohol and stale cigarette smoke coming from Oscar. Hardly alluring.

Leann frowned at her old lover. "I want to know if you told the police about my father's gun collection."

Oscar's leer disappeared, and a scowl twisted his face. "I don't know what the hell you're talking about."

"Yes, you do, Oscar. You looked at those guns when you used to come over. There's no other way the police would know about them. They weren't registered. You *must* have told them!"

"You're crazy! I never told those cops *nuthin'*!" Oscar stepped onto the front stoop, right in front of them.

Leann put her hands on her hips, like an old-fashioned housewife scolding a straying husband. "Don't lie to me, Oscar. It *had* to be you! Now, admit it!"

"I ain't admitting nuthin'! You're crazy, Leann! Are you trying to get me in trouble with the cops or something? *Damn you!*" Oscar raised his arm and moved toward Leann, who was holding her ground amazingly well.

Kelly immediately moved in front of Leann. "Back off, Oscar!" she warned.

"Who the hell—" Oscar held his aggressive stance as he peered at Kelly. "Wait a minute . . . I know you. You're the bitch that helped Zoe run away!" He drew his arm back again.

Kelly pushed Leann back as she quickly pulled her cell phone out of her jeans pocket. "You hit me, and I swear I'm calling the cops, Oscar!" she threatened, brandishing her cell phone. "I've got cops and lawyers for friends, and your butt will be in jail before you sober up. There's a witness standing right here."

Oscar's face twisted in anger, his arm holding still. "You *bitch*!"

"You think I'm kidding? I'm not." She pressed 911, then brought the phone to her ear as she slowly stepped back, her other arm outstretched in front of a wide-eyed Leann, who followed her lead and backed up.

Oscar quickly broke his belligerent pose and scowled at Kelly, then Leann. "You two better get outta here before I get really mad. And don't come back!" he threatened as he retreated into his house once more and slammed the door.

Kelly clicked off her phone, then grabbed Leann's arm and briskly escorted her away from the Yeager front yard and back to her car. Leann got in and started the engine, while Kelly hopped into the passenger seat.

Leann didn't say anything for a couple of moments as she drove out of the neighborhood and back into city traffic. Finally she spoke in a quiet voice. "Well, I've never seen him like that before. I guess all of Vera's stories are true."

Kelly looked at Leann, wondering what to say. Surely Leann must realize what a foolish thing it was to confront Oscar on his own doorstep. Didn't she? Kelly wasn't sure. Leann's sudden surge of courage was a good thing, and would help her through what was bound to be a grueling police investigation. But courage needed to be tempered with common sense.

From the back of her mind, Kelly's inner voice spoke up quietly. *That's good advice. Make sure you follow it yourself.*

Kelly discarded the thought of scolding Leann for her rash idea. Clearly that would be like the pot calling the kettle black, as Jayleen would say. Kelly's sleuthing efforts in the past had included many rash escapades. Finally she settled on a milder reprimand.

"Promise me, Leann, that you will never try to confront Oscar Yeager again."

Leann's mouth curved up at the corners a little. "I promise, Kelly. And thank you . . . for coming with me. I appreciate that."

"You're welcome." Kelly let out a long breath, feeling the tension seep out of her muscles.

"I told you Oscar wouldn't hurt me."

Kelly turned and stared at Leann as she drove through late morning traffic. Kelly didn't know what to say to such a statement, so she said nothing. She simply closed her eyes and took a deep breath.

"**Hey,** I didn't expect to see you here this afternoon," Burt said as he walked into Lambspun's main room. "I thought you'd be holed up in your cottage, working away."

Kelly looked up over her laptop and smiled at her friend and mentor. "I felt the need for some warm and fuzzy surroundings while I worked, considering the stressful morning I've had." She took a deep drink of coffee from her mug.

Burt settled into a chair beside her, which told Kelly he had something to say. "Don't tell me Megan blew up," he teased.

"That would have been easier to handle. No, this morning I rode shotgun on Leann's crazy adventure to confront Oscar Yeager." She gave Burt a wry smile. "Let's just say Oscar was none too pleased with her visit."

Burt sat up straight. "Good Lord! Did he threaten you or Leann?"

"Of course." Kelly shrugged. "That's what guys like Oscar do. It's a knee-jerk response to being challenged."

"What in heaven's name was Leann thinking?"

"She was convinced that Oscar was the one who told police about her gun collection. Apparently her lawyer told her that since the guns weren't registered, there was no way for the police to trace them to her. Someone must have told them about the guns. Believe me, I tried every way I could think of to dissuade Leann from doing that, but she was determined to 'ask Oscar to his face.' She was convinced she could tell if he was lying." Kelly let out a sigh. "Thank goodness I showed up with Lisa's dress when I did. Leann was heading out the door."

"I'd say Leann was damn lucky you were there. What'd you do? Stand in front of her?"

"Yeah, and pulled out my cell phone when Oscar threatened us. He had his hand back, ready to swing. That's when I threatened *him*. I warned him I had cops and lawyers for friends and his butt would be in jail fast if he hit me. Then I pointed to Leann as witness." She winked.

Burt found his smile again. "Good girl," he said with a chuckle. "Smart move."

"I tell you, Leann is back to her feisty former self, all right. It's a good thing, because it can help her get through the police investigation. That reminds me, have you heard anything from Dan? What did he think of that information about Vera?"

"Yes, he called a few minutes ago. He was *very* interested in hearing about pharmacist Christine and her comments concerning Vera. In fact, he planned to question Christine tonight when she reports in to work at Super Duper."

"Excellent. You told him that she and Vera were really old friends, right? He doesn't want her gossiping back to Vera."

Burt smiled. "Yes, I told him. Don't worry, Dan will handle it. But there's more. When I told him what the pharmacist had said about Vera, Dan was quiet for a minute. Now I know him. That means Dan was sorting through stuff in his mind. Then I asked him exactly how they'd traced the gun to Leann. Was it registered to her father? That's when Dan admitted the gun wasn't registered. They'd had a tip Leann had a gun collection. That's why they went there. And we know Leann acted dazed and confused by their questions."

"They were tipped off about the gun?" Kelly exclaimed. "It had to be Oscar. Leann was *right*!"

"Actually, no. Leann is wrong. The tip came from someone else."

Kelly frowned at him. *"Who?"*

"Vera," Burt said, watching Kelly's reaction.

Kelly sat up even straighter, and stared off into the adjoining yarn room over Burt's shoulder. Vera. *She told police about the gun collection?* But she'd said she never noticed the gun case on Leann's wall. Clearly, that wasn't the truth.

"Wait a minute, Burt. I remember Vera telling Mimi and me that she'd never noticed a gun case on Leann's wall. Clearly she did if she told police about it. Why would she lie to us?"

Burt shrugged. "I don't know, Kelly. Maybe she didn't want people to know that she fingered Leann."

Snippets of conversations crept from the back of Kelly's mind now. Forgotten snippets, appearing innocuous until now. Now they began to coalesce into ideas. Lizzie had said that Oscar lost all of Vera's money in a bad business deal. Vera hated him. And Vera blamed Zoe, too. Zoe kept badgering Vera, urging her to trust Oscar with the money. Zoe had mistreated Vera, according to Lizzie.

"You know, Burt, learning this about Vera has jogged loose some other information I'd heard about her. Lizzie told me that Vera hated Oscar Yeager because he took her only savings and lost it all in some business deal. And Lizzie went on to say that Vera blamed Zoe for badgering her into trusting Oscar. And Zoe even took the only piece of family jewelry Vera had. Lizzie said Zoe browbeat Vera into letting her take it because she needed money when she left Oscar." Kelly caught Burt's gaze and watched his eyes light up.

"Oh, really? Well, that's certainly interesting to hear. I'll be sure to tell Dan. I could tell he had some questions about Vera, from the tone of his voice. After all, she was also the one who told them about Leann and Oscar's affair."

"Right, I remember her saying that. Now I'm wondering if Vera was merely helping the investigation or planting seeds of suspicion about Leann," Kelly said. She stared off into the yarn room again as another memory fragment surged forward, demanding attention. "Oh, and I almost forgot. I spoke with lawyer Lawrence Chambers last week about an appointment, and he mentioned one of my friends had called and asked him questions about Colorado inheritance laws." She paused for effect.

Burt raised a shaggy gray brow. "Don't tell me. Vera."

"Yeah. She'd asked me to recommend a lawyer so she could make a will. Mr. Chambers said she never mentioned a will. But she did take the time to tell him she was convinced that Zoe's husband Oscar was sure to be convicted of her murder. Then Chambers repeated Vera's comments about Oscar's abusive past."

Burt stared off at the windows, then nodded. "That's very intriguing, Kelly. It seems that Vera has been busy with more than salvaging Zoe's seamstress business. You know, I think I'll give Dan a call right now." Burt rose from his chair, then looked down at Kelly with one of those fatherly smiles that always warmed Kelly's heart. "Thanks, Sherlock. You've done it again. Most people wouldn't remember comments like that, but you do. And it's the small pieces of information that help detectives put cases together."

"You're welcome, Burt. Let me know what Dan says," she said as Burt started to walk away.

"I will. And I'll be curious to know if pharmacist Christine confirms what she said about seeing Vera that night. After all, Vera told police that she was home all night, sewing."

Kelly clicked back to her spreadsheet. "Give me a call when you hear from Dan."

"You bet, Kelly," Burt called over his shoulder.

Eighteen

"**Hey,** Jen. Can you give me a fill-up, please?" Kelly said as she leaned against the café counter. "I've got a bunch of errands to run this morning before I get to work on my accounts."

"Sure thing," Jennifer said as she picked up the coffeepot and poured a black stream into Kelly's mug. "Since you're already going to be out, could you do me a big favor? Could you take my bridesmaid headband over to Vera at the shop, please? The ribbon is coming undone, and I didn't want to try an amateur repair."

"Sure, Jen. No problem." Kelly took a deep drink of coffee.

"Thanks a bunch. I have it here with me. I was going to take it over this afternoon, but Pete and I have a chance to cater an afternoon tea for some faculty wives at someone's home. We'll be busy straight through this morning into the afternoon."

"Don't worry, I'll take care of it. What happened to the headband? Don't tell me you and Pete were playing 'Catch the Bridesmaid,'" Kelly joked.

Jennifer started laughing. "What was that again?"

"It's a new game Lisa and Greg started. Ask her about it," Kelly said, then took another drink of nectar. *Ahhhh.* Caffeine.

"I haven't had a desperate call from Megan this morning, so I'm assuming Curt and Jayleen's two-day parent tour helped her relax. Today is all relatives, all the time." Jennifer started loading breakfast dishes from the counter onto her tray.

"Haven't heard a thing, so I'm betting that Megan sees the finish line ahead and knows she can make it." Kelly leaned against the counter. "Everything starts tomorrow. We've got lunch reservations at Babette's. Bridesmaids, Megan, mom, sister, and Mimi. Then wedding rehearsal in the canyon, then dinner at Jayleen's."

Jennifer lifted the tray to her shoulder and turned toward the alcove section of the café. "I'm so glad Curt decided to contribute his aged prime steaks to the rehearsal dinner instead of the reception. Pete and I are salivating already."

"I'll say. That's a lot more manageable number than the nearly two-hundred-plus reception guests. There's no way Curt had enough prime beef in his freezer for that." She fell into step beside Jennifer.

"It will be a lot more fun at Jayleen's. And way more relaxed, too."

Mimi suddenly rounded the corner from the hallway and spotted Kelly. "Kelly, I'm so glad you came by. Do you have a minute?"

Kelly checked her watch. Errands to run. Accounts to

finish. She was on the home stretch. "Just a couple of minutes, Mimi. I've got a busy schedule today."

"This won't take more than that. Follow me." She beckoned Kelly down the hallway toward the shop.

"I'll drop off the headband, Jen. See you tomorrow," Kelly said as she followed after Mimi, who was heading to the workroom ahead. "What's up?" she asked as she entered.

Mimi was unfolding a soft blue bundle. "I fixed your shawl, Kelly, and I want you to try it on so I can see if it looks all right." She held up the fuzzy blue triangle.

Kelly stared at the shawl's triangle, visually comparing both sides. She blinked. "Whoa, Mimi, they're even! You *fixed* it! How'd you *do* that?"

"I used some weighted crystal beads that I stitched into the bottom edge about an inch apart on the left side. It was just enough to pull the scarf down another inch or so, with the help of some steaming. That was all it needed to appear even. It's still a little shorter, but you don't notice it now."

"Mimi Magic," Kelly said with a grin. "You continue to amaze me."

Mimi beamed. "Here, try it on. Let me take a look."

Kelly deposited her mug, then held up the shawl, seeing if she could feel a difference. "You know, I think I can feel it, but I'm not sure," she said, wrapping the shawl around her shoulders.

Mimi scrutinized Kelly from the back. "You don't even notice the difference, Kelly. Go take a look in the mirror on the restroom wall."

Kelly scurried into the restroom and checked out her rear reflection in the wide wall mirror. Mimi was right. She didn't even see a difference.

"It looks great, Mimi. Thank you so much for riding to the rescue once again," Kelly said as she returned to the workroom. She carefully removed the shawl and handed it to Mimi.

"It was easy and fun to do, Kelly. Now I'll steam it once more, then put it in a box with your name at the front, so you can pick it up tomorrow."

"Sounds perfect," Kelly said, checking her watch again. Time was passing. "I'd better get on my errands. See you later. And thanks again, Mimi." She grabbed her mug and waved good-bye as she sped down the hallway.

Kelly knocked once, then opened the sewing shop front door and stepped inside. She'd spied Vera working away at the sewing machine. "Hi, Vera," Kelly said as she walked into the workroom. "I'm making a quick drop-off of Jennifer's headband. The ribbon came undone, and she didn't want to try her own repair."

Vera quickly rose from her sewing perch. "That was good of you, Kelly. I'll be happy to fix it. I made several of those headbands."

Kelly handed over the plastic bag. "Here you go. I agree with Jennifer. I wouldn't want to try fixing those delicate ribbons and flowers. Better to let a pro do it."

"It should be easy," Vera said, slowly removing the headband from the bag. The ribbon had unwound from one end of the band and was hanging down. "Oh, this won't take long to repair," Vera said as she examined it. "If you don't mind waiting, I'll fix it right now. It should take no more than five minutes. Let me get my thread."

"That would be great. Then I can take it to Jennifer while she's still working at the café." Kelly settled into one of the wooden chairs beside the worktable. Having an idle opportunity to chat with Vera, Kelly decided not to waste it. An idea teased from the back of her mind. A simple question. *Why not?*

Vera walked over to a tall dresser and opened the top drawer, then she drew out a box and settled at the long worktable beside the windows. Meanwhile, Kelly sorted through various ways to approach the subject she wanted.

"I imagine everyone is getting all excited for the big weekend," Vera said, threading a needle with thread that matched the ribbon.

"Yes, indeed," Kelly replied. "Thank goodness Megan is as organized as she is. So far, there have been no major crises at the last moment."

"Megan is a very nice girl," Vera said, wrapping the ribbon around part of the headband. Then she stitched it in place from the underside. "I've enjoyed working with all of you. Leann has said the same thing."

Kelly recognized her opening and grabbed it. "Well, it's been a pleasure working with you and Leann." Then she let her voice grow concerned. "I'm so very sorry that Leann's been drawn into that police investigation. It's such a shame. I don't see how the police can suspect her."

Vera looked up quickly, needle poised over the headband. "What makes you think the police suspect Leann?"

Kelly deliberately widened her eyes and leaned forward. "Because I overheard Leann say that the police wanted to question her a third time. At the *police department*! She had to find a *lawyer*!"

Vera looked shocked. "But that can't be. Oscar is the one who killed Zoe, not Leann. Police simply have to find him guilty. They *have* to." She sewed another few stitches, then repeated, "They have to. They have to."

Kelly observed Vera closely. Her focus on Oscar's guilt was almost obsessive. "I think so, too, Vera. But don't forget that Leann's gun was the murder weapon. Plus she doesn't have an alibi for that night. Leann says she was at home sewing, but no one saw her. However, there were witnesses who saw her storm into Zoe's class earlier that night and accuse Zoe of *stealing*!" Kelly wagged her head dramatically. "I just wish there was some way to prove she was at home. Maybe a phone call or something. Or someone saw her car. Maybe you called her to ask about some sewing. Or maybe you dropped something over there that night. You worked with her. Think back, Vera. Maybe you remember something."

Vera shook her head solemnly. "I'm afraid not, Kelly. I never left home that night. I was working on a suit for a regular customer."

Kelly heaved a dramatic sigh. "I wish there was some way to show that Leann is innocent. It's so *awful*."

Vera returned her attention to the headband. "Well, I trust the police will see that Oscar is the one who killed Zoe. Countless people can witness the bruises they saw on Zoe's face and arms regularly. And the police know that Oscar had been to Leann's house, so he knew where to find a gun. I pointed out those very facts to that nice Detective Morrison just last week when I called him. He's so kind. He always updates me on how the investigation is going. I'm sure he'll arrest Oscar shortly."

Kelly watched Vera stitch the dangling ribbon underneath Jennifer's headband. Meanwhile, she marveled at Vera's ability to lie so smoothly. She was certainly a skilled actress.

Ever since her conversation with Burt yesterday, Kelly had found herself growing more and more suspicious of Vera. Little snippets of conversations around the knitting table returned to tease her. When Kelly first met Vera, she'd appeared shy and mousy. Was that an act? Ever since Zoe died, Vera had appeared strong and decisive. Vera had stepped into Zoe's business without missing a beat, finishing Zoe's customers' garments on time. Now it looked like Zoe's business had become Vera's business. "My customers," Kelly remembered Vera saying recently. *Her* customers. Not Zoe's anymore. *Hers.*

Was that a case of Vera stepping up to the plate and handling a difficult situation well or something more? She'd also stepped in and handled all the details of Zoe's funeral. *She* was the contact between the family and the police. Vera once again stepping up to the plate and handling another difficult situation.

Kelly recalled Mimi's comment that Vera was "unbelievably composed" considering what had happened. No tears at the funeral. Of course, many people did not or could not cry in front of others at their loved ones' funerals. They did their grieving in private. Kelly understood that. But Vera's composure seemed different somehow. Was it possible that Vera had already thought these situations through? Had she planned what she would need to do and how she would do it?

Vera slid the needle underneath the headband, tucking in the thread. Kelly watched her quiet competency. Vera had displayed what appeared to be sincere shock at the thought that Leann could be considered a suspect. Had Vera already plotted out that possibility and decided it served her purpose of ensuring Oscar took the blame for Zoe's death? If poor Leann wound up accused of being an accomplice, well . . . that was too bad. *Collateral damage.*

Vera held up the headband. "There now. Good as new."

"Beautiful, just like before," Kelly declared, giving Vera a big smile as she took the headband. "Now where did I put that plastic bag?" She looked around and spotted the bag on the end table beside the sofa.

"You don't mind if I return to the alterations, do you?" Vera said as she returned to her sewing machine. "My customers are expecting their garments on time."

"You go ahead, Vera, I've got to return to my accounts, too. Work is always waiting," Kelly said as she went to retrieve the plastic bag.

When she lifted the bag from the table, she couldn't help noticing the bank statement that was spread out there. The names at the top caught Kelly's eye immediately. Not Vera's name. Zoe and Oscar Yeager's names. Their address, and their bank statement. Right beside the statement, there was a check register. It was partially open with a ballpoint pen sticking out.

Kelly glanced back at Vera, who had her back turned and her head bent over the sewing machine, light gray fabric sliding between her fingers and through the needle to the low hum of the machine. Kelly's curiosity got the better of her, and she reached over and opened the check register just enough to see that there was a finished check still on the register. To be paid to a fabric company, dated today, and signed . . . *Zoe Yeager*.

Kelly stared at the check, then quickly stepped away from the table, deliberately rattling the plastic bag as she hastened toward the door. "Thanks so much, Vera. I'll be glad to pay you for the repair."

Vera glanced over her shoulder with a smile. "No charge, Kelly. I was happy to help. Give my best to the happy couple, will you?"

"I certainly will, Vera. Take care," Kelly said as she opened the door, then hastily sped down the steps.

"Burt, I'm glad I caught you," Kelly said into her phone as she drove through traffic. "I've got something to tell you, but first, did Dan call you? Did he question pharmacist Christine?"

"Yes to both, Kelly," Burt's familiar voice came over the phone. "Apparently she repeated everything she told you and Mimi. Vera came in and dropped off the slacks she had altered. Christine remembered it was the same night Zoe was killed because she and her husband were leaving on their trip the next day."

"Thank goodness for Christine's good memory. What did Dan think?"

Burt chuckled. "He was more than interested to learn that, Kelly. I could tell from his voice. Dan's putting together all those little pieces of information and contradictions accumulating around Vera and making sense of them. He also confirmed again that Vera told him she was at home sewing the evening Zoe was killed."

"Did you tell him what Lizzie and Lawrence Chambers told me?"

"Yes, and Dan really appreciated all the new information," Burt replied. "I could tell he was already suspicious of Vera."

"He's planning to question Vera again, right?"

"He certainly will. But Dan wants to see what Morrison thinks first."

"Well, you can tell him that I was just at Vera's shop dropping off Jennifer's headband for repairs. Since it was simple, she suggested I wait, so . . . well, I couldn't resist asking a question."

"I'll bet." A smile in his voice.

"I told her how upset I was that Leann had to get a lawyer, and that the police questioned her a third time, and of course that means she's a suspect . . . all that. Then, I asked her to think back . . . maybe she had dropped off some sewing at Leann's that night. And Vera looked me straight in the eyes and said that she never left her house that night."

There was a pause on Burt's end of the line. "You know, Kelly, I think I'll give Dan another call or leave him this message. You just caught Vera in another lie. Maybe Dan and Morrison would like to see if she'll lie to them again."

Yes! Kelly exulted inside. "I'll be willing to bet she does, Burt. Vera is clearly convinced she's pulled the wool over everyone's eyes. No one suspects her. Now she's effectively taken over her dead sister's business, and . . . wait till you hear this. I saw Zoe and Oscar Yeager's bank statement on her end table and their checkbook."

"Oh, really?"

"Oh, yeah. And I couldn't resist. I looked in the checkbook while Vera was sewing and found a written check dated today to a fabric distributor and signed by Zoe Yeager."

"You're kidding."

"No, I'm not. I'll bet Vera's been slowly draining those bank accounts. Oscar would never find out until the money was gone. He's too busy drinking. I'm sure Vera figured Oscar would be arrested for Zoe's death, and there would be no impediment to her complete takeover."

Burt paused for a moment. "I'm sure Dan and Morrison will want to hear this right away. Vera is perpetrating fraud, so now they have a reason to take her in for questioning. Good job, Sherlock!"

"I would hope so," Kelly said, relieved that Burt had confirmed her suspicions. "Maybe being face-to-face with Lieutenant Morrison will shake her. He can be really intimidating when he wants to be."

Burt chuckled. "He never intimidated you, Kelly."

"You're right, Burt," Kelly said as she nosed her car into the driveway between her cottage and Lambspun. "But I don't scare easily. Even Oscar Yeager doesn't scare me. He came close, though." She laughed.

"By the way, I told Mimi about your visit to Oscar with Leann and all that, and . . . well, she must have told Jennifer or Lisa, because she said they were all upset at you for doing that. So prepare yourself to be scolded."

"Hey, I'm used to that, Burt. Talk to you tomorrow, okay? Let me know if Dan goes to see Vera."

"Will do."

Kelly turned off her car's ignition, grabbed her purse, and headed for the cottage. She was in the home stretch now. With the rest of the afternoon and evening to work, she'd definitely finish the Warner accounts. Then she could take a few days off with a clear conscience.

Kelly stood up and stretched, a long deep stretch, arms over her head. *Ahhhh.* She was finished at last. Now she could actually relax a little. Housemann's accounts, all done. Warner Development accounts, all done. She checked her watch. Nearly eight o'clock. Maybe she could simply relax the rest of the evening in front of the television and watch the Rockies play ball. *Who were they playing this week?* The Arizona Diamondbacks. Now, *that* should be a good game.

Kelly was about to settle on the sofa when her cell phone rang. Could that be Burt? Did Dan question Vera already? She retrieved her phone from the desk and noticed Lisa's name and number flash.

"Hey, Lisa, what's up? You and Greg chasing each other around the house?" Kelly asked, laughing softly.

"No, we're not, but we'd both like to chase *you*," Lisa said in that fussy schoolmarm voice Kelly recognized. "Whatever possessed you to go over and confront Oscar Yeager on his own doorstep? That is *so* risky! Megan's been having fits since she heard."

Oh, brother. Let the scolding begin. "Hey, I didn't go over there to confront Oscar. I simply accompanied Leann. She was bound and determined to ask Oscar about the gun. So I went with her kind of, like . . . protection."

"Yeah, right. A lot of protection against that beef bag, Oscar," Lisa sneered. "Damn, Kelly, it's taken Marty and Mimi and me, all three of us, to calm Megan down. Of all the times to go off and do something reckless . . . I cannot believe it! Megan was all relaxed today, getting ready to go over to Marty's house with her relatives for dinner, and then she talked to Mimi." Lisa gave a dramatic sigh.

"Well, then, blame Mimi," Kelly teased. "She shouldn't have told you guys. Then no one would be the wiser. Nothing happened."

"Nothing *happened*! Mimi said Oscar was going to *hit* you!"

Kelly decided she would have to have a talk with Mimi. This grapevine phone thing was sounding like that silly childhood game where gossip gets repeated and exaggerated with each version.

"He's all bluff." Kelly decided to fudge a little. "I simply stepped in front of Leann and took out my cell phone. Then *I* threatened *him* with jail time if he did anything. I said I had cop friends and lawyer friends, and his butt would be in jail so fast his head would spin. He scurried back into his house like a rat."

Lisa was quiet for a few seconds. "Still, you were reckless to do that."

"Tell Marty what I just said. Then he can reassure Megan. I certainly didn't mean to upset anyone. I was simply trying to protect Leann. No telling what Oscar would have done if I wasn't there."

"Promise me you won't do anything that reckless again, okay?"

"I promise," Kelly said, fingers crossed.

How could she promise something like that? One person's reckless act was someone else's necessary action. It was all subjective. But from now on, she was instructing Burt not to tell Mimi of those escapades.

"Okay, okay. Try to stay out of trouble between now and the wedding, okay?"

"I swear, Commander!" Kelly joked, hand held high.

"Yeah, yeah . . . I hear you laughing."

"Listen, why don't you chase Greg around the house for a while? Blow off all that tension," Kelly teased.

"I just might do that." Lisa started to laugh. "See you tomorrow at Babette's for lunch. Mimi's bringing Megan and crew with her SUV. If Megan isn't all calmed down by then, you can finish the job."

"You got it, Commander," Kelly said before clicking off.

Kelly headed back to the sofa. Now she *really* deserved to relax. But Carl chose that moment to get up off his doggie bed and stretch.

"You want to go out, Carl?" she asked her dog, who was already at the patio door. "Okay, go out and chase squirrels. It's a really warm night." She slid the glass door open, and Carl raced outside into the dark.

Kelly closed the door and returned to the sofa, clicking on the television. Finding the Rockies and Diamondbacks game, she settled into the cushions . . . for a couple of minutes. Then a loud knock sounded at her front door.

Brother . . . she would never get to relax and see that game. This was probably Jennifer and Pete, ready to fuss at her.

Louder knocking this time. And a muffled voice yelling something. *Was that her name?* "Coming!" Kelly called as she went to the door. She flipped back the lock, and the door burst open.

Steve charged into the cottage. "*Kelly!* Are you all right?" he cried, grabbing her by the arms. "Megan called and told me that some guy *hit* you! Who is that sonovabitch! Where can I find him?" Steve stared at her, wild-eyed with anger.

Kelly caught her breath. She'd only seen Steve this angry once before—when a twisted killer had tried to kill Kelly in Bellevue Canyon.

"*Steve! I'm okay!* Nothing happened. He didn't lay a hand on me! Honest. Megan got it all wrong. She got upset and called everyone. I'm okay. I'm okay."

Steve peered at Kelly, scrutinizing every inch of her face, then held her at arm's length, peering at her. "You sure? You're not just saying that?"

Kelly laughed softly. "I'm sure. See, I'm all good. No bruises. No marks, except from softball." She turned her arms over for him to inspect.

Steve stared at her for a long moment, as if memorizing every feature of her face. "The interstate is jammed, so I've been driving back roads to get here and see what happened. My phone was dead." He closed his eyes for a second and let out a long breath. "I got Megan's call when I left Sam's office, and I could barely hear her. There was lots of noise going on . . . people talking . . . but she was all upset, saying this guy was a wife beater and he *threatened* you! I tried to call you, but my phone battery died. Damn, Kelly! I was going *crazy*!"

Kelly reached out and placed her hands on Steve's chest. He was coatless, shirtsleeves rolled up, tie off. "Nothing happened to me, Steve. I was never in any danger. Megan got all upset because she's on overload with the wedding, that's all. I'm sorry if she scared you. You can see I'm okay."

Steve stared into her face once again, then took Kelly into

his arms. "If anything had happened to you, Kelly, I don't know what I'd do. I'd probably go out and kill the guy."

Feeling Steve's arms around her again sent a fire racing through Kelly's veins. *Yes. Oh, yes.*

Kelly slid her arms around Steve's neck and melded her body to his—just like she used to. She looked into his eyes, darkening with the same passion she felt, and whispered, "You can't do that. You'd be arrested, and I'd lose you. And I don't ever want to lose you again."

Steve pulled her to him and claimed her mouth in a long deep kiss, as they held each other in their arms. Kisses turned more passionate until they slowly made their way into the bedroom, releasing each other long enough to dispense with all clothing so they could join in that perfect embrace. *At last.*

Nineteen

It was the sound of Carl barking outside that awoke Kelly. Morning light streamed through the window. It had to be after seven o'clock from the angle of the sunbeams that fell across her bed. Her warm bed. Her no longer empty bed. She and Steve lay together, bodies curved against each other like they used to. Bare skin against bare skin.

Kelly snuggled in Steve's embrace, releasing a long sigh of contentment. A little muscle somewhere deep inside her chest released. Steve was back with her. Where he belonged. Last night, they had celebrated his homecoming. All night. In fact, Kelly couldn't remember sleeping. Merely relaxing between making love. Maybe they could stay in bed all morning.

Kelly liked that idea, and provocatively moved against Steve. Warm skin getting warmer. She got his attention quickly.

"Ummmm, stay right there," Steve's husky voice whispered. "I want to feel you like this another minute before I have to get up."

"Who says we have to get up?" Kelly tempted, deliberately moving her hips against him again. She had his full attention now.

Steve laughed softly and moved his mouth beside her ear. "I promised Sam and Baxter that I'd meet them this morning to go over some specs. Believe me, I'd like to spend all day right here, but . . . I gotta go."

She felt his warm lips on her neck and that familiar fire flooded her veins again. Kelly shifted in his arms so her mouth could meet his. Steve gave her a soft quick kiss. "That's not good enough," Kelly protested. She could feel Steve's reluctance as he pulled his body from hers.

"Don't I know it, but it's gonna have to do for now," he said as he threw back the covers and got out of bed.

"But I've missed you," Kelly tempted with another seductive smile as she sat up.

Just then, Carl started barking a quick staccato bark. His "Steve" bark. Carl had obviously heard Steve's voice and knew his "Beloved Steve" was in the cottage.

"See, Carl misses you, too," Kelly said, laughing.

"Tell the Big Guy that I'll play with him tonight," Steve said from the bathroom doorway. "Then you can show me how much you've missed me," he teased with a grin before he closed the door. Then the shower sounded, water splashing.

Carl kept barking his yelp, and Kelly decided she needed to thank the Big Guy for not complaining about the lack of attention last night. She left the warm bed and quickly pulled on some panties and a tee shirt. As much as she'd like to stay in their cozy nest, Kelly had people expecting her this morning, too. At least her clients weren't among them.

She grabbed Carl's doggie dish from the kitchen and filled it with a double ration. A reward for being such a considerate dog and allowing his two favorite people uninterrupted time for each other.

"What a good dog," Kelly said as she slipped past a jumping Carl and out onto the patio. She deliberately slid the glass door shut so Carl wouldn't go bounding into the bedroom and surprise a naked Steve. Kelly could attest to what a rude shock cold doggie noses were on bare skin. "Double portion for the Big Guy today," she said as she set the doggie dish on the concrete.

Carl dove in, gobbling down his breakfast, while Kelly stroked his sleek black coat.

"What a good dog you are," she cooed. "*Good dog, Carl.* You didn't even bark last night."

Carl glanced up briefly, as if to say: "I barked. You two didn't hear me." He shoved his face back into his dish, gobbling down the rest of his kibbles.

Kelly refilled his water dish and watched Carl slurp up several mouthfuls, then he trotted off to check the fence perimeter. Kelly went back inside and started a fresh pot of coffee. Soon, the familiar delectable aroma floated on the air. By the time the brew was ready, Kelly heard Steve moving around the bedroom, obviously looking for his clothes. She poured a mug for herself and filled a carryout mug for Steve.

He walked out of the bedroom, all dressed, if somewhat wrinkled. Kelly went over to him and offered the mug. "Are you going to stop by your apartment and change or plead casual Friday," she teased.

Steve took a deep drink of coffee, closed his eyes, and said, "Man, have I missed your coffee." He took another deep drink.

"Is that all you missed?" Kelly gave him a wicked grin.

Steve returned her grin. "I'll show you what else I've missed tonight." He leaned over and gave her a quick kiss. "Better go while I still can," he said with a laugh, and backed toward the door.

"Don't forget, the rehearsal is four o'clock at Jayleen's in the canyon," Kelly said, following him to the front door. "Then we're staying at Jayleen's for rehearsal dinner. The whole wedding party with parents. Curt's ranch house is filled with additional relatives."

"I'll meet you there. After this meeting, I'll go over to the apartment and pack. Can't forget that groomsman tux." Steve sped down the walkway toward his car, then looked back at Kelly. "Do you think the guys would notice if I skipped the bachelor party?"

"Yeah, I think they would." Kelly laughed, then savored the strong coffee as she watched him drive away.

"**Hey,** Kelly, I was about to call you," Burt said as Kelly walked into the Lambspun foyer. Burt dropped two more skeins of rust-colored wool into the open trunk that sat on the foyer floor. Fall colors spilled out of the trunk. Earth brown, tropical forest green, burnt orange, cranberry red.

"Perfect timing, then," she said as she walked through the foyer toward the main room. "Let me drop my knitting bag first."

"Not many customers yet, so we can talk in here," Burt

said as he pulled out one of the chairs beside the long library table.

Kelly dumped her bag and settled into a chair beside Burt. "I take it Dan has called you."

"Oh, yes." Burt nodded. "And I think you're going to be interested in what he had to say."

"I'm all ears," Kelly said with a grin. She took a long drink of caffeine, then set her mug aside and leaned toward Burt. "Did they question Vera?"

"They sure did. But before they even went over to her shop, they first got permission from Oscar Yeager to obtain copies of his bank statement for this month, September. Oscar was totally clueless about his accounts. Seems Zoe did all the banking. Anyway, Dan and Morrison obtained photocopies of all checks written since the beginning of the month, and would you believe that Zoe Yeager came back from the grave to sign seven checks after her death?" Burt smiled slyly.

"My goodness, we should call the tabloids," Kelly said. "That would be a front-page story. Tell me, how much are we talking about in total?"

"Nearly three thousand dollars. That's felony fraud. The photocopies definitely showed a noticeable difference in Zoe's signature." He shook his head. "I'll bet Vera practiced signing."

"I'm sure she did. Vera impresses me as someone who carefully plans before she acts. Methodical." Kelly took another drink of coffee. "So what did the guys do next?"

"Well, they got a search warrant for the sewing shop and Vera's apartment. Dan presented it to her when he and Morrison went over to question her at the shop."

"Oh, brother, I bet that caught her by surprise."

Burt nodded. "Yes, it did. Dan said she turned white as a sheet, then became very agitated when they told her they were going to take her to the department for questioning. She tried to convince them that Zoe had authorized her to pay for those fabric expenses. Dan said he explained to Vera that it didn't matter what Zoe Yeager authorized *before* she died. She was dead now, and all of the Yeager assets belonged to Oscar Yeager as her husband. Only he could authorize expenditures for the sewing shop." Burt gave Kelly a wry smile. "Apparently, that's when Vera lost it. Dan said her face got all red and she started yelling that Oscar didn't deserve the money. It belonged to her. She was the one taking care of the business. Zoe couldn't have built it without her. Oscar was a no-good drunkard, and Zoe had cheated her for years. They had stolen all her money years ago. *She* deserved the money . . . they owed it to her . . . and on and on like that. Dan said she was practically spitting, she was so enraged. Her face was purple. He was afraid she'd burst a blood vessel or something."

"Oh, boy," Kelly said softly, leaning back into her chair. "That sounds like a total meltdown. Clearly, Vera has drifted into her own reality where she could justify her actions. What happened when they took her to the department? Did they ask her anything about the night Zoe was killed?"

"That's when Morrison took over. Dan said Vera had already been read her rights, but she told them she didn't need a lawyer. It was all a mistake. So Morrison started asking her questions about Zoe and the shop, then worked his way to the night Zoe was killed. Apparently Vera repeated that she'd never left her apartment that night. Then Morrison told her they had a statement from someone who saw and spoke with her that same night at the drugstore only two blocks from the Presbyterian Church parking lot where Zoe was killed."

Kelly leaned on the table again, mimicking Burt's hunched pose. "What'd she say? I'll bet that shocked the daylights out of her."

"Ohhhh, yeah." Burt nodded. "Dan said Vera blanched again and just stared at Morrison for a minute, eyes round as saucers."

"Did she try to deny it?"

"Nope. That's when she asked for a lawyer," Burt said with a knowing smile.

"I'll bet she did. I'm sure she was convinced she'd fooled everyone. She'd covered all her tracks, and figured she had gotten away with murder. Then she's caught by her own lie."

"Now we'll simply have to wait and see what happens. She's being held at the County Detention Center on felony fraud charges with other charges pending. A court-appointed attorney is visiting her this morning. We'll see what happens."

Kelly sank back into her chair. "Vera's one smooth liar, I'll say that. And she was so believable. That made it easy to overlook her."

"There are some people who blend into the scenery so well they almost disappear. You don't even notice them at first. Vera's like that. She never drew attention to herself."

"You know, I actually liked Vera. She seemed such a nice person, hardworking, unassuming. Plus, we all felt sorry for her after Zoe died."

"I liked Vera, too. We all did. None of us suspected she had this simmering resentment against Zoe and Oscar brewing inside, distorting her judgment, and waiting to explode."

"I'll bet Vera will want to go to trial. She truly believes she can fool anyone, and she has. She fooled all of us. I have to admit, she is one of the most convincing liars I've seen so far. There was nothing that gave her away. No mannerisms, no look in her eyes. She is one excellent actress."

"And of course, that plays well with a jury. If it gets to a jury trial. That's the tricky part. There will only be circumstantial evidence against her for Zoe's murder."

"It would be the same with Oscar Yeager," Kelly retorted. "There are many people who would testify that Oscar beat Zoe. And Lisa and I witnessed his threats. But there would be no proof he was in that parking lot that night."

"There's no proof that Vera was, either, but the cleaning lady did say she saw a *woman* outside Zoe's car late that night. Not a man," Burt reminded her.

"That will have to be the deciding factor, I would think," Kelly mused out loud. "Oscar may be a brute, but given what we've learned about Vera, I truly believe she killed her sister."

"I do, too, Kelly. And there may be another piece of evidence that could definitively put the blame on Vera. The guys found a dark hooded jacket in Vera's closet, and they're taking that to the crime lab. If there's even one speck of Zoe's blood hiding there, the lab techs will find it."

Kelly released a long breath. "Let's hope they do, Burt. I don't like to think of killers getting away with their crimes."

"Oh, Vera won't get away with anything," Burt replied. "She's definitely going to jail on those felony fraud charges."

"Okay, then. Let's see what happens with the crime lab."

Kelly took a long deep drink of coffee and tried to push the thought of scheming killers from her mind. Today was a happy day. A Megan and Marty day.

As if he'd read her mind, Burt grinned. "Are you ready for the festivities to begin?"

"Oh, yeah. And I have some really good news to share which should add to the general festive mood." Kelly returned his grin. "Steve and I are back together. *Together* together. You have my permission to tell Mimi. And anyone else you bump into today." She winked.

Burt closed his eyes and exhaled a dramatic sigh. "Thank God. It's about time." He pushed back his chair. "I'm going to tell Mimi right this minute." He came over and gave Kelly a kiss on the cheek and a fatherly pat on the shoulder. "We're all back to normal at *last*," he said with a grin, then hurried out of the room.

Kelly simply smiled to herself and sipped her coffee. *Back to normal?* Kelly had to agree with Jayleen's earlier statement. After this last year of crazy changes, Kelly wasn't sure if she'd recognize normal if it walked right up and bit her.

Kelly savored the sauvignon blanc and took another bite of Babette's delicious crepe. She watched Mimi show Megan's mother and sister Babette's glass display case filled with delectable and tempting French pastries, all wickedly delicious. They "ooooed" and "ahhhhed" appreciatively.

"Your mom and sister are having a great time, Megan. I'm so glad you picked Babette's." She raised her glass.

"It was Jennifer's suggestion," Megan said, toying with

her crepe, then taking another sip of wine. "She figured an afternoon of chocolate would mellow everyone out."

Lisa snickered. "I love it. So true." She finished off her salad.

"Actually, I think Curt and Jayleen's Sightseeing Express did more to relax your parents than anything," Jennifer observed, glancing toward the dessert display. "Babette is just finishing the job." She raised her glass of white wine. "To Curt and Jayleen."

All of them joined her salute. Megan finished off the entire glass, poured some more, then nibbled her crepe.

Kelly noticed Mimi and Megan's mother were chatting with Babette's staff, obviously choosing a dessert. "Hey, guys, while we have a moment to ourselves, I thought I'd spread the good news. I already told Burt this morning." She glanced around the table and opened her mouth, but . . . Jennifer spoke up first.

"You and Steve? Please tell me yes."

Kelly grinned. "Yes. Last night. He stayed the whole night. So everyone can relax now." She leaned back into her chair and sipped her wine while she watched her friends' reactions.

Jennifer closed her eyes. "Obi Wan is very pleased."

"*Yessss!*" Lisa exulted, fist pumping the air.

"Ohhhh, my *Gawd*!" Megan crowed loudly, throwing her head back, wine sloshing from her glass. "*Finally!* Now we can really celebrate!"

Kelly simply laughed.

"I've gotta text Greg," Lisa said, digging into her purse.

"Me, too. Pete, not Greg," Jennifer said, riffling through her purse.

"I've gotta tell Marty!" Megan exclaimed, spilling all of her wine this time as she fumbled for her purse.

"Megan, you should finish that crepe," Kelly said. "It's not like you to leave food on your plate. And this is Babette's, remember?"

"Oh, yeah," Megan said, taking a quick bite and swallowing. "Hey, Babette's French! This calls for champagne! *Babette!*" she called, waving toward her mother and sister. "Get some of those chocolate things and ask Babette for a bottle of champagne! We need to celebrate Kelly and Steve, too! They're back together!"

Mom and sister stared at Megan with a quizzical look, but Mimi nodded with a smile while Babette disappeared into the back room.

Kelly simply relaxed, sipped her wine, and laughed at her friends. She was glad she had been able to add to the merriment. *Let the festivities truly begin.*

Kelly slid her knife through Curt Stackhouse's aged prime beef. Practically no resistance. She speared the rare morsel, dripping with juices, and popped it into her mouth . . . then savored. "Oh . . . my . . . Lord, this is so good," she said after she'd swallowed.

"You can say that again."

"Don't talk while I'm eating."

"Yummmm . . ."

"Does Curt take in boarders?"

"Somebody take Greg's plate. He used to be a vegetarian. This isn't good for him," Jennifer teased as she sliced another morsel of her steak.

"And kudos to the grill cook," Pete said, raising his glass to Jayleen, who sat next to Curt at the table.

Jayleen's entire great room was packed with the Smith-Harrington wedding party and families. A succession of smaller tables had been put end to end and sideways to form a squared-off U shape. Kelly and all her friends filled the bottom of the U and around the corners, which made it easier for them to talk to one another. Always a consideration when the gang got together.

Kelly glanced at Steve beside her. He was tearing into his steak like it was his last meal. Wolfing it down. The gang was finally together again, really together. Laughing, talking, savoring good beers and fine wines, eating everything in sight. Could Marty and Greg food jokes be far away?

She looked toward the ends of the U. Marty and Megan anchored both ends, their respective relatives lining each side. Since both families were right across from each other, conversation and laughter bounced back and forth.

"Can anyone tell if Megan's eating her steak? She barely had any of her lunch," Kelly asked before she took another scrumptious bite of her own.

"I worry about that, too, Kelly," Jennifer added. "She's been tossing down champagne and wine. And chocolate mousse. She had two of those at Babette's."

"I think I saw her eating," Lisa said, peering toward Megan's end of the table. "It's hard to tell. She's never in her chair. She's constantly moving around talking to people."

"Good. That means she won't notice if I steal her steak," Steve threatened before downing his last bite.

"Dude, don't even try it. Marty has a steak knife, and he'll fight to the death to protect anything within six feet of his plate."

Curt guffawed across the table. "Hell, Steve, there's bound to be another steak in the kitchen. Lord knows how many Jayleen grilled."

"I lost count," Jayleen said with her familiar grin as she sipped her cola.

Steve tipped back his Fat Tire ale and licked his lips. "I'll take a rain check on that, Curt. Besides, it would be more fun to snitch a slice of Megan's just to watch Marty's reaction."

Greg's head popped up from staring at his plate. "*Genius!* Man, have we missed having you around."

You're not the only one, Kelly thought to herself with a smile.

"I imagine we'll be seeing more of you, Steve, now that you've got more reason to visit Fort Connor," Burt teased next to Kelly.

"You imagine right, Burt." Steve saluted him with his beer before drinking.

"Wait till you boys see those bridesmaid dresses," Mimi said from beside Burt. "They're replicas of Megan's beautiful strapless white wedding gown. But in colors. Kelly's is royal blue." Mimi gave Steve one of her Mimi Knows Best smiles.

"Strapless, huh?" Steve said, his gaze sweeping over Kelly. "That's coming off."

Kelly snickered, watching Steve's comical leer and her friends nearly fall off their chairs laughing. Burt spilled his wine; so did Mimi, Pete, and Jennifer. Lisa dribbled beer down the front of her blouse, while Greg spewed Fat Tire halfway across the table. Jayleen hooted loudly, and Curt nearly *did* fall off his chair, he laughed so hard.

"Maybe we should wait till after the wedding," Kelly suggested with a sly smile.

"No promises." Steve grinned at her, then pushed away from the table. "I'm making a run for Megan's steak. Greg, you distract Marty."

"You got it," Greg said as he wiped the back of his hand across his mouth and stood up.

Kelly sipped her wine and watched Steve and Greg stalk Megan's steak. Greg distracted Marty, as promised, and Kelly watched Steve slice off a hunk of Megan's unattended steak, holding his prize aloft for a moment to several cheers. Greg was about to repeat the stealth maneuver, Kelly noticed, until Marty—true to form—realized what was happening. The fiery redhead leaped from his chair, steak knife held high, and proclaimed ownership over all beef at his end of the table.

Kelly joined her friends' laughter, watching both sets of relatives join in the fun. Wedding festivities had turned medieval. She wondered if the English Wars of the Roses had started off like this.

"Hey, Kelly-girl." Jayleen grinned at her from amid the noisy hoopla. "My ranch house door will be open during tomorrow's wedding reception. Just in case you and Steve want to slip away for a while."

Kelly returned Cowgirl Jayleen's grin. "I'll keep that in mind, Jayleen."

Twenty

"Man, I could use a cup of coffee right about now," Kelly said as she stretched her jeans-clad legs in front of her.

"I'll make some." Jennifer sprang from Lisa's maple rocking chair near the fireplace in the great room and walked into the kitchen.

It wasn't cold enough for a fire yet, but it would be soon, Kelly thought as she scooped up a handful of cashews from one of the plates on the coffee table. The other three plates were empty. Cheese ball, pizza rolls, hummus dip with veggies, all gone.

The four friends sprawled across the furniture in Lisa and Greg's great room. Kelly gathered her empty Fat Tire bottle and an empty wineglass and followed Jennifer. "I think we can safely say your parents and sister had a great time at the rehearsal dinner, Megan. I'm not surprised they left here early. They looked really tired." She dumped the ale bottle into the recycle bin and started loading used wineglasses into the open dishwasher.

"Yeah, your dad's eyelids were drooping," Lisa teased from her favorite armchair.

"Well, don't you guys fall asleep on me," Megan declared from her perch on the sofa. "I'm not a bit sleepy."

"You are *so* wired," Jennifer said from the kitchen as she started the coffeemaker.

"I cannot believe you're still standing after all that champagne," Kelly said, collecting the remaining empty glasses from the coffee table.

"It's adrenaline," Lisa decreed with a sage smile. "By this time tomorrow after the wedding, she'll crash. Marty, too."

"Then we'll crash together." Megan giggled and gobbled down some cashews. "Wow, I wish we had more of those appetizers left. I must have inhaled a dozen of each."

"That's because you didn't have your steak," Kelly teased, loading more glasses into the dishwasher. Spying a half-empty glass across the room, she went to retrieve it. However, Megan beat her to it.

"Boy, those cashews made me thirsty," Megan said before tossing down the rest of the greenish mixture.

"*Megan!* That was your sister's margarita," Kelly scolded.

"Oh, Lord," Jennifer said from the kitchen. "Tequila doesn't mix with champagne, wine, and beer. At least it didn't when I tried back in my bar-hopping days."

"Give her a glass of water," Lisa decreed from her chair. "Dilute all that liquor she's been drinking."

"I have *not*!" protested Megan as she handed Kelly the empty glass. "I've been drinking champagne and wine." She gave a sniff.

Kelly filled the empty glass with cold water and handed it to Megan. "That coffee smells ready. Whatever you do, Megan, don't drink any. The last thing you need is caffeine."

"Amen," Jennifer said as she poured a cup for Kelly. "Why don't you take a hot shower, Megan. It'll relax you, and you can fall asleep."

"But I don't *want* to go to sleep," Megan protested. "I told you, I'm wide awake."

"Well, *I'm* getting sleepy," Lisa teased from her comfy armchair.

"Don't you dare," Megan playfully threatened.

Kelly took a big drink of coffee. Clearly, it was going to be a long night. "Megan has been going nonstop all day and all evening," she whispered to Jennifer. "She's bound to crash sometime, isn't she?" Kelly took another deep drink, inhaling the caffeine.

"One would hope," Jennifer said with a wry smile. "It would be better if it's tonight rather than tomorrow, but we'll have to wait and see."

Kelly watched Megan and Lisa tease and joke with each other, then she checked her watch. Again. It was already after eleven o'clock. She and Steve had plans of their own for tonight. She took another drink of coffee, pondering. Megan was still going strong. Running on adrenaline. Meanwhile, what was left of tonight was slipping away.

Just then she heard a beep from her cell phone, signaling a text message. Kelly pulled the phone from her jeans pocket, thinking Steve might have texted her. Instead, the message was from Burt. Short, succinct, and satisfying.

Zoe's blood found on Vera's jacket sleeve. We've got her.

Kelly read the message again and smiled. Vera had tripped

up herself. She never noticed the tiny blood drops. Easy to miss on a dark jacket. Kelly shoved the phone back into her pocket, glanced over at her friends, then made a decision. She drained her cup and set it firmly on the counter.

"Megan, you're a sweetheart, and I love you to death. But you'll have to excuse me. Steve and I made some plans of our own for tonight, so I've gotta go. See you guys tomorrow at Megan's house before we leave for the canyon." She gave her friends a big smile and headed for Lisa's foyer, where she'd left her cowboy boots.

"Going to get your man, huh?" Jennifer teased with a big grin.

"But he's at the bachelor party with the guys!" Lisa called after her.

"*What?*" Megan bounced up from the sofa. "You're going to the Sunset Saloon?"

Kelly pulled on her boots. "I sure am. Don't worry, Megan. We'll set the alarm for tomorrow." She gave her friends a wicked grin. "We'll be sure to wake up in time for the wedding." With that, Kelly was out the door.

"**Who's** that blond girl talking to Steve at the bar?" Pete asked, looking across the crowded cowboy saloon.

"Who knows?" Greg said, tipping back his Fat Tire. "Steve's a chick magnet."

"Good thing Kelly isn't here," Pete said with a crooked smile.

Marty laughed. "You got that right. Man, am I glad they got it together before the wedding. No more walking on eggshells around them." He shook his curly red head, then took another drink of his dark stout.

"And no more sad country songs," Greg said louder as Steve returned to their table. "You can dump those off your playlist, right? Even Kelly won't want to ride with you."

"Hey, some of them are good songs," Steve joked as he set his beer on the table and reclaimed his chair. He glanced around. Tables were full, and so was the dance floor. Couples of all ages were doing the Texas two-step, some better than others. He took a long drink of his Fat Tire. "Man, this place is packed."

"Friday night busy," Pete said as he looked over his shoulder. "Hey, here comes Curt." He waved over his head.

Steve jumped out of his chair and offered it to Curt when he walked up. "Hey, Curt, have a seat. What can I get you?"

Curt settled into the chair, removed his Stetson, and placed it on his knee. "Thank you, son. I'll take a shot of whiskey. I just moseyed on down here to see how you boys were doing," he said with a sly smile as Steve headed for the bar. "Checking to see if my nephew was sober enough to take his vows tomorrow."

Marty grinned. "I can still remember my name, so that's a good sign."

Curt looked around the saloon. "I thought Bill and Jeff and Randy would be here."

"They were here for a while, danced with a couple of girls, then left to check out some more bars," Marty said with a smile.

"Ah, the single life," Greg teased. "Enjoy tonight. Because tomorrow you'll be a married man."

Curt snorted. "How long have you and Lisa been together?"

"Uhhhh, let me think . . . seven years."

"That sounds married to me. As good as," Curt retorted.

"Whoa . . . I don't believe it," Pete said, turning around in his chair. "Look who's coming."

Marty, Greg, and Curt all turned toward the saloon's entrance as Kelly walked through the barroom crowd, heading toward the bar.

"Hey, it's Kelly!" Marty grinned, waving at her over his head. Kelly waved back, trying to make her way past two cowboys who were obviously trying to get her attention.

"I'll be damned." Greg rocked his chair up and waved at Kelly, then pointed toward the bar, where Steve was waiting for the bartender.

"Well, well, that takes a lot of guts." Curt chuckled. "I'm not surprised. Those two have a lot of catching up to do."

Steve dropped a bill on the bar top as he watched the bartender pour the aged whiskey into a glass. Suddenly he heard an oh-so-familiar voice beside him.

"Buy you a drink, Cowboy?"

Kelly. He felt his pulse speed up as he turned and saw her smiling at him. *All right.* "You sure can, Cowgirl," he said with a grin.

"You shootin' whiskey? Damn, I wanted you sober tonight."

She leaned on the bar like he was, only a few inches away. Laughter in her eyes, and that light he'd missed for so long. He was afraid he'd never see it again.

"This is for Curt. I'm wide awake."

"Aren't you tired of playing with these cowboys? Why don't we go home and play?"

Just then, another voice sounded close by. A higher-pitched female voice. Steve looked over Kelly's shoulder. *Aw, crap!*

"Uh-oh . . ." Pete said, rising out of his chair. "Blonde approaching on Kelly's starboard bow." He set his beer aside and dug out his smartphone.

"What? You've *gotta* be kidding!" Greg sprang from his chair. "That's the chick who was at the bar talking to him. *Crap!*"

"Oh, no . . ." Marty set his beer on the table and stood. "Kelly just got here. *Jeeeez!*"

"Blondie is about to make a big mistake," Curt opined sagely, staring at the bar.

A tall guy wearing a denim shirt, jeans, and a Stetson paused beside Pete, then pointed at the four of them staring at the bar. "What're you guys looking at? The blonde or the brunette? I've had my eye on that tall one ever since she walked in the door."

"The tall brunette is making up with her boyfriend at the bar, but that blonde could throw a wrench into the whole thing," Pete said, holding up his smartphone while he filmed the drama about to begin. "Uh-oh . . . did she just touch Kelly?"

"Damn!"

"Why? Are they gonna fight?" Tall Cowboy asked, eyes alight. "Good. Then maybe I can make my move. Hey, Charlie!" he yelled at another table. "Check it out!" He pointed toward the bar.

Kelly turned and noticed the blond girl. Blondie stood, hands on hips, talking to Kelly.

"Uh-oh . . . Kelly's giving her the 'look,'" Greg said, shaking his head.

"Oh, man . . ." Marty said. "This is not good."

Tall Cowboy's eyes lit up. "What'll the brunette do?"

"If Kelly gets really pissed, there's no telling."

"Hey, Charlie." Tall Cowboy waved at his table of friends. "We're gonna have a little action here. I've got twenty on the brunette." He dug out his wallet from his back pocket as his friends laughed and turned their attention toward the bar.

Blondie was still talking at Kelly, while Kelly watched her with a mixture of semi-annoyance. Steve was leaning on the bar, shaking his head.

Charlie walked over, took off his Stetson, and both he and Tall Cowboy dropped twenty-dollar bills inside. "I'm betting on the blonde. I've seen her here before, and she's feisty." Then he held the hat out to Greg, Marty, and Curt.

Greg sneered. "Feisty, huh? Kelly eats feisty for breakfast." He dug out his wallet and dropped a twenty into the hat. "Twenty on the brunette."

"Hey, anybody else wanna bet on the blonde?" Charlie called out, his friends gathering around. Several of them pulled out their wallets as they laughed and dropped money into the hat.

"Aw, hell," Marty said. "I can't pass on a sure thing. Twenty on the brunette. Blondie is outgunned." He pulled out his wallet.

"Outgunned, huh? I like it," Tall Cowboy said, eyes dancing.

Curt chuckled. "Blondie is sailing into some pretty dangerous waters in a little sloop. She doesn't know what she's up against."

"Okay, I was in the Navy," Tall Cowboy said. "If the blonde's a sloop, what's the brunette?"

"A *destroyer*," Marty and Greg chimed together as everyone laughed.

"Fast and lethal. She's battle-tested, too," Curt added with a grin. He pulled out his wallet and dropped two twenties into the hat. "I'm bettin' on the warship."

"Hey, I did a stint in the Navy," a skinny cowboy said, checking out the conversation at the bar. "I'll take the blonde. I like the cut of her jib." He dropped some bills into the hat and smiled.

"What the hell is a jib?" Greg asked Marty, who shrugged and shook his head.

Curt cackled. "Don't worry about it, boys."

Pete simply laughed and continued to film the soap opera in progress.

"Look, I was already talking to this guy, so why don't you move your little act down the bar," Blondie declared with a shake of her curls.

Steve leaned his head in his hand. He couldn't believe it. He and Kelly were about to head out to the dance floor, when some half-drunk bimbo decides to make a play for him. *Damn!* Everything was coming together, and now . . .

Kelly stood up, then glanced over at Steve. She had her "I'm getting pissed" look. Steve met her gaze. "Don't hurt her, Kelly."

Kelly gave him a sly smile, then turned toward the blonde again. Steve sat on the edge of the bar stool . . . ready for god-knows-what.

"Hey, honey, I'm talkin' to you!" Blondie said, shaking her curls again. She came up to Kelly's nose.

Blondie's voice had gotten louder, and Steve glanced around. Everybody in this part of the Sunset Saloon was watching the confrontation with obvious interest. He spotted Marty and Greg standing with a group of guys, talking and pointing, like they were . . . no . . . they couldn't be . . . hell, they *were*! They were taking bets! *Crap!*

"I *said* to move on down the bar!" Blondie demanded. "*I'm* with this guy!"

Kelly put her hands on her hips, matching Blondie's pose, and stepped closer. Toe-to-toe. "*Back off, Blondie,*" Kelly said, loud enough to be heard in the betting gallery.

Loud male cheers and hoots of laughter sounded. Kelly leveled her gaze on the woman in front of her.

Blondie blinked, clearly not sober enough to evaluate the consequences of her actions. "Hey! Don't you threaten me!" She reached out and pushed Kelly. Kelly barely moved.

The saloon erupted then in roars of male laughter as more people inched closer to the two women. Steve noticed Marty and Greg's new friends passing the hat around again. *Crap.*

Shouts of "You gonna take that?" and "Don't give up, Blondie!" and "She's gettin' madder!"

"She's drunk, Kelly," Steve told her with a crooked smile.

"I know," Kelly replied, smiling at Steve over her shoulder. Then she turned back to Blondie. In one swift movement, Kelly grabbed Blondie's left hand, spun her around, and squeezed Blondie's palm . . . in just the right place.

Blondie squealed like a stuck pig, while the saloon erupted in hoots of laughter and applause.

"Sober up, Blondie," Kelly said, handing off the squealing woman to a nearby cowboy, who willingly put his arm around the protesting blonde.

"You *hurt* me!" Blondie whined, rubbing her palm.

Steve smiled, relieved that Kelly had disposed of Blondie with good humor intact. His gut unclenched. *Damn.* He tossed down Curt's whiskey and signaled the bartender.

"Hey, I was about to drink that," Kelly teased, pointing to the glass. "I deserve it. Patience under fire, or whatever."

"I'm ordering more." Steve held up two fingers to the bartender.

Suddenly Tall Cowboy strode up to Kelly and dropped to one knee in front of her, doffed his Stetson, and held it over his heart. "Don't waste any more of your time with him, darlin'. He's been out flirtin' with Blondie and leavin' you alone." Tall Cowboy looked up at Kelly with an engaging smile. "Now if you were mine, I'd never leave you alone on a Friday night. No way!"

"What the *hell?*" Steve cried, staring at Tall Cowboy. *Where'd this guy come from?*

Laughter erupted again and bounced around the bar. Kelly glanced around, then fixed Tall Cowboy with a winning smile. "I'll bet you wouldn't, Cowboy," she teased.

Tall Cowboy dropped his hat and placed both hands over his heart. "Darlin', you had me at 'Back off!'" Loud whoops rose around the saloon.

"Aw, hell!" Steve put his booted foot on Tall Cowboy's chest and shoved. *"Back off, Cowboy!"*

The saloon erupted in whoops, jeers, and laughter as Steve stood up and put his arm around Kelly. "How about that dance now?"

"About time." Kelly smiled up at him. They both tossed down their whiskies, then sauntered to the dance floor.

"**Okay,** pay up, pay up," Greg said, rubbing his hands together.

"Hold yer horses," Cowboy Charlie said as he counted out the cash and handed it around.

"It's a pleasure doing business with you boys," Curt said with a smile as he counted his larger wad of cash.

Tall Cowboy, looking none the worse for rolling on the saloon floor, was laughing with his friends and pocketing his cash.

"Easy money," Marty said with a grin as he fingered the bills.

"Thanks, Kelly," Pete said with a laugh, shoving the cash into his back pocket. Then he looked up and his mouth dropped open. "Man . . . tonight's getting weirder and weirder. Look who's coming." He pointed toward the saloon entrance.

"You gotta be kidding," Greg said as he pocketed his cash, staring in the direction Pete pointed.

Marty's eyes popped wide. "I don't believe it! There's Megan!"

"Isn't it illegal or something for the bride and groom to see each other before the wedding?" Greg asked and waved toward Megan, Lisa, and Jennifer, who were weaving their way around several cowboys as they maneuvered through the saloon.

"Howdy, gals." Curt grinned at the three women as they reached the table. "Can't say I'm surprised to see you."

"*Marteeee!!!*" Megan squealed, louder than Blondie, and pirouetted toward her fiancé, arms spread wide. Unfortunately, her balance wasn't the best, and she fell into Marty's arms.

"Whoa . . . Megan!" Marty laughed as he captured his giggling fiancée on his lap. "Sweetie . . . what have you been drinking?"

"What *hasn't* she been drinking!" Lisa proclaimed, giving Greg a hug. "Wine, champagne all day, beer at dinner."

"And tequila," Jennifer added as she and Pete embraced.

"Oh, brother . . ." Greg made a face.

"Megan! You drank all that?" Marty asked in disbelief.

"Uh-huh," Megan giggled. Then she snatched Marty's remaining stout glass and drained it before Marty could retrieve it.

"Not good," Pete said, laughing softly. "Right before the wedding, too."

"Believe me, we tried to stop her, but have you ever tried to stop Megan from doing anything?" Jennifer shook her head.

"Sweetie . . . you are *so* wasted," Marty said, laughing as he cradled a drunken Megan. Megan giggled in reply and kissed him.

"Where's Kelly . . . Steve?" Megan managed, speech slurring.

"You gals missed the floor show," Curt teased.

"Don't worry, I captured it all," Pete declared, holding up his smartphone.

"What happened? Tell us!" Lisa demanded, squeezing Greg.

"You wouldn't believe us if we did. You gotta watch it. Pete, you gotta put that on a file so we can watch on the big screen."

"What was it?" Jennifer asked, still snuggled beside Pete.

"Kelly and Steve were talking at the bar when some blonde came up and tried to give Kelly hell," Pete said with a grin. "You can imagine the rest."

"And you got a video?" Lisa broke into a laugh. "Yesss!"

"My man," Jennifer said with a grin and squeezed Pete in a big hug.

"Where are they?" Megan said, turning around and almost slipping off Marty's lap.

"They're continuing their conversation on the dance floor," Curt said as he rose from his chair, looking across the saloon. "And it looks like they're gonna need some privacy real soon. Judging from how close they're dancing."

Greg craned his neck. "Where? I'll be damned . . ."

"I gotta get this," Pete said, pulling out his smartphone again.

"Well, I'll be moseying back home, folks," Curt said, touching the brim of his Stetson. "I'll see you all tomorrow, I hope." He grinned toward Megan and Marty and headed for the door.

Jennifer glanced toward Megan, who was no longer giggling. She had her hand on her stomach. "How're you doing, Megan?"

"I don't feel so good . . ."

"Uh-oh . . . I was afraid of that," Lisa said, releasing Greg.

"Honey . . . you okay?" Marty asked, staring at Megan's pale face.

"Noooo . . . I feel sick." Megan's face puckered as if she was going to cry.

"I figured this would happen," Jennifer said, walking toward Megan. "It was just a matter of time. We'll stay with her tonight, okay, Lisa?"

"Yeah, we gotta take care of this. Marty, you and Greg will have to bunk in with Pete tonight. Megan's place is full of her relatives."

"You got it," Pete said, giving a sympathetic nod. "Call me if you need a run to the drugstore."

"Come on, sweetie," Marty said, gathering Megan in his arms as he stood up.

"Matter of fact, you can grab some of the pink stuff when you leave here," Lisa said as she followed after Marty, who was making his way through the saloon.

"Will do," Greg promised.

"Keep filming." Jennifer smiled, pointing to the dance floor. "I'll keep you posted."

"Got it," Pete said as he clicked on his smartphone and headed toward the dance floor. "C'mon, Greg, we don't wanna miss this. Two guys are holding their hats up so Kelly and Steve can kiss."

"Just keep filming, Pete," Greg said, following after him. "Just keep filming."

Twenty-One

Kelly stood absolutely still, clutching a small bouquet of white roses, her attention focused on Megan and Marty, who stood on a raised platform a few feet ahead. Megan looked radiant, despite spending half the night kneeling beside the porcelain god, according to Jennifer and Lisa. Marty was grinning from ear to ear. Both bride and groom looked radiantly happy.

Kelly's eyes grew moist, and she blinked to keep any tears away. She didn't want to miss one second of the ceremony. The minister held up the rings, blessing them, before Marty and Megan slipped the wedding rings on each other's fingers.

Kelly peeked at Jennifer and Lisa. Both had tears already. Mimi had been crying from the moment Megan walked down the flower-strewn grassy aisle toward the white-canopied wedding tent. Kelly had spied Hilda and Lizzie and several of Lambspun's regulars seated in the white chairs inside the tent.

Marty's and Megan's friends were mixed in with rows and rows of Smith, Harrington, and Stackhouse relatives. Kelly had noticed smiles were everywhere she looked when she'd followed her fellow bridesmaids up the aisle, Marty and his brother waiting ahead.

She glanced toward the groomsmen, lined up like the bridesmaids around the bride and groom. She spotted Steve look her way. He winked at her, and she smiled just as the minister proclaimed "husband and wife."

Megan and Marty barely waited for the minister to grant them permission before they embraced each other for a real kiss. The wedding guests showed their approval when they broke out in loud applause.

Kelly and the bridesmaids joined the groomsmen and guests and cheered the bride and groom. Having the ceremony outside at Jayleen's gorgeous canyon ranch added to the informal atmosphere. It was a perfect match for Megan and Marty.

The string trio Megan hired struck up the first chords of a beautiful classical piece that sounded familiar to Kelly. The bridesmaids and groomsmen took that as their cue and turned, opening space for bride Megan and groom Marty to process down the long middle aisle of the wedding tent.

Kelly could detect the scent of food wafting through the air, tickling her nostrils. Marty's and Megan's parents had taken the bridesmaids and groomsmen to a full breakfast in the late morning. The best way to ensure no fainting bridesmaids.

The matron of honor and the best man started off down the aisle, signaling the bridesmaids and groomsmen to follow suit. Steve and Kelly paired up, their eyes meeting as they started the slow stroll from the tent.

Kelly moved her mouth closer to Steve's ear as they danced to the familiar melody. Slow dancing. The sun was setting over the Rockies in the distance, and strings of lights had come to life inside the white canopy tent. The deejay was shifting the playlist to slow and romantic.

"That was a beautiful ceremony, wasn't it?" she said.

"Yeah, but not as beautiful as this," Steve said, pulling her even closer.

Kelly laughed softly. "We'd better watch it. Curt already threatened to throw a bucket of water on us."

Steve chuckled. "Good. That'll give us an opportunity to take up Jayleen's offer of temporary accommodations. We could dry off upstairs."

Kelly laughed again and snuggled closer. "I love you," she said softly against his neck.

"I love you, too," Steve whispered. "I never stopped."

"Me, either."

Steve moved his mouth to Kelly's ear. "I don't need to see a ring on your finger, Kelly. You know that. I just want us to be together. For always."

Kelly pulled away just enough to look into Steve's dark eyes. "For always," she whispered, then slid both arms around Steve's neck and kissed him. Steve pulled her closer as they continued to dance to their own music.

La Boheme Shawl

FINISHED MEASUREMENTS IN INCHES:

Approximately 50" wide x 25" long

MATERIALS:

Approximately 1 ball of bulky yarn to get gauge, approx.
165 yards

Needles:

US # 13 circular needles, 32" length (or desired length for
maximum shawl width)

Gauge:

2 sts. / inch

ABBREVIATIONS:

K = Knit   P = Purl
YO = Yarn Over   sts = stitches
P2 tog = Purl 2 stitches together

INSTRUCTIONS:

Start: Cast on 3 sts.

Pattern:

Increase one stitch at beginning of every row to make a
triangle by doing a YO before the first stitch of each
row.

Row 1: YO, knit to end.
Row 2: YO, purl to end.
Row 3: Repeat row 1.
Row 4: Repeat row 1.
Row 5: YO, *P2tog, YO*, repeat from * to next to last stitch. P1.
Row 6: Repeat row 1.

Repeat these 6 rows until piece measures desired length.
Bind off loosely.

Pattern courtesy of Lambspun of Colorado, Fort Collins, Colorado
Pattern designed for Lambspun by Larissa Breloff

Here are the three Best Hot Appetizer recipe winners from my recent Knitting Mysteries Appetizer Contest

Very Simple

For one dozen dates: Take a whole date, stuff it with ½ walnut or pecan. Wrap the date with ⅓ strip of uncooked bacon, and secure the bacon with a toothpick. Bake on a cookie sheet for 20 minutes in a preheated oven at 375 degrees F. Remove from oven, then stand back, because these will go incredibly fast.

Contributed by Grant Case

Hot Cheddar Bean Dip

Mix the following: ½ cup mayo, a 16-oz can refried beans, 2 cups shredded cheddar, a 4-oz can diced green chiles, and 1 tsp hot pepper sauce. Combine all ingredients in ovenproof bowl. (I keep ½ cup of the cheddar to sprinkle on the top.) Bake at 350 degrees F in a preheated oven for 30 minutes or until bubbly. Serve with tortilla chips.

Contributed by Lynne Wesenberg

BANG!
(To start your party off with a Bang!)

Ingredients: 1 round block of Edam or Gouda cheese, peeled; dry sherry; 1-2 cloves of garlic, minced; 1 can refrigerator biscuits. Preheat oven to 350 degrees F. In a 9" glass pie plate, sprinkle sherry and minced garlic over the bottom; sherry should cover the bottom of the pan. Place peeled Edam (or Gouda) in the center and surround with the biscuits, which have been cut in half (semicircle). Looks like a sunflower. Bake for 15–20 minutes until biscuits are golden and cheese is melted. Serve as is. Pull apart and spread cheese on hot biscuits.

Contributed by Maryfrances Charnley